Murder in
Plain Sight

Nikki Broadwell

Airmid Publishing
Tucson, Arizona

Murder in Plain Sight

Formatting by Wild Seas Formatting

ISBN: 978-0-9906697-4-6

Acknowledgements:

Thank you to my friend Helen for suggesting I write a mystery.

1

I felt proud to see my name, Summer McCloud, painted in deep blue above the door. Tarot and Tea was officially mine. The name always made me think of a singing duo: a man dressed in outlandish striped bell bottoms, the woman in a lacy dress and cowboy boots, straight brown hair to her shoulders—probably ironed. I had the feeling I had seen these two on an old album cover somewhere.

I heard someone call my name and turned to see Becky from Daily Bread, the bakery next door, hurrying toward me. She handed me a paper cup with a lid and a small paper sack.

"I brought over your breakfast," she smiled,"coffee with cream and a couple of doughnuts left over from the morning rush." Her freckled cheeks were flushed from the heat of the ovens, wisps of strawberry blonde hair escaping from under the red bandana she wore.

"Thanks, Becks."

"It's a bribe," she added with a sheepish smile. "Can I borrow that old Tarot deck your mother used to use?" She pointed to the window where the worn Rider Waite deck was spread out in a fan shape.

"Sure." Becky had been a client of my mother's, coming in often for readings. Apparently she based her decision to buy the bakery on my Mom's predictions.

"I've got to get back," she said, watching several

people making a beeline toward the bakery. "Bring them by later if you have the chance," she finished. "And I'm making chicken salad for lunch."

I watched her run down the street, apron strings flying. Becky and I had been friends since kindergarten. Both our mothers were witches and we'd grown up commiserating with each other about their rituals and occult practices. As kids we strove to keep it hidden from our classmates. But since my mother's disappearance and supposed death we'd talked about joining the coven that met once a month under the full moon. Becky had already taken the plunge but I was still on the fence.

I thought back to the days before I'd made the final decision about taking over the shop. "You're not planning to sell, are you?" Mrs. Browning had asked, her eyes wide. "Tarot and Tea has been a fixture in Ames for nearly twenty years." And then Valerie Henderson, Becky's mother and one of my mother's best friends, waltzed into the store in her breezy way. I could almost see her riding a broomstick. "Has Lila contacted you through the ether, my dear? I know she would want her life's work to go on."

My mother purchased this property before I was born and remodeled extensively, turning the downstairs into the occult shop with her living quarters upstairs. After I was born she bought the cottage on the other end of town where I lived now, using the second story of Tarot and Tea for storage. Tarot and Tea stood next to Daily Bread and on the other side was a used bookstore called Bookers, run by a man of the same name in his fifties who rarely emerged from within the store. Daniel Booker had an apartment upstairs and seemed to be the epitome of a recluse.

2

Across the street was a music store specializing in old vinyl recordings and next door to that was a secondhand store called Once Again, featuring used clothing, dishware, paintings and furniture. People who came to this part of town were either tourists looking for bargains, on the fringes of society, or old customers of my mother's. The bakery was also a draw and several of my newer clients had discovered the store because of Daily Bread.

I turned to open the door, pushing inward with my hip now that my arms were full of breakfast and a box of essential oils and diffusers that had been sent to my house by mistake. This was the first time I'd included oils in my inventory and hoped for lots of interest. They were expensive and promised all sorts of healing properties both internally and as aromatherapy.

I set the box down and turned on the light. All was as it had been the night before, including the cat that had spent the night in the storefront window. Uh oh.

"Tabby! What are you doing out here? I thought I locked you in the back room." I picked up the enormous animal, cradling him like a baby as I headed into the back of the store pushing through the swinging door into what had been a kitchen. It still contained a small gas range where I could make tea but the other accouterments had been replaced with shelving and more storage. Here was where the cat's litter box, food and water were placed. And of course, all untouched since the night before.

"Poor baby," I crooned, placing Tabby on the floor. I dumped out the small amount of stale kibbles and refilled his dish, watching him take to it as though starving. At least the cat had been kind enough to not use the storefront window for a litter box.

When I walked by the mirror I caught sight of my windblown chestnut hair, stopping to run my fingers through the knots and push it behind my ears. The shoulder length tangle was chestnut, not my mother's golden blonde waves that always made me think of a movie star. Her curves completed that image, curves that my willowy frame did not share. Even though she'd been gone for five years I still had conversations with her in my mind. The platitudes I'd heard after her memorial of, 'she lives on in your memory' made sense to me now.

Lila McCloud's disappearance when I was barely twenty-three had been sudden and unexpected. The police searched the surrounding area for weeks before they concluded that she'd been swept away by the river and drowned. I'd finally come to terms with it after visiting a psychiatrist who put me on anti-depressants. Since the day of her disappearance I half expected my mother to stroll into the store with some outlandish story about being abducted by munchkins or something equally crazy. Why Lila had decided to go for a swim on a cool spring evening when the river was running high was beyond my understanding, but Lila McCloud had never done things in a conventional manner.

With Mom gone I had dreamed for a time about a father who would miraculously appear and take over the role she'd played in my life. But as the years rolled by I lost the desire for a parental figure. And besides, my father was a misty memory. When I had questioned Mom about him she always got a funny look in her eyes and refused to answer. I hadn't seen any pictures, as though she wanted to rid him from our lives completely. When I was a teenager I used to joke that her pregnancy had been an Immaculate Conception. "I wish," she would say, turning away to finish whatever she was doing at the time. I had one half-brother eight years older but his father was another taboo subject. Apparently Mom hadn't bothered to marry either one of them.

The store phone rang, interrupting my musings about the past. I hurried to answer it, wondering if it was the supplier who had failed to bring my latest order of crystals.

"Hi, baby sister," Randall's voice purred. "How are things going?"

Okay this was weird. I had not heard from my brother in five years and the ingratiating tone was not one he normally used. "Hi Randall, what's up?"

"Just thought I'd check in. Everything all right down there?"

I frowned. "Yes," I said warily. "Do you know something I don't?"

Randall laughed. "Isn't it okay for a brother to check on his sister?"

"We haven't talked since the memorial, Randall. But thanks for checking on me."

"You're welcome. I have some business in Ames in the next few days. Can I stay at your house?"

"Of course you can stay. How long will you be here?"

There was a pause before he said, "Not sure. See you soon."

The phone clicked off leaving me staring at the receiver. With eight years between us Randall wasn't around much when we were growing up. In high school he ran with a gang of hoodlums who seemed bent on getting in trouble. I had no idea what his life was like now. According to him he was a respectable businessman who worked in the pharmaceutical industry. I had yet to see pictures of his wife. They'd had a quickie wedding because of an unplanned pregnancy and I hadn't been invited. But then again I hadn't made the effort to travel down to meet her either. And now they had a baby boy.

I looked up to see a dark-haired woman who appeared to have stepped out of the past. Her forties style suit, the heels that seemed out of date, and the fox fur, including the head, wrapped around the woman's neck were not clothing from this era. I was both repelled and intrigued by the design of the stole; the mouth of the animal had been fashioned into a clip to keep it neatly in place, the black bead eyes staring from the triangular face. An image of a terrified fox running for its den went through my mind. Thank goodness they didn't make those anymore.

"Good morning, dear," she said in a clipped accent that could have been French, could have been Italian. "I don't suppose you have a book on culinary potions?"

"Potions? Do you mean recipes or witch's brew?"

The woman laughed, a high sound that seemed faintly sinister. "No, no. I speak of poison, my dear. Something to, perhaps, do away with a bothersome husband?"

I noticed the lines around the woman's mouth and how her bright red lipstick had feathered into them. Like the fox around her neck her dark eyes were unreadable. Pulling myself together I said, "Poison. I'm not sure we have a book on that. We have herbal remedies for ailments," I offered, moving to the shelves. "Here's one called *Books on the Occult and how to Cast Spells*. When

I looked up the woman shook her head.

I ran my hand along the spines. "This one could have what you're looking for," I said, pulling it out. I had never seen this book, *Sixty Ways to Kill Your Lover*, and the title was just plain macabre. I held it out hoping the woman would say no, but instead there was an avid gleam in her eyes.

"There it is," she said, excitedly. "That's the one. How much is it?"

When I turned it over a note fell out but before I could pick it up she'd bent down and slipped it into her pocket. I opened my mouth to say something but when she waved a hand in the air the thought disappeared out of my mind. I turned to the computer on the counter but the book wasn't in the system with no bar code and no price. When I pulled up the inventory for the shop the title was not listed.

"What seems to be the problem?" the woman asked in an annoyed tone, tapping her foot impatiently.

I felt her irritation like a prickling against my skin. "It's not in the system."

"Pick a price and I'll pay it," she said, pulling an alligator wallet out of her vintage Hermes leather bag.

"It isn't that simple," I answered. "I have to account for it and if it isn't in the system that means I didn't purchase it."

"I don't really care whether you purchased it or not," the woman announced. "I would just like to buy it."

Her face was flushed, her eyes dark with anger. It took me one second to pick a price. "Let's say fourteen dollars," I said sweetly.

"Fine," she said, counting out the bills. "Thank you."

I watched her head toward the door, noticing that her

stockings had seams up the back and hers were none too straight. I didn't know they made those anymore.

She had her hand on the doorknob when she turned to look at me over her shoulder. "You look like your mother," she said, and then the door clicked closed behind her.

By the time I opened the door to ask her how she knew my mother she was heading into Bookers. There was something definitely off about her.

It was late afternoon before I had any time to myself. The store had been busy all day, questions keeping me on my toes, but very few people had purchased anything. I'd sold a few crystals, some other stones, a Rider-Waite Tarot deck and several herbal packets, but mostly the customers had browsed, acting as though they were in a library or possibly a museum. Even Mrs. Browning, the gray-haired pleasant woman in her seventies and one of my very best customers, had seemed off, her hoop earrings and usual colorful headscarves and gypsy skirts replaced with drab wool. And she hadn't purchased her usual chamomile tea, instead spending an inordinate amount of time staring at the books as though in a trance. Thank goodness I'd taken the bookkeepers advice and begun a mail order business. Lila's Tarot card and palm readings had been the meat of her earnings and without that I'd had to scramble to make ends meet.

After running my mother's Tarot deck over to Becky and taking the cardboard take-out box of chicken salad she foisted on me, I worked on arranging the essential oils and diffusers, placing them in a prominent shelf where they would attract attention. I told a couple of people about them but no one seemed very interested. I wondered if mercury was in retrograde, the time when the planets sent communication into a tailspin.

I closed up at five, placing the 'Shut' sign in the front window. Not owning a car was an occasional inconvenience but it saved me a lot of money in the long run.

I made sure Tabby was where he was supposed to be before turning off lights and locking up.

The small New England town of Ames was quiet tonight, dry leaves rustling under my feet as I walked the few blocks into town. Most of the houses here had been built in the late 1700's and early 1800's, the mullioned windows reflecting the outlines of the oaks and maples in the dusky light. Some were saltbox style with a sloping roof in the back, others were simple with a front door in the center and two chimneys; one on either end. They were all graceful and elegant, lovingly reconditioned by their owners. Mature trees dating back to when the houses were built lined the sidewalk, their thick trunks and spreading branches evidence of their advanced age. Even though it wasn't yet September, they were full of color, and many leaves had already dried and fallen off. My boots crunched through them releasing the pungent aroma that reminded me of the dark season coming. We'd had an early bout of cold weather as well as a drought over the summer.

As I drew closer to the business hub of town, the houses gave way to more commercial buildings, some of brick and some of the grey stone that came from the local quarry. The road curved to the right revealing a hardware store, a drugstore and several jewelry and dress shops in the same colonial style. On the other side of the street the market and a flower shop almost filled the block. Most of the buildings had been remodeled many times over the years, but a few were close to original, dating back to close to 1751, the year the town was founded.

The Ames Family Market stood at the corner of Main Street and Ames, named for the family who still ran it. Harold Ames had owned the mill here back in the early days and the original market had been built with wood from the sawmill. The store was brick now and the mill on the Ames River had long since fallen down, but it was still part of the early history of the area.

On the way into the store I passed by the tin buckets of late summer flowers, inhaling the fragrance of the freesias and admiring the tall Iris stems, deep purple blooms peeking out from within the green bulb that encased it. Inside I said hello to Pauline Ames, the gray-haired woman in her seventies who was the current owner, and then went to the pick out something for my dinner.

"Summer!" a voice called out. "How is the store doing?"

I turned from my perusal of Japanese eggplant, responding to Marguerite Power's smile with one of my own. "Everything's fine but I haven't seen you in forever."

Marguerite's gaze slid away. "I've been so busy lately I haven't had time. I'll try and get down your way soon."

I chuckled to myself at the idea of 'down your way' since the town was all of eight blocks long and three blocks wide, my store being on the southern edge of the business district. I knew she lived a block over from the market in a small apartment building that housed several of the older residents of Ames. Many of my customers hailed from there. I had a strong feeling her absence was due to something else but whatever it was she wasn't saying.

When Marguerite walked away I picked up an eggplant, a red pepper and a couple of zucchini squash and made my way to the meat counter.

"What do you need today, Summer?" Mr. Riddle, the butcher had been here for as long as I could remember, his snow-white hair and lined skin a reminder of how many years had gone by. I had memories of the lollipops he used to hand out when I came in the store with my mother.

"Just a couple of lamb chops," I told him, waiting while he pulled them out and wrapped them in brown paper and string.

"Here you go, young lady." He handed me the package. "If you have a mind to, Ethel is giving a little party for our granddaughter on the twenty-seventh. We'd love you to come."

"How old is Cindy going to be?"

Mr. Riddle ran a hand along his chin. "I think she's close to your age."

I laughed. "I'm two years away from thirty—isn't she around twenty?"

He chuckled. "All you young people look the same age to me. You're right. She's turning twenty-one this year. We'll be having wine if I know Cindy. Party starts around five." He looked at me hopefully as though the idea of drinking wine would surely make up my mind for me.

"I'll try, Mr. Riddle."

I paid for my food and headed along the sidewalk, passing by the fire station, the library and the post office before turning right on Randolph. My cottage had actually been the carriage house for an elegant home that had since been pulled down, replaced with a modern monstrosity that everyone in town complained about. The couple who owned it were not around much and I'd heard rumors that Mitzi and Bucky Chesterfield were billionaires and owned several other houses around the country. I had yet to meet them. Luckily there was a high hedge between my little house and theirs.

I'd grown up in the cottage and felt as connected to the house as I did to my friends. It seemed small when I was young with my brother still at home but now two small bedrooms were more than enough.

When my cell phone rang I pulled it out of my purse, saw that Agnes was the caller and slid my finger across the screen.

"Summer, are you home?"

"I'm a block away, why?"

"I have something I have to tell you."

"What?"

"Not over the phone. Can I come by?"

"Sure. I'll be home in five minutes."

The phone went dead and I wasn't sure if the call had been dropped or if Agnes had clicked off. Cell phone coverage here was spotty at best. We didn't have enough towers and something about the quarry and the rock formations seemed to interfere with the signal. I didn't buy this explanation but I barely used the thing so I didn't really care. My mind went to Agnes and her cryptic message wondering what she couldn't say over the phone. Had there been a murder? I laughed to myself at this idea since murders in Ames were few and far between. I couldn't remember the last time we'd had one. This was a peaceful little village that the world had forgotten, one of the reasons I loved it so much.

A few doors down from my house I heard Cutty barking. He always knew when I was close. My neighbor, Betty Franklin, gave me a withering look from where she was working in her garden and I heard her mumble something about out-of-control dogs. I excused her grumpiness when I noticed how close to term she was. She could barely bend over. If her baby didn't come soon she wouldn't be able to tie her shoes.

The thought of having a baby gave me the shivers. My twenty-eighth birthday earlier this month had come and gone with little fanfare. I did go out with men occasionally but I had no desire to get married. Maybe my mother's single life and independent attitude had worked its way into my psyche.

I adored my cottage at the end of the quiet tree-lined street. It contained a lifetime of memories as well as heirlooms that I'd never bothered to go through. The attic was full of them. My door was red now, a color that I'd chosen because in Feng Shui it meant welcome. It was in a book I'd ordered for the store about the Chinese art of harmony. I'd attempted to arrange my furniture to create the flow that the book spoke about but had no real idea if I'd done it correctly—all I knew was being in the house made me feel good.

My house key was under a flowerpot on the stoop and I bent to retrieve it. As soon as I was inside Cutty came hurtling through the dog door in back, wagging all over as he greeted me. I'd fenced in the small backyard so I could leave him when I went to work. He seemed happy with the arrangement but always excited once I returned.

I slipped off my shoes and left them by the door, climbing the two steps up to the kitchen. Cutty watched me pour kibble into his dish and add a scoop of canned dog food. After I fed him I cut up my vegies, slathering them with olive oil and sprinkling sea salt over them before seasoning the chops. Above me on the top of the highest cabinet, Mischief, my black cat, stared down on me, her eyes like green marbles.

I was sitting on my couch reading when someone rapped on my door. It was nine o'clock at night and I was getting sleepy, the sound startling me so much that I nearly knocked over the antique Tiffany lamp in my haste to answer it. I opened the door and peered into darkness, surprised to see Agnes. She seemed distraught, her straight dark hair in tangles as though she'd run in a high wind.

"I had to come over to warn you, Summer," she said breathlessly. "Since you don't own a TV I figured you wouldn't have seen the local news."

I flung the door wide. "Come in," I invited, closing it behind her.

Agnes was very pretty with dark eyes always lined with kohl, her lipstick varying from kiss me red to a deep maroon color. Her hairstyle reminded me of the roaring twenties with clipped straight bangs that stopped just above her eyebrows, the rest of her straight dark hair ending neatly at her chin. Her high-heeled boots made her look impossibly tall as she teetered toward the couch.

"Did you run in those?" I asked, pointing to the red ankle-high boots.

Agnes looked distracted as she pulled her heavy sweater over her head and lowered herself to the couch. "What? Yes, of course I did. Come sit, Summer. You aren't going to like this." She patted the couch next to her.

I stared at her bare arms, fascinated as always by her beautiful tattoos. Saraswati the Hindu goddess of knowledge, music and creative arts, was depicted in sinuous and colorful detail on her right arm. On her left forearm Guanyin, the Chinese goddess of compassion, had been rendered in the traditional seated position, and above her was a satyr, an oddity that didn't really go with the rest of them but was actually my favorite with his goat eyes and horns.

I sat down next to her wondering what could possibly have happened. I hadn't heard any sirens and my cell phone hadn't alerted me to any coming storms.

"Did you have a visitor in your store today, a woman who you've never seen before?"

I frowned, going back over my day. "There was one woman. She was kind of unusual and the book she wanted wasn't in the database. Why?"

Agnes sat forward, turning toward me with an intense gaze. "Dark hair? Older?"

I nodded.

"Her name was Serena Weatherby."

"Was, as in past tense?"

"She's dead, Summer."

"Dead? How?"

"That's the funny part. No one knows. There wasn't a mark on her."

"Why are you telling me this?"

"Because the only clue they could find was the

receipt inside the book she bought from you."

"So?"

"I think they're going to bring you in for questioning."

"You've got be kidding!"

"Jerry was kind enough to warn me."

Jerry Brady was a man we'd both dated in the past who just happened to be a homicide detective on the local police force. I stared at her, trying to take in the situation. "Do they think I had something to do with her death? All I did was sell her a book!"

"There's more. One of the poison recipes included in that book was authored by your mother."

"What? I've never seen that stupid book before. It wasn't even in the inventory on the computer. And why would my mother have a recipe to kill somebody?"

Agnes picked up my crystal paperweight and turned it over in her hands. "It's a good thing I went by the station today," she said, placing the paperweight down on the side table. "Jerry left a wool scarf at my house ages ago and I picked today to take it back. Kind of lucky, don't you think?"

I didn't pay attention to what she said, my mind on my interactions with Serena Weatherby. "She mentioned that I looked like my mother."

The dark window reflected my image back to me as I attempted to collect my thoughts. I saw two lines appear between my brows. I turned away. My heart was beating a little too fast and I felt as though I might be holding my breath. "Is it possible I could be arrested? I don't have enough money for a lawyer." My mind hurtled ahead like a runaway train. A vision of me in handcuffs being dragged off to jail went through my mind. This was no ordinary imagining, it was a real vision of my future and I needed to pay attention to it. If I didn't it, I was sure it would come to pass.

"I don't know what they're planning. Jerry said something about a 'person of interest'. I guess that's what they call a suspect these days. He knew I'd tell you—maybe he wants you to lay low?"

This was the message I needed. I had to get out of here before they picked me up. I was meant to solve this. "Agnes, you're on vacation for a few days, aren't you? Could you watch the store?"

Agnes looked startled. "Take over Tarot and Tea? I don't know…"

"You don't have to sell, just be there to ring people up. Oh, and someone needs to feed the animals. And Cutty needs to be walked. You could take him to your house or maybe you could stay here?" I watched her for a reaction to all these demands, surprised when she smiled.

"And what, my little amateur detective, are you going to be doing?"

"If I tell you I might have to kill you," I said, sotto voice, trying to make light of what I was feeling.

"Shall I say anything to Jerry?"

"I don't want to get him involved—I'm sure it would compromise his position if he tried to help me. I have his number if I need it."

"You'd better get to it. I have a feeling they might come tonight and if not tonight then early tomorrow. Sorry I didn't tell you earlier. Where will you go?"

"I know a place where I'll be safe." I hugged her and promised to be careful.

After Agnes left, I packed a bag. Before I left I hugged Cutty. Mischief eyed me from on top of the hutch in the corner of the living room as I headed toward the back door. "Don't worry, kitty. I'll be back soon," I told her. As I hurried down the dark street I heard sirens approaching. My fast walk turned into a run.

2

After several circuitous detours, I made it to my mother's Airstream trailer parked in a vacant lot on the outskirts of town. I hadn't known what to do with it and so I just left it sitting here, a decision I was glad of right now.

When I opened the door the odor of mouse droppings, and the mustiness of disuse wafted out. I cranked all the windows as wide as they would go. In the tiny closet I found my black Halloween wig from the time I'd dressed as Morticia from the Addams family, a gauzy long over shirt and an ankle length gypsy-type skirt that belonged to my mother. After dressing and adding a pair of enormous dark glasses I left the trailer, locking it carefully behind me. I headed toward the restaurant district to see what might be on the news about the crime.

There were no sidewalks or streetlights in this area of town and I dodged potholes, my mind jumping from one subject to another. Who exactly was Serena Weatherby and why, after buying a book on how to poison someone, did she end up dead? I couldn't imagine any reason for the police to suspect me, but I'd rather hide than be stuck in a holding cell. I shivered watching shadows gather between buildings. My radar was on high alert. I began to jog when I heard shouting and the sound of dishes being broken. A high-pitched scream sent me running and I was very glad when the lights from several restaurants came into view.

I hurried to the familiar bar called Grub and Grins where Agnes and I had met a couple of times in the past. It wasn't my favorite place but most of my customers didn't hang out here so there was less chance I'd be recognized.

Once seated at the long wooden counter I finally let out my breath. "Heineken, please," I asked when the bartender raised his eyebrows at me. I had the strong feeling that he recognized me but he didn't say anything, only turning away to grab the bottle from the cooler. He poured it into a chilled glass and set it in front of me.

The TV screen hanging in the corner caught my eye, the news obviously about Serena Weatherby. "Could you turn up the sound?" I asked the bartender. On the television screen a blonde reporter was talking and pictures were being flashed of Serena in better days. Serena was laughing and young, wearing a light summer dress that gave me a sense of deja vu. After that the camera panned across the entrance into Tarot and Tea.

"Police are looking for suspects in the mysterious death of Serena Weatherby, the blonde reporter said. "She was a stranger in town and found face down in the mud along the riverbank. The only clue was the book she purchased at Tarot and Tea and a note found clutched in the woman's hand. But when police went to question the owner, Summer McCloud, she was neither at the store nor at home. It was just five years ago that Summer's mother, Lila McCloud's clothes were found in almost the exact same spot as Serena's body. The detective I spoke with earlier today had this to say:"

Video feed of my detective friend, Jerry, came on the screen, his expression subdued. *"So far we have little to go on,"* he said into the newscaster's microphone. *"Of course we're doing everything in our power to come up with an explanation of why a woman in her seventies would end up dead next to our river."* He ran his hand through his light brown hair and looked down before continuing. *"The autopsy will reveal how she died, but until we speak with Miss McCloud or anyone else who might have come into contact with Serena Weatherby, our hands are tied. If anyone knows anything or recognizes this woman, please come forward."*

Another more recent picture of Serena Weatherby flashed across the screen, depicting a smiling fiftyish woman—nothing like the woman I'd seen in the store with skin like brittle parchment. The news flashed back to Jerry who looked troubled. *"Please come forward, Summer,"* he said, staring straight into the camera. *"You were possibly the last person to see Serena Weatherby alive."*

I wanted to shout out that I would come forward if I didn't think the cops would take that as a sign of guilt. I looked down at my beer and tried to quiet my hammering heart. Something clicked over in my mind but a second later whatever it was had gone.

"Summer McCloud is being sought in connection with this crime so please, if you've seen her let the police know. Let's hope it's cleared up soon. I'd hate to think we have a murderer in our midst." After this statement from the newscaster a picture of me flashed across the screen—a headshot taken right after my mother went missing. In it I looked slightly deranged, with wild hair and puffy eyes at half-mast. How they'd come up with that photograph was a mystery, and the way it was interjected into the story made me furious. It intimated that I was the reason my mother was never found, and from there it was an easy jump to assume I had something to do with Serena's death.

My hands balled into fists, my heart pounding. Around me I heard the buzz of conversation, people with their heads together discussing this terrible local tragedy. I distinctly heard one woman say, "Summer McCloud has always been a bit off just like her mother but I wouldn't have taken her for a murderer."

"You never know with these quiet types, " the woman sitting next to her answered.

"Can I please have a vodka and orange juice?" I asked the bartender, pulling out my wallet.

A couple of hours later I stumbled back to the trailer, my mind foggy. Once inside I pulled off the wig and sat down. It was time to look for answers, but only after I had a good night's sleep.

I was awakened by the headache pounding in my temples. I rose and heated water on the little propane stove, pouring it into my cup where I'd placed the strong black teabag from the box I'd brought with me. After sipping for a while my headache diminished and my mind cleared enough to ponder the situation. Maybe Serena Weatherby would come up somewhere on a Google search. But before I did that I had to close my eyes again—just for a moment.

Serena Weatherby and my mother walked along the riverbank talking
together in low tones. "How quickly does it work?" Serena asked, pulling the book out of her handbag. "I don't want him to suffer."

Lila cocked her head to one side as though listening.

"I used that recipe on my first husband," she answered, "and he was gone in five minutes and no one was the wiser."

I noticed the title: Fifty Ways to leave your Lover. Wait a second. That was a song title not the book title.

I blinked my eyes open and sat up. Sunlight streamed through the windows and dust motes floated in the beam of golden light puddling on the braided rug. It must be at least ten by now. Serena and Lila were friends? But what did that have to do with Serena's death? And who was Lila's first husband? As far as I knew she never married. Should I trust this dream or chalk it up as a way for my mind to explain the unexplainable?

The vision brought my buried inner sleuth abruptly to life. This case involved my mother—how could I resist? But then I thought of the last time I came forward six years ago. Even with my mother vouching for me I was regarded as a person of interest. The police found the body exactly where I'd said it would be and because of DNA evidence they tracked the killer down. Otherwise I would have been hauled off to jail. Now I was probably on some sort of list of weirdoes who might or might not be the type to kill someone. Since then I'd kept my visions to myself. But despite being their number one suspect I was ready to jump in with both feet.

3

I purchased a throwaway phone at the Wal-Mart on the outskirts of town and pressed in Jerry's cell phone number. "Jerry, this is Summer, Summer McCloud? I need to talk to you."

"You shouldn't be calling me," he whispered. "I'm part of the team trying to find you."

"I know that," I hissed. "I remembered something that might help with the investigation."

"Where are you?"

"I'm not telling you that. I'll meet you under the bridge, you know the one."

"The one where…?"

"Yes, that one."

Jerry and I had a moment under the Larch Street Bridge, but after the one lingering kiss and a few other things that now brought heat to my cheeks, nothing more had happened. At the time both of us had been frightened by the intensity of our attraction and simultaneously backed off. Since then we'd barely seen each other but I trusted him and doubted he would turn me in.

There was silence and then Jerry asked, "When do you want to meet?"

"After dark, say around nine?"

There was a long pause and a sigh. "Okay. Keep out of sight until then. Cops are combing the town."

"Don't worry." I clicked off and threw the phone into the nearest trash bin.

Once I reached the Airstream I lay down on the bed. The night before had taken a major toll and I was still tired. There were several hours to kill before the meeting with Jerry. I closed my eyes.

"Lila, what are you doing?"

"I'm taking off my clothes."

"All of them?"

"Yes, all of them. I'm going swimming. And after that you and I are heading into unknown territory."

"Is that what you call it? I could come up with a better term."

"Like murderer's hideaway?"

Serena laughed before she turned serious. "He deserved it, Lila, you know he did. He molested at least three little boys!"

"They all deserve it for one reason or another," Lila responded, turning away to remove her last article of clothing. In the dusky light her skin looked like pale ivory. "Is this the only reason you marry them? How many is it now? I should call you the black widow, Serena."

Serena watched Lila head toward the water flowing fast and dark. "You helped with all of them as I recall, and you were quite adept with your potions. Didn't you do away with Randall's father? I haven't seen him around for a while. Does that make you spider's assistant?"

Lila doubled over laughing. When she straightened she turned to stare at her friend. "I didn't harm him despite his evil ways. I only warned him off. He'll get his in the end—that's the way the universe works."

Serena's eyes widened as Lila stepped into the river. "Lila, this isn't a good idea. If you get washed away they'll think I did it."

"No dear," Lila called, *lifting her arms as she waded deeper. "They'll know you did it."* Lila let out a tinkling laugh followed by a tiny cry as she was carried quickly into the current.

I woke with an intake of breath. The dream had seemed so real. But Serena looked almost the same age as my mother. And what was all that about murderer's hideaway? My mouth fell open as I realized the implications of what I'd just seen. My mother could be alive.

"So what is so all-fired important to bring me down here at this hour?"

I stared at the man who I considered a friend. Right now he looked anything but with his frown of annoyance, the way he stood with legs apart and fists balled. And the holstered gun hanging on his hip didn't help. I gazed into the shadows cast by the bridge my keen sense of smell picking up the pungent odors of green algae coming from the stagnant water close to shore. "I had a vision, Jerry. Did anyone do an autopsy?"

Jerry made a derisive sound and pulled out a pack of cigarettes.

"Please tell me you didn't start smoking again." This had been an ongoing point of contention between us during the time we'd gone out together.

He pulled out a cigarette and put it between his lips. "I don't actually smoke them."

I chuckled. "Expensive nonetheless."

"So, are you planning to answer me? I don't have all night you know."

"My mother and this woman, Serena, knew each

other. I…it seemed from the vision that my mother helped Serena poison at least one man."

"What?" The unlit cigarette flew out of his mouth landing on the damp ground a foot or so away.

"I didn't get all the details, but my mother was…"

Jerry shook his head. "You brought me down here to tell me about a vision? I need evidence, Summer. And so far all of it points to you."

"What do you have that points to me?" At that moment there was a whoosh and then bats were flying out from under the bridge. Jerry crouched and covered his head with his hands. "Jesus, I hate those things."

"They won't hurt you. They have sonar."

When a minute went by and no more bats emerged Jerry straightened and looked around warily. "I haven't spoken to the ME yet but we found a note that was signed Summer."

"What are you talking about?"

He turned as an owl glided silently by. "It's freakin' eerie out here."

I grabbed his arm. "What did the note say? I never saw that book before Serena bought it. If you want to look at my inventory list you'll see. It's like she planted it in my store."

Jerry shuddered as another group of bats flew out from under the bridge. "Let's get out of here."

"Where can we go?" I scanned up and down the walkway above the bridge. I didn't see anyone but it was a popular walking trail, leading from one end of town to the other.

"The squad car is parked on the other side of the bridge." He pointed in a northerly direction.

"I guess if any cops see me with you they'll just

think you're bringing me in?"

Jerry smiled for the first time. "If I wasn't such a damn fool I *would* be taking you in. But I have to say I don't believe you murdered this woman. It isn't in your nature."

"Thank you for that at least," I said, taking the hand he held out. He hauled me up to the walkway and we both hurried to his car.

He opened my door and went around and slid behind the wheel, pushing the seat back to give himself more room. "Listen, Summer, I need a lot more information to clear your name. If you let me take you in I can protect you."

"Protect me from what? From conversations I've overheard, a lot of people think I did it—that news reporter certainly seems to. This is a small town--if I'm sitting in a jail cell everyone will be convinced of my guilt. That was the first time I'd ever seen that woman."

Jerry pressed his lips together. "There are those on the force who want to pin this on someone as quickly as they can. We haven't had a murder here for years and the town is in an uproar about it. I don't want you picked up by some yahoo cop who doesn't know what he's doing. You could get hurt." A minute of silence went by before Jerry's gaze met mine. "I think about you a lot, Summer. I wish we hadn't…"

"Hadn't come to our senses?" I shook my head. "We're too different, Jerry. It wouldn't have worked."

"Why do you say that? Because I'm a cop?"

When our eyes met I felt the pull of him just as I had in the past. Sometimes he had the look of a little boy; his lost expression always got to me. It was the same with animals and I'd brought home many a stray over the years. Before I could stop myself I was imagining how good it would feel to have his arms around me. I shook myself. "Because I have visions and you live in a world that doesn't accept visions," I finally answered.

He placed a hand on my knee sending shivers up my leg. "I admit I have a hard time with your visions but I could get used to them."

I pushed his hand away and reached for the door handle. "Who was the note addressed to and who signed it?" I asked before letting myself out.

"No salutation and only your name after the message."

"I need to see it." I stared at him hard, willing him to agree.

Jerry looked troubled, his eyebrows pulling together. "It's in the evidence locker, Summer. I can't just go and get it."

"Please, Jerry. I'm trying to figure this out—you know I didn't do this."

He sighed and looked away. "I'll do what I can but how can I get in touch with you?"

"I'd tell you where I'm staying but I'm afraid someone else would find out. For now I have to keep it a secret. If you have a message give it to Agnes. I can meet you anywhere."

"Agnes?"

"She's staying at my house. She said you warned her about this. Aren't you two…?"

"That lasted approximately one day, Summer. She's weirder than you are."

I laughed. "Thanks a lot."

Before I could get out of the car Jerry reached for me, his arms going tight around my back. "Don't worry," he whispered, his breath warm on my neck. "We'll get to the bottom of this."

I tensed up and then relaxed into the embrace. It felt as good as I imagined and I didn't want it to end. "Thanks, Jerry," I finally said, pulling away. "I'll see you." I pushed the door open and climbed out.

"Be careful," I heard him say just before I slammed the car door shut. I nodded once before pulling the hood of my sweatshirt over my hair.

In the Airstream later I thought about the feel of his chest against mine, his steady heartbeat and the spicy smell of his aftershave. I shook my head but the feeling inside my body refused to go away. This was a complication I didn't need right now.

4

Early the next morning I looked up Serena Weatherby on the computer. I had to get my mind off what Jerry and I had been up to in my dreams and focus on the fact that I could be railroaded for a crime I didn't commit.

Her name brought up several long articles regarding Jonathon Weatherby. He was a very rich man in his early eighties who was well known as an entrepreneur and for donating large sums of money to certain businesses and charities. Apparently he had inherited a huge estate from his father when he turned twenty-one and then invested in oil and several other lucrative companies, becoming a multi-millionaire by the time he reached fifty.

I skimmed down through several articles finally finding one that mentioned Serena. It was a news clip of Jonathon Weatherby's sudden unexplained death and mentioned that his wife Serena was his sole beneficiary. There were pictures of Serena and Jonathon together and also pictures of his two grown children, a severe-looking blonde woman named Regina Applegate and a darker haired man, Gavron Weatherby, who both appeared to be in their forties.

Apparently Jonathon and Serena had met on a cruise ship and had a whirlwind romance, marrying a month later. The lavish wedding hit the New York society pages and featured every well-known person for miles around, including several senators. Two years later Jonathon was dead from what was assumed to be a heart attack although he'd never experienced any heart problems. There had been some discussion of foul play but nothing was proven. In the pictures Jonathon looked in the peak of health and was purported to be an avid mountain climber and hiker. Beside him Serena looked tiny, the expression on her face unreadable.

The article went on to say that the children were understandably angry for being cut out of the will and that lawyers had been working to find a way to break it. But the article was months old.

I scrolled further down the Google page finding another article about Serena that mentioned two other husbands who had died accidentally. The details were sketchy at best, the biased writer referring to Serena as the black widow. And when I scanned through the old photos I was pretty sure I saw my mother in at least one of them. "Holy crap," I whispered, closing my computer.

After the visions I'd had recently I wondered if my mother had done it, but Lila was long dead. Regina and Gavron were a better bet since they stood to inherit—or did they? How could I find out what was in that will? I had a dizzy spell and had to sit down. And that's when I had another vision.

"Oh please, spare me the drama," Serena said, *staring at Lila.*

The two women were in the cottage I inherited from my mother. It was obviously summertime since they were both dressed in loose cotton tops and capris that reminded me of Audrey Hepburn movies.

"You can't keep doing this, Serena. I can't let you do it again. It's murder."

"So? You said yourself they all deserved it. I'm

doing the world a service ridding it of these degenerates."

"It isn't up to you to be judge and jury. Why don't you report them to the police?"

Serena made a sound in the back of her throat. "I tried that once and they threw me in jail for libel. It's impossible since these bastards are all as wealthy as Croesus. They do what they want when they want it with no questions asked. If the police question them they pay them off or get them fired."

The vision blurred and disappeared leaving me with an excruciating headache. Why was I tapping into these conversations? I'd never had visions like this before. Mine were usually vague and misty with a couple of landmarks that sent me scurrying in a certain direction. These seemed like they were happening now but I knew that couldn't be true. And what was I supposed to do with the information? The vision proved nothing as far as pointing to Serena's killer.

There had to be a reason why Serena died in Ames. I was determined to read the will and also learn more about my mother and her role in Serena's life. Did Lila keep a journal over the years? I'd never seen her writing in one. Who in town could I speak to about this? Surely Lila's friends would know about Serena.

If they'd been murdering men over the years I had to prove it. But if my mother were indeed still alive, uncovering murders that she participated in would put her in jeopardy. I sat down on the bed and put my head in my hands. When I looked up again I noticed the box sitting against the wall. I opened it and pulled out a folder. Inside I found several letters dating back to shortly after I was born. They were addressed to my mother from someone named Vivienne.

Please leave us alone, I read. We love each other and despite what you think he's a decent man. He's sorry about the baby but he warned you going in. With all your psychic abilities you refuse to see the truth. If you continue with your threats you will pay and believe me, things could get very ugly. Vivienne

I jumped when someone knocked on the trailer door. My heart seemed to rise up in my throat until I heard the familiar voice. "Summer? It's me, Agnes."

I unlatched the door and stared down at my friend. "What are you doing here? Wait a second--did I tell you about the Airstream?"

Agnes pushed by me and pulled the door closed. "Your mother told me about it—said I could stay here during that time. Don't you remember? Mom and Dad were arguing like crazy and drinking too much. I figured this is where you'd be."

I did remember. We had both turned seventeen that year and things were not going well for Agnes. It was only a month later that her parents were killed in a car crash. She lived with us in the cottage until she turned eighteen and then insisted on getting a job and supporting herself. Agnes had been forced to grow up quickly. I nodded. "That was a terrible year all around. So why are you here?"

Agnes's eyes darkened but then she shook herself. "For one thing your brother was there when I got to your house yesterday. Why didn't you tell me he was coming? And your animals miss you, and the store—holy cow! I don't know how you deal with it! What a bunch of..." She shook her head staring at me wide-eyed. "I don't even know what to call them. They're way beyond weird,

Summer; most of them just hang out and read or fiddle with your products and never buy anything."

I smiled. "It's lucky I have such a flourishing mail order business. I'm sorry I forgot to mention my brother. Is he still there?"

"He left today. He said to say hello and he was sorry he missed you." Agnes seemed to be holding something back, her gaze on the floor.

"How did he seem? I still can't figure out why he was here."

Agnes fidgeted with the wool scarf around her neck. "He told me he had business with Brent over at the drug store—you know the pharmacist, right?"

I thought of the middle-aged man who doled out pills like candy. "Brent of the bad teeth? Yes. So tell me the real reason you're here."

Agnes seemed glad to leave the subject of my brother, her arms relaxing against her sides. "Jerry came by your house—said you told him I was staying there. He's worried about you."

"And?"

Agnes looked away. "He tried to get me to reveal where you were."

"But you didn't tell him, right?"

"I had to. He's the only one who can keep you out of jail. He promised to help. Honestly, I think he's in love with you."

Adrenaline surged through my body and I was suddenly shouting. "No, he's not! He's just like all the rest of them! He wants what he wants but I'm not giving it to him!"

Agnes's mouth opened in surprise. "What are you talking about? Sex?"

"I don't know. It's like someone just spoke through me. Did the voice even sound like me? Agnes, I'm scared."

"No, it didn't sound like you. Has this happened before?"

I nodded. "I keep having these visions and they aren't dreams anymore. It's like I'm hearing conversations between my mother and Serena. And believe me they were not on good terms with the men they were with."

Agnes frowned. "Lila was psychic. Maybe she's sending you messages from the other side. Do the visions have anything to do with the murder?"

"Kind of. It seems that Serena killed her husbands because they were hurting children—at least one of them was. Serena and my mother were doing it together."

"Your mother's dead, Summer."

"Is she? Look what I just found." I showed her the letter.

After Agnes read it her puzzled gaze met mine. "Who's Vivienne?"

"I don't know. The envelope had Lila written on the outside."

"There's no date. Where'd you find it?"

I pointed. "In that box over there. It's filled with papers."

Just as Agnes went to pull out another folder the door opened and Jerry came into the trailer, his expression grim.

"Any chance you could knock before you barge in?"

"I saw you through the window and I don't have time to fool around. Two people just arrived at the precinct to claim Serena's body and they didn't strike me as people who cared about her. Fortunately the ME isn't finished with the autopsy so they'll have to wait."

"Let me guess—blonde woman and dark haired man?"

"How'd you know?"

I looked down. "I saw them in my vision," I mumbled. "They're Jonathon Weatherby's son and daughter, Regina and Gavron. Why is this so important?"

"Because they're claiming that Serena killed Jonathon. They're here to clear their names before they get blamed for Serena's murder. They both have alibis. Apparently there was no love lost between them, and with Serena out of the way they admitted hoping to inherit. But there's a slight hitch. There's another child in the mix and Serena left everything to her."

"How old is this child? The woman was in her seventies!"

"I have no idea. But on top of that Serena was in disguise. The ME thinks she was in her fifties like your mom."

"So her child could be around my age?"

"Hard to say. The department has requisitioned the will since it might explain why she was killed. Jonathon's children are doing everything in their power to block it. They say their father wasn't in his right mind when he let Serena cut them out."

"Sounds like I'm off the hook."

"Not entirely," Jerry said reaching into his pocket. "It wasn't easy but I managed to get hold of the note we found." He handed me a square of paper.

I read the words: *Take great care my friend, the enemy approaches.* My name, *Summer*, was on the next line. "Jerry this isn't a signature it's the beginning of another sentence—look." I held the note out.

He frowned examining the note. "You may be right. But why would your name come up at all?" He handed it back.

"If Serena killed Jonathon maybe my mother was warning her that the authorities were on to her. I think she was just about to tell Serena something about me." I waved the note in the air. "Is this what the police consider incriminating evidence? No wonder so many innocent people end up in jail."

Jerry ignored my outburst. "Summer, Jonathon died recently. Your mother's been gone for what--five years now? As soon as the ME is finished we'll know more. What I'm trying to figure out is why Serena was here in Ames in the first place."

My last vision reappeared in my mind—the one where my mother threatened Serena if she murdered anyone else. And in my first vision Serena was with her when she stepped into the Ames River. Maybe my mother was staying in the place they referred to as 'murderer's hideaway'. "My mother might not have drowned, Jerry. I think there's a possibility she's alive."

Jerry stared at me for a full minute before seeming to come to a decision. "I wasn't going to tell you this but something happened that has me questioning her death."

My heartbeat quickened. "What?"

He glanced at Agnes. "I can't go into details right now. The department is keeping it under wraps until we know more."

"But Jerry, this is my mother we're talking about!"

"If she's out there I'm going to do everything in my power to find her."

"So you can put her in jail for Serena's murder?"

Jerry stared at me for a moment before turning toward the door.

"Answer me!" I screamed.

He glanced back. "I'm a cop, Summer. This is what I do." He opened the door and then he was gone, leaving Agnes and me alone in the trailer.

Agnes's eyes were wide. "What's going on?"

I sighed heavily. "I don't know what to think anymore."

"And what about the missing child? If they don't find her what happens?"

"Honestly, I don't know. And whose child is it? It can't be Jonathon's since they married within a month of meeting one another. So how come this child is in the will? Why would Jonathon agree to that? Maybe he adopted it."

"You need to see the will."

I nodded. "Jerry said they requisitioned a copy. And now Jerry wants to arrest my mother. It's hard for me to imagine her not showing herself if she's alive. We were really close."

"But aren't you excited about the possibility?"

"Not if it means she ends up in jail for the rest of her life."

5

After Agnes left I paced around the trailer trying to get my head together. I wanted to dig through that box and read every piece of paper inside it, but right now I had to find a way to get my hands on the will and figure out who would benefit from Serena's death. The department had requisitioned a copy but I doubted seriously that Jerry would let me see it. When my gaze lit on my wig a plan came to mind.

I spent the next hour perfecting my outfit, dressing in oversized clothing my mother had left in the trailer and donning the dark wig which I made even more outlandish by teasing it into a semblance of rat's nest hair. I painted on garish lipstick, making sure that it came outside the lip area looking as though an unsteady hand had applied it, adding a smidgeon of dark eye shadow under my eyes. My mother's dirty worn out hiking boots completed my disguise.

When I walked into the station no one even glanced my way. I guess they were used to bag ladies coming in to complain about one thing or another. I left on my sunglasses even though they were so dark I could barely see.

"Is Detective Brady around?" I asked at the main desk.

The officer looked me over skeptically. "What do you want with him?" she asked.

"He's a friend of mine," I said, knowing this would

bring a laugh. And it did, several other cops within hearing distance chuckling. It was then that I saw Jerry walking toward a desk in the back. "There he is," I said loudly, pointing.

Jerry looked up and then turned away but a second later he did a double take and came toward me. "What are you doing here?" he asked me, looking around to see if anyone was listening.

"Can we speak privately?" I asked in my new hoarse voice that I hoped indicated heavy cigarette usage.

He nodded, leading the way to a private room where he closed the door.

"What in hell are you wearing?" he asked, looking me up and down.

"This is my informant disguise. I came to give you info on one of those perps you've been searching for."

Jerry laughed and pulled out a chair for me. "And what is your information, Miss...what's your name?" he asked, sitting down across from me.

"Mata Hari," I told him without cracking a smile.

Jerry raised one eyebrow and then his expression turned serious. "Why are you really here, Summer?"

"I need to see the will."

"That's impossible."

"Why?"

"Because it's evidence. I can't show it to you."

"Can you at least tell me the name of the law firm?"

"What do you expect to get out of this?"

"Jerry, you think my mother killed Serena."

He frowned and stood up, staring down at me with a hard expression. "If you keep going like this you'll end up in jail. Leave the cop stuff to me."

"I figured this out before you did, Jerry. If it wasn't

41

for my visions you'd still be in the dark."

Jerry shook his head. "Not so. And as far as your mother being innocent we'll just have to see. I'm sure she knows about Serena's child."

"Did the ME find out how Serena died?"

"I can't reveal anything yet. It's part of the ongoing investigation."

His gaze slid away. A sure sign he was hiding something. "Is my mother mentioned in the will? You must have some reason to suspect her."

"Summer, there's a lot you don't know and I'm not at liberty to tell you."

"How can you let me wonder about her? I almost went crazy when she disappeared."

"You said yourself she threatened Serena. And you have to admit she has a wild side."

I shrugged about the 'wild side' comment. Yes, she did, but not wild enough to kill someone. "She threatened Serena *in my vision*, Jerry. I thought you didn't believe in visions!" I was shouting now and someone knocked on the door.

"Everything all right in there?" a voice called.

"It's fine," Jerry called out. He leaned over me, his eyes dark. "Summer you have to stay out of this," he hissed. "It's dangerous. Your mother may have planned this from the get go. She disappeared and let you assume she was dead and from what I can glean, took off with Serena and helped her murder Jonathon. And now it looks like she killed Serena as well. And there's…" He stopped in mid-sentence and stared at the floor.

I wiped my eyes with my sleeve, accidentally removing some of the make-up I'd carefully applied. "Just give me the name of the law firm," I said, standing.

He grabbed my arm. "I mean it, Summer. If you get any more involved in this I won't hesitate to put you behind bars."

I twisted out of his grasp. "Just tell me the name."

Jerry shook his head and sighed. "It's a New York firm called Jacob and Elliot. But I doubt you'll get any information out of them."

I opened the door and meandered my way slowly toward the front of the station, trying to stay in character. When I reached the door I pushed it open and stumbled outside pretending to limp as I crossed the street into the little park. By now I was shaking all over and the wig was making me sweat.

I sat on a bench and watched mothers with babies in strollers and older folks strolling along the pathway. I recognized Mr. Flint and Mary Hardin but they didn't even glance at me. They were both customers of mine and they knew me well. My disguise must be good if it fooled them.

But the positive thought was instantly replaced with fear about my mother. I had to find her before Jerry or some other crazy cop on the force discovered where she was. From Jerry's comments it seemed he knew things I didn't. Something had happened to convince him she was alive.

This disguise was not appropriate for what I had in mind for Jacob and Elliot and so I headed for the one small department store in town. After spending too much money I walked back to Tarot and Tea. I felt scattered and slightly light-headed, something that happened when too much stress piled up. Solving murders was one thing but my mother's possible involvement and the betrayal I felt if this were true was disturbing to say the least.

I thought again of the lead-up to her supposed death, wondering if there was some clue I'd missed.

My mother and I got along pretty well but there were times when she seemed to sink into a kind of despondency and if I tried to talk to her, her anger was right on the surface. I learned to steer clear of her when she was in one of these moods. If Randall was around he confronted her and there were several times I remembered yelling and my mother slapping him. But these memories were from when I was a young girl.

I recoiled as a buried memory wormed its way up from my subconscious. It was summer and we were all at the river. I must have been around eight, which would have made Randall around sixteen at the time. I think my mother might have been drunk, in any case she was belligerent and out of sorts and I was scared of her.

"You're a filthy whore!" my brother had shouted.

My mother looked stunned and then slapped him and yelled, "How dare you speak to me that way?"

"I've seen you with your lovers, mother. You don't even try and hide it. Do they pay you for your favors? You make me sick."

My mother's eyes went wide and then she grabbed Randall by the arm and was about to slap him again when he twisted away. And then he punched her in the stomach and took off. I didn't see him again for two full days. I ran to help her up but she shoved me and I fell down. "Get the hell away from me!" she shrieked before pushing herself up and stumbling along the bank. I watched her disappear around a bend wondering what to do. I sat there for more than an hour waiting for her to return but she never did. In the end I walked home alone. It was several hours before I saw her again.

After that day I began to notice the men frequenting the shop. She introduced them to me as Uncle this or Uncle that and told me to go outside and leave her alone for an hour or two. She would put the shut sign in the window and lock the door. Randall had been right.

When I entered Tarot and Tea Agnes looked up in surprise. "What are you doing here?"

"I need to talk to you for a minute." I whispered my plan to go to New York and talk with the lawyers.

"There's no way you'll get anything out of them." Agnes looked around the store, making sure her voice was low enough not to attract attention. "And by the way, you look really terrible in that get-up."

"But no one recognizes me," I replied, watching all my regulars. "So it must be pretty good. Now, back to New York. I'd like to drive if you'll lend me your car. It's only a few hours from here if the traffic isn't bad on 95. I have a great plan."

Her eyes narrowed. "I hope you change clothes before you head into a fancy office." She went to the register to check someone out as I pretended to peruse the shelves. A minute later she was back. "You can borrow my car but please try not to wreck it. New York traffic is insane. And take my phone." She held out her brand new I-phone.

"Agnes I can't do that. You need it."

"In Ames, Connecticut?" She scoffed. "I can get along for a day or two without it. I have my computer and there's a store phone."

"Thanks." I put the phone in my bag accepting the keys she retrieved from her purse. I hugged her. "You're a really good friend."

"Be careful!" she called out just before the door closed behind me. Why was everyone compelled to say those two words? Did they think I wasn't going to be careful or was it some sort of magical talisman that they hoped would keep me safe?

I drove her 2005 Honda Accord back to the trailer and packed a small bag with the clothes I'd just purchased. It was two-thirty in the afternoon by the time I left Ames. Arriving in New York during rush hour was probably the stupidest thing I'd done in a long time. But something told me not to wait until morning.

It was around six thirty when I noticed a seedy motel off the main highway and decided I had to stop. Traffic was bumper to bumper with no end in sight. I pulled off the road and into the trash-strewn parking lot and turned off the car. The lobby was not as bad as the parking lot indicated, and had been recently remodeled. I only hoped the rooms had been too since this place looked as though it was built before the beginning of time.

Surprisingly there was Wi-Fi in my room, allowing me to search for Jacob and Elliot. When I found the address I entered it into Agnes's phone. It would take me forty minutes to get there if traffic was light, which of course it never was.

For some reason I thought of the box of my mother's papers that I hadn't had time to go through and cursed myself. Surely there was information in there that could lead me straight to her. For a second I feared the box would be gone when I got back but I put it out of my mind. Who knew about the trailer besides Jerry and Agnes? And neither one of them would be snooping into my mother's personal effects—or so I hoped.

Just for fun I Googled my mother, Lila McCloud,

surprised when I got several hits. None were current however. They all mentioned Tarot and Tea and Lila's old website that dealt with astrology. But when I went to the URL the site was gone, as I knew it would be. If she were truly alive what in the world had she been doing these past five years? I had a hard time imagining a strong enough reason to abandon a daughter, or a son, for that matter.

My mind turned to my plan for tomorrow. I was to be an heiress, someone who had not come forward earlier—Serena's other daughter who she had adopted out when I was barely five years old. I was sure I would get nowhere with this but possibly I would learn something more about the will. And maybe, just maybe they would reveal information about my mother. I went to bed feeling optimistic. My dreams were filled with strange images of my mother and some guy I didn't recognize and Lila and Serena brandishing sharp knives and chasing men down across wide expanses.

In the morning I was not feeling the same enthusiasm as I stumbled into the bathroom to stare into my bleary face. I patted on face make-up that I rarely used to cover the circles under my eyes, brushed on mascara and applied dark eyeliner that I mostly reserved for nights out. I dressed in the outfit I'd picked out—a classy black skirt that hugged my curves but wasn't so tight that it gave the wrong impression, with a sheer pale ecru blouse that came with a camisole. Over this I wore a fitted DK dark blue jacket that flared in at the waist. This little item had cost me dearly but it was worth it. I pulled on pantyhose and then stuffed my feet into the heels I'd bought to complete the look of what? Wealth? I hadn't worn heels this high since my high-school prom.

Dressing like this reminded me of my time in New York. I was a year out of college and working at a publishing house in New York when my mother disappeared. I'd begun to hate the rat race of the city and had just found out that in order to move forward in my career I would need to get an MBA, a prospect that did not interest me in the least. My degree was in English and I'd hoped to become an editor. When I thought about it now the timing seemed serendipitous, as though my mother had planned it all in order to provide me with the shop.

I breathed out a long sigh, glad that those days were over. If I hadn't inherited the shop I'd probably still be here fighting traffic and dealing with the crazy pace of the city. I much preferred running a shop in Ames and being able to wear loose fitting Indian shirts, casual jeans and skirts to work. And there was no one telling me what to do since I was the owner and the boss.

I had used hot curlers in my hair for the first time in years and now tried to brush it into some semblance of a hairstyle, realizing after a few minutes that it was hopeless. Finally I pinned my hair up and applied the bright lipstick I'd found in Agnes's car. I stared at the stranger in the mirror making a little moue with my new red mouth.

Once in the car I wended my way through backstreets following the bossy voice of the GPS and trying to avoid the major thoroughfares still packed with morning traffic. I knew this part of the city since the publishers I worked for were just two blocks over but I didn't trust myself to remember the ins and outs of it all. Not surprising, I couldn't find a parking place anywhere close to the east mid-town glass fronted high-rise and finally pulled into a parking lot a half-mile away. When the attendant told me how much the hourly cost was I nearly fainted. Prices had doubled in my absence.

I headed down the sidewalk toward the heart of the financial district, trying to keep from tripping or stumbling or simply twisting an ankle. And the mincing steps I had to take to avoid ripping the seams of the form fitting skirt didn't help the problem. By the time I reached East Fifty-Sixth Street my feet were killing me, my thighs burning and I had begun to sweat. But there was nothing to do about it.

Before I had time to practice what to say I was standing in front of the building that housed Jacob and Elliot. I took a deep breath and let it out slowly before pushing open the heavy glass door.

As soon as I entered the office I felt small and insignificant. Was this the effect they were going for when they constructed the high molded ceilings and paneled the walls with heavy mahogany and placed gigantic ornate mirrors here and there? I tried to maintain some semblance of dignity (which was in short supply for me even on a good day) and walked up to the desk. I put on what I hoped was a haughty expression and introduced myself to the immaculately dressed blonde woman sitting there.

"I'm Theresa Manning and I'm here to speak with the lawyer assigned to the Serena Weatherby estate. "

"Do you have an appointment?"

"No, but I'm sure he'll want to see me."

"Well, actually he is a she and Ms. Elliot is very busy this morning." The woman smiled revealing blindingly white teeth.

"I think she'll want to see me since I have a claim on the estate."

The woman stared at me and then picked up a phone and pressed a button. I couldn't hear what she was saying but I figured it went something like: 'There's a weird woman out here who claims to be involved in the Weatherby case. What should I do with her?'

She hung up the phone and stood. "Come with me," she commanded, heading quickly toward a closed door on her spike heels. I marveled at her poise.

She opened the door and ushered me inside the lushly appointed room. Soft muted gray-brown carpet cushioned my shoes as I made my way across what seemed an endless expanse of open space. The walls were dark like the reception room but instead of mirrors, artwork lined the walls—vaguely familiar landscapes and still lifes done in oils. Maybe they were originals.

"Miss Manning, won't you take a seat?" The impeccably dressed woman in her early fifties pointed to one of two heavy mahogany chairs facing her wide desk. What was with all the mahogany?

I did as I was told, seating myself in the chair on the right. I tried to cross my legs but gave up when my skirt rebelled. I took in her tweed suit, the understated gold cuffs clamped at her earlobes. Her smooth salt and pepper hair came to her chin and was perfectly waved. She wore a large diamond and a wide band of gold on her left ring finger and on her right, an oversized ring in gold with a large emerald, several small diamonds surrounding it. Again, beautifully understated, but obviously extremely expensive. Butterflies fluttered through my stomach.

She folded her hands on the desk and leaned forward. "And what can I help you with today?"

The way she said the words put me instantly on the defensive. She was definitely good lawyer material. "I came because I had to insure my claim," I said in the strongest and most commanding voice I could muster. "You see I'm Serena Weatherby's daughter. She gave me up for adoption when I was five years old."

"Do you have proof of this?"

I tried to stop myself from fidgeting, clasping my hands together in my lap. "Um, no. I didn't realize I would have to have proof. My mother intended to leave me money. She told the couple who raised me. I have a letter from her if you'd like to see it." I pulled the forged document out of my bag and handed it across the desk.

Ms. Elliot took the letter and put on a pair of close-up glasses, perusing it carefully. I thought about the time I'd put into that letter, the pathos I'd dredged up and placed on my fake mother's guilty lips. It was full of apology and guaranteed that I would receive my share of money once she was no longer on the earth. The problem was the signature. If they had one on file this would never fly.

She handed the letter back regarding me impassively. "Anyone could come in here with a letter like this. Do you really think this holds water in the legal world of today?"

I let out my breath. At least she hadn't yet asked for my identification. "Can you at least check the will and see if I'm listed?"

She scoffed and shook her head. "You do have guts, I'll give you that. I don't know what you're after but as far as the will goes it's private. It's been read to those who have a claim and you, my dear, are not listed within those pages."

I finally got my legs crossed and then leaned forward. "Can you at least tell me if a woman named Lila McCloud is in the will and if she came for the reading?"

The woman's eyes widened fractionally. "Why would you think I'd reveal this information to you?" She stood abruptly, glowering down at me. "I think it's time for you to leave, Miss Manning, if that's your real name, which I doubt. I don't know what you're after but I should have listened to my better judgment before letting you in here."

Apparently I'd hit a nerve. She ushered me quickly out the door and closed it behind me. I didn't glance at the receptionist, imagining only too well the smug expression she had on her face. Instead I kept going toward the doors and exited with my head held high, walking crisply to the elevators. Once the elevator doors closed with me inside I slumped against one wall feeling a drop in energy as though I'd run several miles.

6

For some unknown reason I decided it was a good idea to head to a bar I knew near the financial district and order a stiff drink. And the worst part of it was it was barely noon. I sipped the Cosmo the bartender had recommended, feeling my nerves begin to settle. Why I ordered a second one was beyond my understanding. Maybe it was the kindness of the bartender, his flirtatious manner making me feel slightly better about myself. We did keep up a lively repartee for a while until other customers came in.

By the time I got back to the hotel room I was feeling the effects of lack of sleep, alcohol abuse and the let down of what I'd hoped would be a way to get my hands on the will. I should have known, I told myself sternly, but it didn't help. Around four o'clock I pulled out Agnes's phone and called my store.

"Well?"

"Didn't go well," I told her. "The only thing I can say is that I'm pretty sure my mother is a beneficiary."

"And how did you come to that conclusion?"

"When I mentioned the name Lila, Ms. Elliot's eyes widened."

"Widened eyes. So that's your proof?"

"Please, Agnes, give me a break. I'm exhausted and hung over."

"Hung over?"

"I started a bit early," I admitted.

There was a long silence and then Agnes asked, "When are you coming home?"

"Tomorrow morning."

"Good. I'll be glad to get out of here. This place is seriously weird and seems to be getting weirder."

"What do you mean?"

"Some guy came in this morning and introduced himself as Ephraim Weatherby—asked if I was Summer McCloud."

My heart sped up. "He must be related. What did he look like? What did he want?"

"After I told him my name he left."

"I need a family tree," I muttered, thinking about the box of papers in the trailer. "On second thought I'm getting out of here right now. I have stuff to do at home and if I have to work at the store I won't get the chance."

"Just make sure you return my phone."

"How late will you be up?"

"I don't go to bed until eleven. Why?"

"I'm coming by."

I packed up my little bag and stuffed in the clothes I'd worn today, replacing them with jeans and a sweatshirt. And then I went to check out.

"You look terrible."

I stared at my friend. "Just let me in, please. I've had a hard day."

Agnes moved aside and I went past her into my living room where I sank into an overstuffed chair. "Cutty?" I called out. He was in my lap a second later, licking my face as he wriggled happily.

"You have to move back now," Agnes said. "Cutty misses you and your life on the lam is definitely getting you nowhere."

"I will but tonight I have to go through that box of my mother's papers."

Agnes came over and sat down on the couch. "After seeing that letter I'd say that's a good idea. Someone was threatening your mom."

"I know but there was no date—it could be twenty years old."

"Did your mom keep a journal?"

"Not that I know of but she obviously felt it was important to save those papers. Maybe she hoped I'd go through them some day. I'm interested in this Ephraim guy. He could be the murderer."

"Why would you say that? He seemed like a perfectly harmless older man."

"How old?"

"How do I know? Maybe seventy?"

"If Serena and my mother killed his brother he had a motive to kill Serena. I wonder what he wants with me?"

"I told him you'd be in the store tomorrow."

I leaned back and closed my eyes. "Oh great. Now I have to field a murderer who might want to kill me too."

"You're being melodramatic, Summer. If he did do it why would he want to draw attention to himself by killing you?"

I sighed and pushed myself up. "I guess you're right. I've got to get back to the trailer. If I stay here much longer I'm sleeping on the couch. Oh, here's your phone," I said, holding it out. "I almost forgot to give it back."

Agne laughed. "The entire reason you came by."

"There was also Cutty," I said, reaching down to fondle his ears. "I'll be back home tomorrow," I crooned in my best doggie-loving voice. "Thanks for everything, Agnes. I think it's safe for me to use my phone again so I'll give you a call as soon as I learn anything new."

Agnes smiled and reached for me, giving me a warm hug. "Be careful," she said again. "And let me know if you find any other clues in that box."

"Sounds like you might be catching the sleuthing bug," I smiled, heading out the door.

I walked the distance back to the Airstream in the dark, hoping this wasn't the night I'd be stabbed or shot. When I finally reached the trailer the door had been jimmied and when I hurried inside the box of papers was gone. And I was sure I could smell my mother's distinctive perfume lingering in the air.

7

I could barely sleep that night after trying unsuccessfully to latch my door. I finally jury-rigged a bungee cord and pulled out my mother's old baseball bat, placing it next to me on the bed. Whoever had taken that box could be lurking around just waiting for a chance to kill me. I thought of Ephraim wondering what motive he might have for taking my mother's papers. But how could he have known about the trailer or about the box? In the wee hours I thought again of the whiff of my mother's scent, dismissing it as impossible, but by the time I woke in the morning I wasn't so sure.

After making the strongest tea I could choke down I pondered things. That box had been taken by one of three people: Agnes, who I knew hadn't done it, Jerry, who would have had more finesse when he broke in, or my mother. And if it was my mother she was trying to hide something. I just hoped it wasn't her guilt.

I wolfed down a cracker with peanut butter, dressed and then stuffed everything of value into my backpack before heading to the store. On the walk to Tarot and Tea I called Jerry on my cell.

"What did you find out in New York?" he asked.

I could hear him chewing and knew he hadn't left home yet. I had the strongest urge to go over to his house just to feel his arms around me again, but from his tone I had a feeling he wasn't in a caring mood. "Not much except I think my mother is named in the will."

"Did the lawyer tell you that?"

I decided to skip the widened eyes explanation. "Not in so many words but her body language gave it away."

Jerry was quiet for a second or two and I heard the clatter of dishes. "I didn't think anything would come of talking to the lawyer. Are you planning to leave it alone now?"

"Jerry, you didn't break into my trailer did you?"

"Break in…? No, of course not. Are you telling me someone did?"

"I…well, yes, someone did and they took my mother's box of papers."

I heard the sink water come on. "You didn't tell me anything about a box of papers."

"I'm sorry. I kind of forgot about it with everything that's been happening. I found a letter addressed to my mom but other than that I didn't get a chance to look through it."

"What did the letter say and who wrote it?"

"It was from someone named Vivienne and she threatened my mom. And there was no date."

Jerry was quiet for a few seconds before asking, "What does your intuition tell you?"

"Since when do you believe in my intuition?"

I heard a sigh before he said, "You've been having visions, Summer, I just wondered if you'd had one about this."

"Sorry, no. I've narrowed the break-in down to my mom. But the way she felt about this trailer makes me wonder about the lock being broken like that."

"If a person is desperate they'll do whatever they have to do. Obviously there was something incriminating in there."

I felt like kicking myself for not moving that box somewhere safe. "I don't like what you're implying, Jerry."

"Who else knew about the trailer, Summer? You have to face facts."

Heat rose into my cheeks. If Jerry had been standing in front of me I might have slapped him. "I'm going home tonight," I told him, anxious to get off the phone.

"Good. I hate to think of you out there. It's not a safe area."

"Now you tell me. Why didn't you speak up the other day?"

I could almost see him shaking his head. "Do you have any idea how stubborn you are? If I'd mentioned something like that you'd have dug your heels in even further."

I looked up at my storefront and shifted the phone so I could get into my purse to retrieve my keys. "One more thing--Jonathon Weatherby's brother came by the store yesterday asking for me. If he comes today do you want me to call you?"

"Yes. And try and keep him there until I can get there."

I rang off and opened the door, breathing in the familiar incense and spice scents that lingered in the store. But another aroma was mixed in with the others and I recognized the *L'Occitane Rose et Reines* perfume. I stopped dead in the doorway, peering into the dark corners. Tabby meowed and rubbed up against my leg, startling me. Hadn't I impressed upon Agnes how important it was to leave him in the back room? I headed toward the back wondering if my mother was sitting at the little table with a cup of tea, but when I pushed open the door there was no one there.

On the table was a square of paper that read, My darling girl, I had to let you know that I am among the living. It won't be long now.

I read and reread the note, holding it up to my nose and turning it over and over in my hands. I felt hot and then cold all over. My mother was alive. Tears filled my eyes. When I heard the chime of the bell and looked up at the clock I realized I'd been standing in the back room for nearly twenty minutes. The lights in the store were still off and I had done nothing to prepare. I hurried into the front to see Mrs. Browning frowning at me from the doorway.

"Come in," I invited, smiling. "I got in a bit late today. How did Agnes do in my absence?"

"She isn't you, dear, but then again, you're not your mother, are you?"

"Why did you say that?" I asked sharply, adrenaline shooting through my veins.

"Say what, dear? I was merely trying to make the point that we don't always have exactly what we wish but in the long run it all works out for the best."

I thought of the Rolling Stones song, *You can't always get what you want*, feeling a strong urge to share the note with her. "I'm sorry, Mrs. Browning. It's been a difficult few days." I turned on the lights and closed the door behind her.

"Have you been cleared of the murder yet?"

I turned from where I headed toward the register. "I…yes, I've been cleared."

"Glad to hear it," Mrs. Browning said as though discussing the price of milk. Without another word she headed toward the shelves.

I checked the register trying to discover how many sales Agnes had made but my mind refused to go any further than my mother's note. My mother was here-- close by. And the note said it wouldn't be long now. What was she waiting for?

I looked at my e-mail orders and jotted them down to fill later. In the meantime several other customers came in. I made a few sales, ringing them up in a daze. No one seemed to notice my lack of attention or the blank stares I must be giving everybody. By eleven the store had cleared out some and when the door opened emitting a tall older man I knew exactly who it was. He came straight toward me where I stood behind the counter.

"Are you Summer McCloud?"

I nodded. "You must be Ephraim Weatherby."

"Yes, I am. Do you know why I'm here?"

"Could you wait one second, Mr. Weatherby? My phone is on vibrate and I have to answer this. It's a supplier," I lied.

I headed toward the back of the store as I punched in Jerry's private line. "He's here," I whispered when Jerry answered. And then I hung up and headed back to the front. But when I got there Ephraim Weatherby was gone.

Jerry arrived ten minutes later, his face red as though he'd been running. "Where is he?" he asked, his gaze searching the store.

"I guess I scared him off when I called you."

"What did he say?"

I shook my head. "Nothing. He only asked if I knew why he was here."

"Did you?"

"Maybe he wanted to talk to me about his sister-in-law's death or about the child? I have no idea."

"You look kind of pale, Summer. What else is happening?"

I opened my mouth and closed it. How did this man know me so well? Did I trust him enough to tell him about the note from my mother? Absolutely not, my little voice shouted inside my head. "I'm fine. Just tired, that's all."

"If he shows again let me know," he said, turning toward the door. "Maybe I'll drop by your house when you get home from work."

"Jerry, I don't know if…" But by that time the door had closed behind him.

There was no one in the store now and so I hurried into the back to get a snack of some kind. I picked up a handful of nuts and an apple. When I went into the front Ephraim Weatherby was standing in the doorway, and the expression on his face was anything but pleasant.

"You called the cops," he said in a low tone. "Why would you do that?"

My nerves ratcheted up. "I didn't call them. Jerry is a friend of mine and drops by from time to time."

"I believe that like I believe there's no global warming."

At least he was an environmentalist, I thought desultorily. Maybe I would die at the hands of someone who actually cared about global climate change. I chuckled.

"What's funny?"

"On, nothing. Just how ironic everything is. So tell me what you want from me?"

"I want to know if you spoke to Serena before she died."

"She was in the store and bought a book. But that's the extent of it. Why?"

"Did you know your mother and Serena were in a coven together?"

I headed toward the counter that held the register, hoping the thick wood would absorb the bullet before it reached my body. "I could have guessed since they were best friends."

"How did you discover the friendship?"

"I have visions now and again. I saw them together in one of them."

Ephraim smiled. "So no direct knowledge then."

"I think I remember her from when I was a little girl. Why are you asking me these questions?" I had begun to shake, another weakness of mine when I got stressed.

"Your mother has some personal papers of mine. Would you happen to know where they are? I can rip this place apart if you don't tell me."

I stared at him. "There's nothing here at the store. I did have a box of my mother's papers but someone stole them."

Ephraim watched me from under bushy gray eyebrows. He reminded me of a bird of prey with his hooked nose and hooded eyes. He looked dangerous but there was also something familiar about him.

"Do you expect me to believe you?" he asked, advancing on me as he reached into his pocket. I flinched then, sure it was a gun and that in a minute I would be lying dead on the floor.

At that moment the door burst open and Jerry ran in, his weapon brandished. "Get on the floor!" he shouted.

A shot rang out rendering me unable to hear. I was on all fours crawling for safety when I heard another muffled shot. When I turned Jerry was falling backward as if in slow motion, his face contorted in pain. Ephraim's baffled gaze met mine, a gun in his hand. He turned and limped toward the door.

I crawled toward Jerry who was lying on his back with his eyes closed, a dark stain spreading across his shirt near his left shoulder. I stood dizzily and ran to call 911. "Cop has been shot!" I yelled into the phone before giving them the address.

I kneeled next to him trying to stop the bleeding until the EMT's arrived and then I locked up the store and rode with Jerry in the ambulance, my hand clasping his. His eyes remained closed except for once when they met mine. He seemed like he wanted to say something but couldn't get the words out. When we got to the emergency room he was whisked away. I stayed in the waiting room for two hours before someone had the courtesy to tell me what was happening.

"He's going to be fine," the doctor told me. "We got the bullet out. Luckily it didn't hit anything vital. He'll be sore for quite a while though. What worries me more is the head injury. He needs to be monitored for concussion for a day or two. Would you like to see him?"

I nodded, following him down a long hallway and into a darkened room. Jerry had his eyes closed but as soon as I walked over to the bed he opened them. I took hold of his hand. "Doc says you're ok," I told him, trying to smile.

"That bastard got away."

"Don't worry about that now. You need to concentrate on healing."

"He's the one, Summer. He killed Serena."

"How do you know that? It seems weird that he'd

risk it all to come and talk to me."

"He had a gun and he could have shot you." Jerry winced and relaxed back against the pillow. "I'm just glad you're all right." He squeezed my hand and looked up at me with his sad puppy-dog expression, melting my heart.

I bent over him and kissed him lightly on the lips.

"Visiting hours are over," the perky nurse said, arriving in the room. "You can come back tomorrow. "

"I'll be out of here by then," I heard Jerry mutter as I walked out the door.

"Jerry got shot?" Agnes sounded frantic on the other end of the phone. I was headed back to the store to make sure the cat was in the back and to pick up my mother's note.

"He's fine, Agnes. He's in room 213."

"I was alone with that dude yesterday. I had no idea he was dangerous!"

"I don't think he's dangerous by nature. He wanted something that I didn't have."

"What did he want?"

"My mother's papers. But they were stolen while I was in New York."

"Summer, this entire thing is getting out of hand. I don't think you should be alone and especially with Jerry in the hospital. I'm coming over. Do you own a gun?"

"No! I don't have a gun. I don't need a gun. Stop freaking out."

"Don't go back to the store. If I were you I'd close it for a while. Is there blood on the carpet? Did Ephraim get shot too?"

"I don't know but I have to check on the cat and

make sure he's locked up. I'll see you in an hour or so."

"I'm coming to pick you up," she announced before she clicked off.

I entered the store warily wondering if my mother had returned. I checked around for blood but apparently none of it had made it to the worn Persian carpet next to the desk and counter. I was glad of that at least. In the back I folded the note and stuck it in my bag before making sure the cat had food and water. "Sorry, Tabby. I promise I'll be back early tomorrow." I rubbed him until he began to purr and then I left the room and closed the door. I checked everything over before I went out the front door, making sure to lock it. I had just put the keys in my bag when Agnes rolled down the street at the wheel of her Honda.

I climbed into the passenger side. "Thanks for this. I've done a lot of walking today."

"I didn't go see Jerry. I thought it might be awkward since…"

"Since what?" I asked, staring at her.

"Well, you know. He seems interested in you and I don't want to get in the middle of it."

"Agnes, you're his friend and I'm his friend. How awkward can that be?"

"You know what I mean."

"No, I really don't. But I have something you might be interested in," I said, pulling the note out of my bag. "I found this in the store earlier today. It's from my mother."

The car swerved sideways as Agnes tried to get a look at it.

"Be careful! I'll read it to you." Once I finished Agnes didn't say a word. It was a full minute later that she turned to me. "What does she mean 'it won't be long now'?"

I shrugged. "I have no idea but I figure it won't be long until I find out."

Agnes laughed and pulled the car to a stop in front of my house and cut the motor. "How can you be so calm?"

"I may appear calm but inside I'm running in circles. I would love to have a glass of wine tonight."

"Your drinking is beginning to concern me," Agnes said, looking me up and down. And then she grinned.

I tried to smile. "Something about the events of the past few weeks has changed everything. Maybe the next time Jerry and I go out to dinner…"

"So there is something going on."

"I didn't say that! I just thought I might take him out once he's better—you know, to thank him for possibly saving my life?" I shook my head and climbed out of the car, heading toward my front door.

Behind me I heard Agnes lock the car, her footsteps hurrying behind me. "Do you have wine?" she called out. "Because if not, I can run by my house and pick some up."

A half hour later after making a quick trip to her house, Agnes handed me a full glass of wine and poured one for herself. Cutty lay on the couch between us, snuggled against the pillows. Mischief looked like an Egyptian statue on top of the refrigerator, her haughty demeanor indicating she was still put out by my absence. I was sure she'd forgive me by bedtime and lie next to me in her usual spot. It was so nice to be home.

"Did being in New York make you miss it?" Agnes asked.

"Not at all. I had a tiny apartment and my job…well, I told you what they expected of me." I shook my head. "It was kind of weird that my mother disappeared right when I had to make a decision.

Agnes raised her eyebrows. "Like maybe she disappeared for you?"

I shrugged. "Mom knew all about what I was going through. I talked to her nearly every day."

"What did she advise?"

"She never gave me advice, just listened and encouraged me to find my own way. Tarot and Tea always felt like my home away from home. It was easy to slip into the role. But my mother being gone was really hard for me."

I thought about Lila's ability to make people laugh and how she taught me to stock shelves and talk with customers. She even read my palm a couple of times telling me things that were hard for me to believe at fourteen. "You will solve crimes, Summer. And I see a very handsome man in your future." My mom slanted a gaze at my face and then shook her head. "You're too young to understand but we can do this again in a couple of years."

I loved that part of my life with her. But then there were the times when she'd been drinking. I looked over at Agnes. "When I was a teenager she was sometimes drunk and I had to take over."

Agnes looked down. "I remember those days. You didn't talk about it directly but I knew something was off. You never confided in me. I thought you'd decided we were no longer friends or something."

"I tend to go inward when I'm upset, Agnes. You're more of an extrovert and might not understand the tendency. What about your career?"

Agnes swiveled to look at me. "Do you mean my foray into the world of law?"

"That's the one. Do you miss it?"

Agnes scoffed. "I never would have made it through law school. I'm much better suited to painting and growing things and selling beautiful art and flowers. I'm an artist at heart. I can't even remember why I tried in the first place."

Agnes worked at Flowers and Frills, a gift shop that catered to the wealthier segment of town. People flocked to the store partly because of Agnes and her *avant- garde* appearance as well as her ability to sell them exactly what they wanted. Mabel, the owner, a woman in her sixties, adored Agnes and treated her like a daughter.

"I'm glad we're both doing what we want to do now instead of following someone else's dream."

"What happens if your mother comes back?"

I felt a little jolt in my heart region when I tried to imagine being ousted from the job I loved. Could the two of us get along well enough to share? "I don't know. It would be hard for me to turn the reins over now. Maybe Mom could do readings—the customers would love having her back."

"Good plan but I hope for your sake she's down with it. She's never been one to sit on the sidelines." Agnes picked up the bottle and poured herself another glass, leaning back before taking a sip.

I was contemplating her words when my cell phone rang. I didn't recognize the caller I.D. but something told me to answer it anyway.

"Is this Summer McCloud?" a raspy male voice asked.

"Yes. Who is this?"

"You don't need to know who I am. I know who murdered Serena."

"Who?" I asked stupidly.

"You'll need to do more than ask to get that information. I think it's worth some money, don't you?"

"Well, I don't have any, so…"

"Nothing in the bank? I think you do, Summer. Why don't you think about how much it's worth to you to clear your mother's name."

"Wait--what?" But the caller had hung up. A chill went down my spine.

Agnes raised her eyebrows in question.

"I think that might have been the man who murdered Serena."

"What did he want?"

"He wants me to pay him for information. And he knows about my savings account. I'd call Jerry if he wasn't in the hospital."

"He has a phone in his room."

It was my turn to stare. "I thought you said you didn't visit him."

Agnes actually blushed. "I lied. I didn't want to upset you."

'Why would I be upset?"

"I…I wasn't sure how you'd feel about it."

"Are you interested in him?"

"Not really and besides, the only person he talked about was you."

Agnes folded her arms across her middle and sat up straight, regarding me from her dark lined eyes like some kind of genie. All she needed was a turban to complete the exotic impression. Maybe I should hire her to do readings at the store. "Do you have the number?"

"Just call the hospital and ask for room 213."

I laughed to myself remembering telling her his room number.

"He left this morning," the nurse told me when I called. Jerry had told me he wasn't staying long but I certainly thought they might keep him for more than a day after being shot and operated on. I dialed Jerry's private number, surprised when he answered. I'd thought he'd be in bed asleep.

"Summer, are you okay?"

"Me? Why wouldn't I be? Why aren't you still in the hospital?" I heard my defensive tone, questioning him as though I was his mother instead of expressing concern for his wellbeing. There was silence on the other end. "Are you still there?" I asked.

"I'm here but I'm wondering what's going on with you."

"I don't really know except someone just called and basically blackmailed me into paying money to find out who killed Serena."

"What? I knew something was going on."

"Are you psychic now?"

Jerry laughed. "I have my moments, especially concerning you. Tell me what happened."

After I relayed the conversation Jerry said, "Who would know you have a savings account?"

"I have no idea. Maybe it was just a lucky guess. The account was set up by my mother and I took it over after she disappeared."

"How much are we talking about?"

"Ten thousand give or take?"

"And why isn't it invested?"

I sighed. The account had been a source of irritation ever since my mother's death. I didn't know what to do with the cash and didn't have the time or the inclination to pay someone to help me with it. "I haven't felt like doing anything about it. But back to your other question—someone who knew my mother might know about the account."

"Any man friends you can think of?"

I scanned into the past. "There were lots of men, Jerry. I think she had a pretty healthy sex life. But I do remember one in particular. I got the feeling they knew each other from a long time before. I heard them arguing but I never paid much attention."

"Come into the station tomorrow morning and we'll go through a sketch artist. This could be important."

Before I could say good-bye Jerry had hung up.

For one crazy moment I had the feeling that the man on the phone was my missing father. It could explain his knowledge of my bank account. Damn. I was sure that missing box of papers held every piece of information I needed.

I turned back to Agnes who was obviously waiting for an explanation. After telling her what Jerry had said we polished off the bottle of wine. Before she left we hugged and then her worried gaze met mine.

"Please be careful, Summer. And don't leave your door unlocked like you usually do. I'm glad Jerry knows about this."

"I'll be fine," I told her, but inside I was shaking.

8

"Can you remember how he wore his hair? Was it brown or blonde? Face shape?"

I was sitting at Jerry's desk at the police station in front of the sketch artist, Jerry throwing questions at me, one after the other. "It was a long time ago. His hair was brown, I think, and maybe he had hazel eyes?"

Jerry pulled opened a book of mug shots and handed it to me. "Check through these and see if anyone jumps out. They go back a lot of years."

I scanned through it as the sketch artist tried to make sense of my meager descriptions. I was moving rapidly from page to page when I saw him. "Jerry, this is the guy—this is the man who used to come around!" I pointed at the picture of a man in his thirties or thereabouts. He was good-looking in a gangster sort of way, with thick brown hair that fell over his wide forehead and a mustache. He actually looked a little like a younger version of Tom Selleck. His eyes were wide apart and intelligent and even though it was a black and white photo I thought they were hazel. He was frowning in the picture but there were laugh lines around the edges of his eyes.

Jerry leaned over my shoulder. "Jesus, Summer. You look like him."

"I do?" I looked more closely suddenly noticing what he was talking about. It was mostly the shape of the eyes and the wide forehead. "Who is he?"

Jerry glanced at me. "You mean besides being your father?" He bent to check the name. "It says here his name is Frank Messer. Does that strike a chord?"

"No. I never heard my mother mention that name."

"Well, if he isn't your father I'll eat my hat."

I laughed. "Which hat are we talking about? The cop's hat or the baseball cap you wear?"

Jerry ignored me, reading through the info next to Frank Messer's name. "Says here he was wanted for armed robbery and assault. He did time, Summer."

Jerry looked at me as though this news would be upsetting but I never met the man.

"He was released six months ago after doing twenty years," he continued. "The prison is in upstate New York."

"That would explain why my mother intimated he was dead. Do you think he killed Serena?"

"What motive would he have?"

"I don't know. Maybe he was trying to protect my mother for some reason."

"I wish she would come forward," Jerry said, letting out a sigh. "And I'm sure you do too."

"About that…" Before I could tell him about my mom's note someone called to him from a desk toward the front and he hurried away.

"Guess you don't need me anymore," the sketch artist said, putting away his things.

"I suppose not, but thanks anyway."

"No problem. It gives me a chance to use my skills." The lanky young man smiled and then walked away toward the front of the station.

I looked down at the mug shot, my mind wandering

into the past. Did I remember this man or was I imagining things? Were he and my mother still involved? Maybe the arguing was because of his criminal behavior. I could easily see him with my mother with his good looks and devil-may–care expression. Maybe I'd meet him after all. And then I thought of the raspy voice, the nasty way the man on the phone had spoken to me. Could a father talk to a daughter like that? Jerry's voice brought me out of my little reverie.

"Let's get you out of here. How about some lunch? I'll treat."

"Sure," I answered. "Italian?"

"Yes, and I'm planning to imbibe."

"At lunch?" I stared at him, shocked. Jerry was a stickler for not drinking on the job.

He grinned. "I'm still on medical leave and it's been a difficult few days." He pointed toward his left arm, which was in a sling due to the shoulder injury. "I thought we could both use a moment to relax," he continued. "And besides it's getting close to three o'clock. I'm hungry." He reached down and hauled me to my feet and I followed him out of the precinct. "I have a few things I want to discuss," he said cryptically, opening the passenger door to let me in.

I sipped my wine, watching Jerry shovel pasta into his mouth. It was like the man was starving. And maybe he was after being in the hospital and having nothing good to eat for a couple of days. I took a bite of my ravioli and waited for him to bring up whatever was on his mind. So far he hadn't said more than two words. A minute later I got my wish.

"So, Summer, what do you think we should do

next?"

The question was so ambiguous I wasn't sure how to answer. Was he talking about us, or the murder case, or what? "Um…are you talking about Frank Messer?"

Jerry took a sip of wine and placed his glass on the red and white-checkered tablecloth. "Your mother and Frank is what I was referring to. If they're together we need to find them. Any ideas?"

"You, an accomplished detective, are asking me for advice?"

He raised one eyebrow and cocked his head to the side. "I'm beginning to have faith in your little voice."

"Really. Hmm. I highly doubt that, knowing you as I do, but in answer to your question, my mother left a note for me at the store. She's definitely around."

He frowned. "Why haven't you shared this?"

"I didn't have a chance before now. My concern is who threatened me. Could that have been Frank? Because I have a hard time believing he would act like that to his own flesh and blood."

"You don't know anything about him, Summer. Talking to your mother is the best way of finding out about Frank. Tell me about this note."

"All it said was it wouldn't be long now."

"Before you see her?"

I nodded, washing down my pasta with a sip of red wine.

"Where would your mom go if she was here and trying to stay out of sight?"

I didn't have to think about it. "The trailer."

"Do you mind if we take a ride over there after lunch?"

Once we reached the trailer I watched in horror as Jerry unholstered his gun. He gestured for me to stay in the car as he climbed out and approached the Airstream at a crouch. He flung the door open and disappeared inside, his head appearing a minute later. "She's not here!" he called.

I hurried out of the car joining him in the trailer. There was a sheaf of papers on the little built in table and when I picked them up I realized it was a copy of Serena's will. "Look at this!" I handed it to Jerry who took it and flipped through the pages.

"Look's identical to the one we have at the station."

He folded it and would have put it in his pocket if I hadn't grabbed it back. "This is my copy and I plan to read it through very carefully."

We pulled the trailer door shut as best we could and got back in Jerry's car.

"How 'bout we go over to my house. That way I can make us coffee and we can talk without being overheard."

I gazed at him trying to discern his expression. There was something behind his words that didn't seem about my mother or the case. "What do you have in mind?"

Jerry shrugged. "Just thought we could talk a bit. It feels like we've been skirting around whatever is going on between us."

"This murder has kind of taken precedence, Jerry."

His eyebrows pulled together. "You're telling *me* this?" He turned the key in the ignition of his vintage Mercedes sedan, shifted and pulled away from the Airstream.

"I didn't mean to embarrass you. I thought we were just friends."

Jerry cheeks turned red. "I'm not embarrassed, only disappointed. "Okay, maybe I'm a little embarrassed. I thought women liked to talk."

"I'd like to spend more time with you. Maybe a bit more warning next time?"

"So yes or no on the espresso?" he asked, slowing down. The turn to his house was about five hundred yards ahead.

"Espresso?" I laughed. "Yes."

Our eyes met and when I saw his expression something shifted in my chest. Yes, I was very attracted to him but it seemed like this whole wooing thing was coming out of left field. "What's with you today? It seems like you're thinking something but not telling me what it is. I've been caught up in this stuff about my mom so maybe I'm not reading minds as clearly as usual." I grinned but Jerry didn't react to my lame attempt at humor.

"You're right," he finally said. "I've been thinking about us and what the next step might be."

"I'm attracted to you, Jerry, but it's hard to think about that right now. Can we take it slow?"

He met my gaze before pressing down on the gas. We made the next left turn and roared away in a cloud of black smoke that I decided not to mention.

His sixties brick ranch style house was in a neighborhood of newer houses on large lots a few miles from the main business district. I liked the low-slung look of it. In the sunken living room off-white wool carpeting contrasted nicely with Jerry's black furniture and leather couch and chair. A large flat-screen TV took up one wall and several abstract paintings in bright colors lined the wall next to it. At the end of the room was a fireplace without a mantel. It all had a very masculine feel.

Jerry made cappuccinos while I sat down on the couch to read through the document. Merrily Weatherby would inherit with my mother listed as a secondary beneficiary. If my mother and Merrily were both gone the bequest shifted to my mother's first born, Randall, my brother. What? I looked up but Jerry was still in the kitchen steaming milk. I read on.

Apparently Serena had supplied Merrily's foster parents with money over the years. Jerry came into the living room and held out a cup before sitting next to me.

"I'm sure Jonathon was none too happy with this child having his last name," I said, taking a sip.

"We discussed this before. He could have adopted her, you know."

"Did you see that Randall is a beneficiary?"

Jerry nodded. "In the case of your mom's death, yes. He's the male progenitor."

"Has he been contacted?"

"How would I know? It's up to the lawyers to do that. It takes a long time for an estate to be settled, especially when there's a question about who's alive and who isn't. I'm sure a private eye has been hired to find the daughter."

I kept on reading but there wasn't much more to read. Jonathon had left everything to his wife and with a few small exceptions, Serena had left it all to her daughter. No wonder Jonathon's children were pissed off. "Do you think Jonathon's children can contest it?"

Jerry shrugged using his one good shoulder. "If I were them I'd try. I'm sure Jonathon intended to leave them something. Wish we could have seen the previous will, the one Jonathon changed just weeks before his death."

"How do you know about that?"

"Jonathon's children mentioned it."

"Seems kind of suspicious, doesn't it?"

"Happens all the time when there's a new wife on the scene."

I looked down at the document. "My mother's address is listed as the shop. I wonder why?"

"Maybe she's moving around and doesn't have a permanent address."

"What about Frank? If he's the one who threatened me he's not a nice man."

"Nice? He did twenty years for assault and armed robbery."

"Yeah, but to treat your daughter like that is another matter altogether."

Jerry let out a bark of laughter. "You're funny, Summer. You really think a criminal would care about a daughter he doesn't even know? When you hear from him again I want you to set up a meeting."

"*If* I hear from him again."

"You'll hear from him. Greedy bastards don't give up easily."

I put the will down and we chatted about this and that for a while until Jerry put his arm around my shoulders and pulled me close. Just as he was leaning in for the kiss my phone rang, startling both of us.

"Perfect timing," he muttered.

I recognized the number, put it on speaker and answered. "How much do you want?" I asked before the caller had time to say anything.

There was a heavy sigh and then a voice rasped, "All of it."

"Are you insane?"

"Get's your dear mother off the hook, doesn't it? And what about your possible guilt?"

"They decided I didn't do it. Who is this? Is your name Frank Messer?"

"Put the money in an envelope and leave it in the park on the bench in front of the oak tree at midnight and don't bring along your boyfriend."

"It's too late for me to withdraw that much money!"

There was a pause before he said, "Tomorrow night then, and everything I told you still applies."

Something about the inflection struck a chord, but I couldn't place what it was.

"Damn," Jerry said. "I'm going to call the station and try and trace that number. As far as you meeting this creep alone tomorrow night, it ain't gonna happen."

"Do you think I'd go alone? I have no idea who this guy is but he seems to know all about me."

"I'm betting on Frank Messer. Who else would know your mother and all about your bank account? This guy is watching you and that freaks me out. I want you to stay here until we catch him."

"Here?"

"And don't worry," he said as though reading my thoughts. "I promise to be a perfect gentleman. I have a guest room."

I let out the breath I'd been holding. "I'll have to pick up my stuff from the cottage. Can I bring Cutty?"

"Sure, why not? The yard is fenced."

"I hope this is over soon. My nervous system isn't going to take much more of it." I held out my hand that was shaking, my eyes meeting his.

Jerry took hold of my fingers and pulled me toward

him, leaning in for the kiss that had been interrupted. I had no trouble kissing him back and when his one good arm came around me I melted into the embrace.

Jerry was as good as his word, letting me go after our one very long kiss and pulling me to my feet. "Let's go get your things and your dog so you can settle in. You have work tomorrow and so do I and tomorrow night will be a long one."

He drove me to my house and came inside as I went through my closet to gather some clothes together. I pulled my bag down from the shelf and shoved things in, heading into the bathroom to grab my toothbrush. When I came back Jerry was sitting on my bed rubbing Cutty's ears.

"I like your little house."

I smiled. "Me too. If my mother is alive I hope she doesn't kick me out."

"You can always move in with me."

"What are you saying? We've barely begun to…"

Jerry shrugged and stood up. "I care about you Summer. I've felt this way for a while now."

"But moving in? That's kind of a drastic step, isn't it?"

"Just a suggestion for the short term. Don't freak out about it." He turned and headed out of the bedroom and I heard him open the front door.

I stood there holding my bag and trying to make sense of whatever was going on in his mind. One minute we were barely friends, a minute later we were kissing and now…moving in? I couldn't contemplate it right now. I turned off the bedroom light, called to Cutty and followed Jerry out the front door, locking it behind me.

Once we reached his house he showed me to the

guest room. I expected a kiss or a hug but he just said goodnight and headed into his bedroom. I was mildly disappointed but also aware that I was the one who had set the boundaries. I thought about the earlier kiss. I wanted to know if he'd felt the same intensity I had, but now it was too late unless I knocked on his door. And before I could question it that was exactly what I was doing.

Jerry's eyebrows were raised in question when he opened the door. "Are you okay?" I asked.

His mouth quirked. "What makes you ask?"

"Jerry, this isn't really very funny."

"No? So what did you expect, my princess--the royal carpets rolled out, music and fanfare because you let me kiss you once?"

"That isn't fair!"

"You're the one setting the rules."

"Do you want to discuss this or are you going to give me the silent treatment?"

"I'm not in the mood for talking." And then he closed the door in my face.

I was close to tears when I walked into the guest room. I barely registered the antique four-poster bed covered in an old-fashioned quilt. I didn't know much about Jerry or his family. When we'd gone out before we'd talked about how he decided to join the police force—because his father was a cop--and then mostly concentrated on the here and now. This was his house and these were his things and as I walked around the room picking up photos I began to get a new sense of him.

Many of these photos were taken when he was

younger: playing football, driving for the first time, or so it seemed from the thumbs up he was giving the photographer, birthdays with his large and loving family, a picture of Jerry and some girl next to a lake, Jerry smiling rakishly into the camera. What a cutie he'd been.

I had put on my P.J.s and was crawling into bed when I heard the quiet knock on the door. When I opened it Jerry was standing there in his boxers, his left arm cradled in the sling against his body. His upper body looked strong and muscular and I had to suppress an urge to place my hand on his chest.

"Just want to say I'm sorry," he said. "I know you've been stressed out. Now isn't the time to throw you a curve. But to be honest I do really like you, Summer, and I like having you here in my house."

I smiled and when he reached for me I hugged him back trying to be careful of his arm. "I'm sorry too," I told him. "Maybe after all this…"

He held up his hand. "I promise not to rush you. Goodnight." And with that he turned and disappeared into his room and closed the door.

Jerry was gone by the time I got up the next morning but he'd left a note explaining how to work the espresso machine and the microwave. He signed it *J* with a flourish and added a P.S. *I'll call if I find out anything about that phone number.*

I put Cutty in the fenced back yard a lot larger than mine, then made an espresso, glad that I didn't have to be at work as early as he did. As I sipped I wandered around his living room looking at the family photos I'd never noticed before. Apparently his family was enormous. From the gatherings it looked as though he had several sisters and a couple of brothers. Irish Catholic? I thought about my freewheeling mother, my lack of any kind of religious upbringing. I appreciated it but sometimes seeing photos like these made me long for something I couldn't name. I shook myself free of the encroaching maudlin mood and headed to the bathroom to take a shower.

I reached the store late after searching for an extra house key to Jerry's house for over an hour. I never found one and ended up leaving Cutty in the back yard with water and food and then locking the front door as I left.

As soon as I opened the register and checked on the cat I dialed Jerry's number.

"What's up?"

"I couldn't find a key so I left Cutty in the back."

"Sorry. I forgot to leave you one. I traced that number by the way. It's a throw-away phone."

"Too bad."

"Yup, but I figured as much. Did you manage okay with the espresso?"

"Yes, but I never would have without the instructions. Good coffee, by the way, but espresso doesn't seem very cop-like."

Jerry laughed. "Italian mother, what can I say? Got to run—see you later."

The phone clicked off suddenly as though he'd hung up on me. I had to remind myself that he was a cop and on the job.

It was a few minutes later that my brother Randall walked into the store.

"I thought you went home," I said, staring at him. He looked rumpled and unkempt, unusual for him.

"Did you hear that our mother might be alive?"

"I did hear that but I haven't seen her yet. She left me a note a couple of days ago."

Randall sighed, running nervous fingers through his very short hair. "Who saw her, Summer? I mean someone needs to have seen her for a rumor like this to start. Do you know where she is?"

I shook my head no and continued my opening procedure. There was something very odd about my brother's behavior. "Did you get everything done in town that you'd planned?"

"Everything except finding her."

I looked up noticing the haunted expression in his eyes. "What's going on, Randall?"

He started and then pulled himself together. "Nothing other than being shocked that Lila has come back to the living. But you don't seem that surprised."

"I've known for a couple of days. She's named in Serena Weatherby's will."

Randall frowned. "Really? How much money are we talking about?"

"I actually don't know. The money all goes to Serena's daughter but the wording suggests that if something happens to the daughter Lila will inherit her share."

"Serena. I remember that chick. She was a piece of work."

"You saw her when you were little?"

"Not that little. She and Mom were doing some weird shit back then."

"What were they doing?"

"Occult stuff—you know—magic and potions? A lot of strange people used to come and go. Listen, I've got to get going. If you see Mom tell her I need to talk to her."

He turned and headed to the door and before I could ask another question he was gone.

Randall had always been a mystery to me. When I was a little girl he constantly teased me and it wasn't the kind of teasing that you knew was all in fun—no, this teasing was pure meanness like telling me I was stupid and ugly and that I may as well go drown myself now before I got any older. Right now I didn't trust him. And if he wasn't staying at my house where was he staying? He looked as though he'd slept in his clothes and this from a person who had always been fastidious to a fault.

The next person to arrive was a man I'd never seen before who looked a bit like Ephraim. I wondered if this was yet another brother of the dead man but then I realized I'd seen him around town for the last several months. He must just be new to the store. He looked to be in his early seventies, nicely dressed with a tweed jacket that hung from his gaunt shoulders as though he'd bought it when he was heavier.

"Tell me about these essential oils," he asked, his kind brown eyes on mine. "Is there one that is used for an aphrodisiac?"

I joined him by my display. "Jasmine is good and Frankincense and also sandalwood. If you'd like to smell them the ones in front are all samplers. They also come in blends." I didn't want to question him further on what he had in mind but I did want to explain that these would not act like Viagra. Before I could say anything he picked up all three and headed toward the counter to pay.

"You're Summer McCloud," he said, reaching into the back pocket of his gray trousers for his wallet. "I'm Douglas Weatherby. I knew your mother a very long time ago." He looked somewhat wistful, his gaze going into the distance. "She was a lovely woman and I have to say you take after her."

"Thank you," I answered, taking the money he held out. "Are you related to Jonathon Weatherby?"

"I'm his brother," he told me, smiling.

"I met your brother Ephraim the other day," I ventured, looking up.

"Ephraim? I don't have a brother by that name. I guess you're aware of my sister-in-law's death. One of the reasons she came to Ames was to see me."

"Really? She bought a book from me the day she was killed."

He nodded. "She was writing a book and needed research materials."

"Fiction or non-fiction?"

"It's a memoir--the story of her life."

He chuckled and then coughed, pulling a heavily starched blue handkerchief out of his breast pocket. I saw the DW stitched neatly in one corner. There was something old-worldly about this man.

"Have the police come up with any leads?" he asked me, replacing his handkerchief carefully.

"Nothing that sticks. The main thing I've heard is that she was a lot younger than she appeared."

Douglas gazed into the distance. "Serena was always dressing up to appear like someone she wasn't. She was an actress at heart--a fascinating woman. Did you know she was a prima ballerina?"

"No, I didn't. Do you think she killed your brother?" I blurted out before I could stop myself.

He looked stunned. "I know she was upset by Jonathon's proclivities but I highly doubt she murdered him. Serena and I were very close."

From how he said this and the way his eyes softened I thought they were probably more than close—more like lovers. Another puzzle piece slipped into place.

He replaced his wallet and then picked up his package. "Thank you, young lady. I wish your mother were still around. I would love to say hello."

I opened my mouth to tell him that she might be around soon but by that time he was gone, leaving me with more questions than answers. A snapshot of my mother, Serena and Douglas went through my mind— they were wearing bathing suits and on a beach together. They all looked very chummy. But I had to let it go when the bell chimed and two more customers came in.

I closed up the store during a lull at lunchtime and ran to the bank to at least pretend I was withdrawing money. I did take out five hundred dollars, which I placed in the official-looking envelope they provided me with.

There were two customers waiting to get in when I returned and I apologized for shutting the store, explaining that I had an errand to run that couldn't wait. They were regulars and didn't mind, chatting to one another as I unlocked the door and then heading into the shelves to peruse the new books I'd received this week.

By the time five o'clock rolled around I was feeling the effects of a restless night's sleep in an unfamiliar bed and the stress of worrying about Jerry, my missing mother and now Randall. The interlude with Douglas had been oddly refreshing for some reason, making me doubt my earlier assumption that Serena had killed Jonathon. I hoped that eventually I would find out the truth.

I closed up and walked the twelve blocks to Jerry's house knowing that tonight's sleep would be even worse. The route took me over the river and as I walked across the bridge I had a vision. Serena was walking along with a man and then suddenly fell forward to land in the mud. He did not bend down to help, only staring at her still body for a couple of seconds before jogging in the other direction. I came to myself with a gasp.

When I knocked on Jerry's front door he opened it quickly as though he'd been waiting for me. "Sorry about the key. I had one made for you today." He pointed toward the kitchen table where the brand new key lay shining under the light.

Cutty bounded off the couch and ran to greet me. "Thanks, Jerry, but I doubt I'll be here for long. I figure you'll arrest the killer tonight."

Jerry laughed. "Don't count your chickens. We have no idea what this guy is up to, only that he seems to know you pretty well. As far as catching him I don't like to make assumptions—things go awry when I do." He moved to the stove and stirred something in an iron frying pan. "Do you like spaghetti?"

"You know I do. Shall I make a salad?"

Jerry nodded turning back to fiddle with the knobs on the stove. "Salad makings are in the refrigerator."

During dinner I related my vision.

"You can't remember his face?"

"I never saw it. And if he's the killer he didn't do it then."

"The ME thinks she was poisoned earlier. But if your vision is accurate he's the guy. Who else would run away like that and not even try and help? He knew what was going on."

"You do realize this was a vision, right?"

Jerry gazed at me in silence and then shrugged, his mouth turning up at one corner. Did he believe in visions now? "How did Serena get poisoned?"

"That's the question."

I cleared the table and did the dishes as he put the food away. And then he went into the living room and turned on the television. I wasn't used to the noise and became more and more frazzled as the football game continued, the loud announcers droning on and the yells of the crowd. I tried to ignore it but by the time I had finished in the kitchen I was ready for quiet. "I think I'll go read," I said, coming over to the couch.

He leaned over the edge of the couch and grabbed my hand. "Do you want me to turn it off?"

"This is your house, do what you want. I'm just not used to the noise."

Jerry let me go and rose to switch off the T.V. "I'd much rather talk than watch the game. I don't like the Steelers anyway, and they're winning."

I sat down next to him feeling uncomfortable and tense. I wasn't sure what to talk about or where to put my hands or whether I wanted to pull my legs up under me or cross them. "I learned something new today," I began, turning toward him. "Jonathon had a brother named Douglas but Ephraim isn't his brother."

Jerry frowned. "How'd you figure that out?"

"Douglas came into the store this morning. I think he and Serena had an affair, and according to him she wasn't capable of killing Jonathon."

"Did he say he had an affair with her?"

"Not in so many words," I answered, feeling annoyed. "He said he loved her."

Jerry turned away and stared at the blank screen. "Maybe he's the man in your vision, the one who poisoned her sometime earlier."

"I don't think so. He's in his seventies and the man I saw in my vision was a lot younger."

"You can tell age in a vision?" Jerry laughed.

"Yes, as a matter of fact. What happened to beginning to trust my visions?"

Jerry shook his head his gaze going toward the floor. "I'm looking forward to having a long chat with Lila."

"She's still a suspect?"

"Maybe not for the murder but she's in this up to her eyeballs."

"Douglas knew her too. He said she was a beautiful woman."

"He thinks she's dead?"

"Yeah. I didn't want to get into it with him."

"Good thinking. Until we have a handle on all of this the less people know the better."

We sat quietly for a while until Jerry picked up my hand and twined his fingers though mine. "How would you feel about sharing my bed for the short time until we leave for the park?"

I felt the usual shiver his touch engendered but I was still annoyed by our earlier conversation. "You have a way of pissing me off, Jerry Brady. Right now I don't want to be anywhere near you."

He seemed surprised, his eyes clouding. "I can't help how my mind works, Summer. I have to look at all the facts and half of what you tell me is corroborated by nothing."

"Except my visions, that is. If you want to continue whatever this is we've begun, you need to take me seriously."

He frowned. "I'm doing my best, but we've got a murder investigation, a missing woman who may or may not be alive and someone threatening you. I want to keep you close tonight."

His fingers tightened around mine and when I gazed at him he had a very bewildered expression on his face. My anger disappeared. "I'm about ready to jump out of my skin."

Jerry raised one eyebrow, a pirate-like expression that was definitely a turn-on. "You know what can help with that."

It was my turn to blush and I felt the heat rise from my chest into my cheeks. I shook my head, trying to look him in the eye.

"Fine," he said grudgingly. I'll set my cell phone alarm so we don't oversleep."

Jerry stood and I followed him into his bedroom.

"Oversleep. That's a laugh and a half," I said, lying on my back on one side of the bed with my head on the pillow. Jerry lay down next to me and took my hand. We were both fully dressed so that when it was time we could grab our coats and go.

"Don't worry, this is as far as I'm taking it," he said, closing his eyes. A second later Cutty jumped up and curled next to my outside leg. I let my mind wander, mulling over my feelings. Jerry and I had stopped just short of becoming intimate the last time. And here we were again, poised on the edge of a precipice.

I hadn't had a serious relationship since Mike, the guy I'd been madly in love with before I met Jerry. I'd met him in college and we'd moved in together in New York before I got the job at the publishing house. He was in law school and a hunk and a half. I'd dated since then but whenever I revealed my true nature the men always backed away. They didn't want a weird girlfriend who insisted she had conversations with her dead mother and sometimes had visions.

I knew I shouldn't let Mike and his selfishness ruin what was going on in the present but I'd trusted the guy implicitly until the day he dumped all my belongings out in the hall and had his locks changed. We'd been shacked up off and on at his apartment for six months before he decided to call it quits. And since he never talked about his feelings I'd assumed all was well. It took me a year to get over it and especially since I was unable to get any closure.

It wasn't long after that that my mother disappeared and I moved back to Ames. And the pain of that on top of Mike's unfeeling break-up nearly did me in.

I let the past go, turning my thoughts to finding the killer and my mother. My mom had to be involved in this but until I spoke with her I wanted to keep an open mind. Possibly after tonight we'd know the truth.

Jerry was snoring lightly now and I turned to gaze at him. He was a good-looking guy with his high cheekbones and mussed-up hair. He had the little boy look now that he was asleep, the one I found irresistible. I had an urge to run my fingers through his hair but I restrained myself. I moved closer enjoying the coziness of the three of us together, Jerry's hand warm in mine, Cutty at my feet, and before I knew it I had dozed off.

When Jerry's alarm went off I'd been in the middle of an intricate dream that featured everyone I'd recently met, including Ms. Elliot of Jacob and Elliot. There was a feeling of confusion and frustration, with people appearing and disappearing as though merely wisps of smoke. I opened my eyes and sat up, my nerves shot through with adrenaline. Jerry had his back to me, buckling on his gun.

"I can't believe I fell asleep."

"You were snoring."

"I don't snore."

Jerry chuckled. "Maybe it was Cutty I heard. Are you ready for this?"

"I don't know. I'm scared."

"I'll have your back, don't worry."

"I only have five-hundred dollars."

"You can't capitulate, Summer. I'm planning to arrest him."

"He might not be the murderer."

"Murderer or not, what he's doing is extortion and that's a federal offense." Jerry gazed at me with his eyes narrowed and then left the room. I heard him pick up his keys from the kitchen table. I grabbed my jacket from where I'd placed it on the chair next to the bed and followed him out to the car.

Jerry parked a couple of blocks away. He told me go ahead as he slunk into the shadows in cop mode. I noticed he'd dressed all in black. I was shaking all over as I approached the benches. But why would the guy kill me? He was only after the money.

When I reached the bench where I was supposed to meet raspy voice I sat down and waited, peering into the darkness. I waited for about fifteen minutes and then placed the envelope in the middle of the bench and backed away, heading toward where we'd parked the car. If Jerry didn't catch him tonight he would be five hundred dollars richer and we would have nothing.

By the time I reached the car I was shaking all over and felt weak and sick to my stomach. I panicked when I tried to open the car door and found it was locked. Where was Jerry? I crouched next to the back tire listening for his footsteps, my ears straining. I heard a heavy footfall, my mind conjuring an image of what raspy voice must look like and what he would do to me. I held my breath and moved closer into the shadow of the dark car. When a hand come down on my shoulder I let out a piercing shriek that could have awakened the dead.

"It's okay," Jerry hissed, helping me up with his good arm. "The guy didn't show."

"What about my money? There's five-hundred dollars in that envelope that I can't afford to lose."

"Listen, Summer. I want you to take my car and go to my house. I'll stay here and wait for him."

"How will you get home?"

"I'll call the precinct for back-up. Don't worry, I've got it handled."

"Didn't you tell me that counting your chickens isn't a good thing?"

"You're trembling," he said, pulling me close. "It's cold out here and you're not dressed warmly enough."

"Thanks, Mom."

"Take the damn car and go home," he whispered, handing me the keys. A second later he disappeared into the shadows, his gun drawn.

I climbed into the driver's seat and started the diesel Mercedes. As I rolled away I was sure I saw a hunched figure running along the edge of the park. I sucked in my breath and pushed down on the gas, roaring away in a cloud of dark smoke.

It was four a.m. before I heard Jerry come in. I was on his bed curled up in a ball, fear playing tricks with my mind. I jumped up when I heard him, rushing from the room and throwing myself at him. He held me with his one good arm, the other one pressed between us.

"Who was it?" I finally asked.

Jerry shook his head. "Never saw him. When I got back to the bench your envelope was gone."

"What took you so long?"

"I called Sam, my partner, and we went for a beer."

"You left me here worrying and went for a beer? I haven't slept a wink."

"Sorry. I had to decompress and I wanted to talk this over with Sam. He has good instincts."

"I'm going to bed," I announced, heading toward the guest room.

"You can stay in my room if you want."

I shook my head and kept on going, calling to Cutty once I opened the guest bedroom door.

I didn't wake in time to make it to the store by nine. Hardly surprising considering how little sleep I'd had. Again Jerry was gone. The man seemed to live on adrenaline. I had a vague uneasy feeling about the night before as I made my coffee and hurried to get dressed. What really happened out there? I gave Cutty his breakfast and then shut him in the back yard before hurrying east in the direction of the store.

Luckily when I reached Tarot and Tea there was no line outside waiting to get in. I unlocked the door, surprised to smell my mother's perfume again. What was she up to now? I thought about that box of papers, my mind going to what Douglas had said about the book Serena was writing. Were her notes in the box?

Lila was not in the store and there was no note from her. I had no customers all morning, surprised until I remembered the exhibit that had just arrived at the local museum. It was the impressionists, a traveling show that would be in Ames for only a week. I tidied up and replaced books from where my customers had left them haphazardly on chairs.

Around eleven customers began to arrive and by two the store was buzzing with activity. I figured it was because of my proximity to the museum. I made several very good sales and had no time to spend fretting.

Agnes arrived just before closing, blowing in on a wind that whipped through the store, scattering calendars off the shelves and the papers off my desk. I looked out the window at the storm clouds brewing, feeling the drop in pressure. I couldn't believe I hadn't noticed until now.

"I came to give you a ride home. It's freezing out there and about to start raining. The weather channel said we could have hurricane force winds tonight."

I thought of all my stuff over at Jerry's, my dog. But tonight I really wanted to be home. I figured that the main threat to me was gone now, although I doubted that Jerry would agree with me. "I have to pick up Cutty from Jerry's house," I said, waiting for her eyebrows to rise, but she only shrugged and led the way to her car.

When we reached Jerry's house I used my key to open the door, surprised to see Cutty locked inside instead of out in the yard where I'd left him. "Jerry?" I called out, but there was no answer. I headed into the bathroom and then into the bedroom to grab my stuff and was out again in ten minutes.

"I'm not going to even ask what's going on with you and Jerry," Agnes said, her gaze meeting mine. "But as a friend I caution against going too fast. He has a reputation, you know."

"What kind of reputation?"

"Ladies man."

"Really? I never heard that."

"Why would you? You live in a dream world of your own making, Summer. I tend to listen to conversations going on around me and I know several women he's dated and ditched over the years."

I turned away from her feeling chastised and then watched tree limbs whipping around in the high wind. "Not that it's any of your business, but we haven't done anything more than kiss."

Agnes turned the key to start the car and then pulled away from the curb. "That's probably a good thing."

She was right. If we had gone further and then he'd dumped me it could send me tumbling into the darkness where I'd been after my mother disappeared. I'd been there after Mike as well and I didn't want to go there again. Both times had taken a round of anti-depressants as well as months of counseling before I was on my feet again.

"I saw your brother today. I thought you said he went home."

I turned, surprised. "Where'd you see him?"

"He was going into the drug store. And there was someone with him but I couldn't get a good look at who it was."

I laughed. "My mother?"

"I don't think so unless she was wearing a very good disguise. This person was kind of hunched over wearing a heavy coat with the hood pulled up."

"I have no idea why he'd still be here. I saw him a day or two ago—he came into the store and he didn't look like himself. Honestly, Agnes, I don't know my brother very well."

Agnes swiveled toward me and opened her mouth to say something and then seemed to think better of it. She pursed her lips and looked away.

9

I lit several candles just in case the electricity went out and was listening to branches scrape against my roof when my cell phone rang.

"Where are you?" Jerry sounded distraught.

"I told you I wasn't planning to stay, Jerry. Agnes picked me up at the store and brought me home."

"Jesus, Summer. You scared the hell out of me. I thought something had happened to you!"

"I thought my clothes and Cutty being gone might clue you in. You are a detective, right?"

Jerry didn't laugh at my attempt at humor. "I'm coming over. You shouldn't be alone, especially during this storm. We still haven't found that guy and tonight would be the perfect opportunity for him to break into your house."

A shot of adrenaline raced through my body. "I won't turn you away," I said meekly, realizing how foolhardy I'd been.

I went into the bedroom to put on something more appealing, thinking that perhaps my faded and ancient pajamas might not be appropriate for his visit.

When my cell phone rang a few minutes later I answered, thinking it was Jerry again, but this time a raspy voice said, "Where's the rest of my money?"

I swallowed, trying to come up with an answer. "The bank wouldn't let me withdraw it. They said…"

"Bullshit. That account is in your name."

"How do you know that?"

"You don't get to ask the questions, little girl. I expect the rest of it tomorrow night and if you don't come through this time there will be consequences. Same time same place." And then he clicked off.

When Jerry arrived I was shaking all over. He took one look at me and went into the kitchen, pulled the milk carton out of the refrigerator and poured some into a pan. I watched him place it on a burner. "Do you have any hard alcohol?"

"Under the sink," I answered weakly. I couldn't take in a deep breath.

A few minutes later he handed me a steaming mug. "Drink this," he ordered, sitting next to me. "It's brandy and hot milk, the best thing to soothe nerves." And that's when the lights flickered and went out.

When he moved some of the candles to more useful places I noticed the sling was gone. "Arm all healed?" I asked.

He sat next me his thigh pressing against mine. "Not completely but that sling was getting in my way. Now tell me exactly what the guy said."

His proximity made me feel safe despite the roar of the wind and the crack of tree branches breaking. Rain beat against the windows, staccato shots. "He expects all of it tomorrow night and if I don't give it to him I think he plans to kill me."

Jerry put a comforting hand on my shoulder. "This storm may be a blessing in disguise. It's supposed to last through the weekend."

"Will you stay?"

"Tomorrow's Saturday and I'm off. But even if I wasn't I'd assign a cop to watch over you. This guy is a serious wackadoodle."

I laughed but it came out like a croak. "Any ideas on who it might be?"

"You say Ephraim was lying about his identity? He's at the top of my list. And next to him there's Frank, your father. Anything else happen that you haven't told me about?"

"My brother came into the store but that's hardly relevant."

"I thought he lived in New York."

"He does but he came up for business." I took another sip. "He told me he remembered Serena and my mother palling around from when he was little—said they were into the occult but he didn't elaborate."

"The occult. That covers a wide range of practices. Do you remember anything?"

"Mom did readings—you know, Tarot and palms, but I'd hardly call that the occult."

"Maybe some people would."

"I hope you don't think she would try and extort money from me."

"Hard to imagine. What I find puzzling is how much this person knows about you. Obviously he or she either knows your mother or knows you very well."

"My mother and Serena were up to something but I don't think it's what it seems. And why hasn't Lila come forward? Did I tell you she was in the store again? I smelled her perfume."

Jerry put his arm along the back of the couch behind me and stared toward the candle flame. "What in hell is she up to?" he muttered. "And that Douglas guy—you said he lives in town?"

"Yeah. I've seen him around. He's a nice person,

Jerry. And from what I could tell he loved my mother too."

"I thought you said he had an affair with Serena?"

I turned away wondering if I should admit my source for this information. "I had another vision," I mumbled.

Jerry took this in stride, not even scoffing. "And?"

"Serena, my mother and Douglas were together at the beach. And for some reason I had the idea that they were like a threesome or something."

Jerry shook his head and laughed. "This gets more interesting every day. You think your mom was into kinky sex?"

"Is it kinky to have a three-way?"

Jerry pressed his lips together as though trying to keep from laughing. "Um...I'd say yes, especially for that generation."

"I don't know about that. Think of the seventies—free love and everything?"

"Your mother is too young to have been part of that."

"Douglas is older. All I'm saying is that Mom has a different attitude about men and relationships. She never married even though she had two children from two different men. And I know she was sleeping around when I was in high school." Something banged against the roof and both of us started. "I hope that isn't the oak tree coming down," I said, jumping up. I'd thought about having an arborist take down a limb or two but decided that the price was too high. If it fell on the roof I would definitely be paying more than what the arborist had mentioned.

"I'll check it," Jerry said. The candle flickered as he donned his slicker and opened the door. I could hear the roar of the storm like a freight train going by. He pulled the door shut, muffling the sound.

Ten minutes later he was back, slipping off the slicker and hanging it on the coat rack to drip dry. "One of the branches came down but it didn't do much damage as far as I could tell. I'll check it properly in the morning. Why don't we get you to bed?"

I let him lead me into the bedroom but when he began to unbutton my sweater I came out of my stupor and pushed his hands away. "I can manage from here. There's a blanket in the chest under the window."

"I'm not sleeping out there." Jerry stared, willing me to argue. "Someone could crawl through that window and by the time I got in here you could be dead."

I looked at the window and then back at him. The expression on his face was deadly serious. I nodded and then grabbed my P.J.'s off the bed and went into the bathroom to change.

By the time I came out again Jerry was under the covers lying on his back with his eyes closed. His clothes were folded on the chair against the wall. My bed was a double and he was a big man but when I crawled in next to him I had plenty of room. I fell asleep to the drone of the wind, Jerry's regular breathing and the occasional slap of rain against the window. It was one of the best night's sleep I'd had in a long time.

When I woke in the morning I was alone except for Mischief curled up beside me sound asleep. I heard Jerry whistling in the kitchen and smelled bacon frying. My mouth watered. I didn't bother to dress, heading into the kitchen in my PJ's to see what he was up to.

"Hey, sleepyhead." He smiled and flipped over a pancake.

I looked at the clock surprised to see that it was nine-thirty. "I can't believe I slept this long." I poured coffee from the half-full carafe and then opened the refrigerator. "The electricity came back on."

"The storm is petering out. Should be done by this afternoon, I'd say. Can you get the butter?"

I pulled out the butter dish and the maple syrup and then set the little table with forks and knives and plates, adding paper napkins. I sank into a chair and took another sip of coffee. "The storm being over actually makes me even more nervous. What am I going to do?"

"You're going to let me handle it," he said, placing two pancakes on my plate. "Consider me police protection."

I laughed. "Pretty nice when police protection sleeps in my bed with me."

Jerry waggled his eyebrows up and down. "Could be even better," he said. "Said protection could soothe said victim's nerves in a way that is foolproof."

I smirked and forked up a piece of pancake, shoving it into my mouth. "Foolproof, you say? Hmm."

"You doubt me?"

"Are you waiting for me to say 'prove it'?"

Jerry grinned and brought me two strips of bacon. "I like this nitrate and nitrite free stuff. Do you get it at the market in town?"

I nodded, my mouth too full to answer. At this moment I loved this man. Not only was he amazingly good looking, but he was also a good cook and funny. But then I remembered what Agnes had said and my excitement disappeared. I had dared to dream about a future with him, but a ladies man? Not happening.

"What's wrong?" he asked, bringing over his plate and sitting down next to me. "Your energy just plummeted."

"What do you know about energy?"

"I'm a human being and we all have it. Is it supposed to be something special?"

"New age people talk about it—you know, things like 'his energy didn't feel right' or 'his energy was off' or 'that guy had seriously bad energy'."

"Is mine off?" He watched me with his boyish puppy-dog look.

"I've heard rumors that you're a ladies man."

Jerry frowned. "What does that mean?"

"It means you like the ladies and you don't ever settle down. You're not to be trusted."

Jerry looked genuinely confused. "Who told you that?"

"A friend." I stuck another piece of pancake in my mouth and tried to ignore the hurt expression that crossed his features.

There was utter silence as he ate and then after his plate was empty he turned to me. "I don't know who said what, but I haven't had a real relationship since we dated. I've gone out with women but it's never lasted for more than two or three dates. As far as being a ladies man I can't see that applying to me. Maybe they have me mixed up with Sam--now that dude goes through women like water through a valley."

I didn't say anything for a while, taking in what he'd told me. Why had Agnes said that? Unless Jerry was lying, which I knew he wasn't, Agnes had made the entire thing up.

"Who told you that, anyway?"

I shook my head. "It doesn't really matter." And then I leaned closer and kissed him. When we pulled apart he took my face between his hands.

"I could spend a lot of time with you, Summer McCloud, and I wouldn't get tired of it. Even your visions are intriguing. I may be falling in love with you."

"Jerry, don't say that. I had a really bad break-up…"

"Mike again? He's the reason you backed away the first time. It's time to put that jerk behind you. I'm here for you now, isn't that enough?"

"Only if you don't disappear on me. I guess I'm kind of emotionally fragile."

"Don't you think I know that?" He shook his head. "I actually pay attention to these things. I respect how slowly you've wanted to take this but I can tell you it's all I can do to hold myself back."

I felt the pull of him, my body overriding what my mind was saying. "What if I don't want to take it slowly anymore?" I whispered.

He gazed at me without speaking for a few long seconds. "You have to make the first move."

I stood up and grabbed his hand. And then I led the way into the bedroom.

10

It was sometime after noon before the two of us rose from my bed. His promise of soothed nerves was an understatement. Even with one arm not quite up to snuff he was able to work miracles. I felt completely relaxed and contented, stretching and yawning as I searched for my clothes. Jerry went to take a shower and then I joined him only because I didn't want to waste water. What went on between us in that tiny shower stall bordered on overkill but I was new to this game, or at least so out of practice that I'd forgotten how wonderful it could be.

But as soon as I stepped out, the ring of my cell phone shattered my peace. Why had I chosen such a strident ringtone?

"Summer? I'm coming over," Agnes said. "I have news."

"Not now. Jerry's here," I told her.

There was a long silence and then she said, "Did he spend the night there? You didn't take my advice, did you?"

"I have to go, Jerry and I are discussing the case."

"I hope you know what you're doing."

"I'm a big girl, Agnes. You don't have to take care of me." Anger bubbled up and before I could say more I clicked off.

"Who was that?" Jerry asked coming out of the bathroom with a towel around his waist. He rubbed another towel through his wet hair, making it stick up in tufts.

"Agnes. She wanted to come over but I told her you were here."

Jerry let out a long sigh. "Thanks. That chick makes me nervous."

"She does? Why?"

"I don't trust her. I've caught her lying about things."

I didn't know what to say about that. Agnes had been my best friend since we were sixteen.

"Is she the one who called me a ladies man?"

I nodded, pulling on my jeans. "I can't understand why she would say that."

Jerry buttoned his shirt and then turned to me. "She came on to me while I was in the hospital. I told her I wasn't interested."

"She was weird about all of that—uncomfortable about going to see you and how I would feel about it."

"Believe me there was nothing uncomfortable about how she acted." Jerry grabbed the gun he'd placed on the bedside table and replaced it in the holster. "She took me by surprise."

"I don't want to hear about it, especially after today. Just as long as you can tell me you're not interested in her."

Jerry took my chin in his hand. "I am not interested in Agnes and I never have been--not then, not now and not in the future," he said, staring into my eyes. "Does that satisfy you?"

I nodded and then went to find a comb. I felt happy and energized but I knew that my insecurity would kick in as soon as he was out of sight. Why did being intimate always lead to insecurity? I had to get it together if I wanted a real relationship. I couldn't be clinging to him like a leach. It's why I'd avoided going there, but it was too late now. Maybe this was a lesson in growing up.

"I have a plan for tonight," he said from behind me.

I watched him in the mirror as I brushed my hair.

"I'm going to stake the place out so we don't miss him this time. I already called Sam."

"When did you do that?"

He grinned.

"You left our love-nest to make a call to your partner?"

"You were sleeping the sleep of the thoroughly satisfied."

I turned around and hit him with my brush.

"I need to go to Tarot and Tea and make sure there aren't any broken windows."

Jerry turned from looking at his phone. "I'll give you a ride. I have to go by the station for a few minutes."

"Meet back here around five?"

"Sounds good. Can I bring a few things over?"

"You mean like food?"

Jerry made a face. "I mean clothes and a toothbrush. You're going to get tired of me using yours."

"And my clothes don't fit you."

"Very funny, now answer the question."

I hesitated for a moment, contemplating boundaries, but in the end the idea of him hanging around for a few days won out. The excuse I told myself was that until we found the killer and whoever 'raspy voice' was I needed his protection. I couldn't think any further than that. "Yes, you can bring a few things over."

11

The trip in Jerry's car revealed the severity of the storm, with downed tree limbs and general disorder along the streets. Rivers of water flowed along the edges of the roads, rushing to the grates where the detritus caught and clogged the flow. Trashcans were upended with trash blown everywhere and roof tiles littered the sidewalks. People were outside cleaning up or on ladders trying to fix shutters or replace windows that had shattered. In town some shops were open but most were closed and few people were about.

Jerry stopped the car in front of Tarot and Tea and leaned over to kiss me. "Don't forget me in the next few hours," he whispered.

"How could I forget you?" I laughed. "I'm still full from that breakfast you made."

Jerry feigned hurt, his mouth turning down. "I hope that isn't the only reason you're letting me stay."

I gave him a look and then opened the door. I watched him drive away. This was not a good time to start a relationship but I knew that saying no to what was going on between us would be impossible now.

The store was fine but I was sure I smelled my mother's perfume again. Maybe it was just lingering in the air like the essential oils. I spent some time with Tabby who I had begun to call Tubby because of how fat he was getting. He loved the attention, purring and rubbing along my leg. After feeding him I checked around for anything that might indicate that someone had been in the store, but this time there was no note.

I sat down at the table in the back and went through everything I knew so far. Tonight would be another chance to capture raspy voice and maybe put another puzzle piece into place. If Jerry didn't catch him my life was in danger—at least that's what the guy had intimated. I heard a knock on the back door and looked up to see Agnes staring in at me. I unlocked the door and let her in.

"Summer, we've been friends forever. I hope this thing with Jerry isn't going to ruin that!"

I gazed at her distraught face, a pang going though my middle. "I'm sorry I hung up on you. I was just so mad. Why didn't you tell me you had a crush on him? It would have made matters a lot easier."

Agnes looked down. "I don't know. I was in some kind of fantasy about him. I asked if you liked him and you said no."

"So instead of telling me how you felt you chose to say he was a ladies man?"

"He kind of is. All the ladies like him."

"That's different and you know it."

Agnes sat down at the table and put her head in her hands. "I'm sorry. I knew how he felt about you but I also thought you weren't interested. I figured maybe he would go for me if he couldn't have you."

I let out a sigh and then sat down next to her. "So what was your news?"

Her eyes met mine. "It's about your brother and you aren't going to like it. I think he's involved in the murder, Summer."

I frowned. "Why do you think that?"

"I saw him again and this time he was with that

Ephraim guy. They were talking together outside The Keg." The Keg was a hotspot that had just opened up at the north end of town, with dancing, pub food and lots of alcohol.

"So he knows Ephraim. What does that prove?"

"Ephraim shot your boyfriend."

"Not on purpose."

"How do you know that? And what was he doing with a gun in the first place?"

"Lots of people carry guns. What do you think the two of them are up to?"

Agnes shook her head, her eyes wild. "All I know is that Randall is very weird. I was scared of him that night he stayed at your house."

I gazed at my friend trying to imagine my brother being scary. He was as normal as they come with his clipped military haircut, medium build and placid demeanor.

"He came on to me, Summer. And he's married, right?"

"What did he do?"

"For one thing he tried to get in bed with me and when I said no he got really mad. I thought he was going to rape me. If it wasn't for Cutty I think he would have. After he stormed out of the bedroom I locked the door."

"My god Agnes, why didn't you tell me this?"

"With all the rest of what's going on? He left the next day and I just kind of let it go. "

I tried to picture the scene but my mind refused. "Do you know if he's still in town?"

"Last time I saw him was around noon today."

I stood up and ran my fingers through my hair, pulling out tangles I'd missed earlier. "You haven't seen

Mom, have you?"

Agnes's gaze was bleak. "I still think she's dead. Someone is fooling with your mind."

"Why would anyone want to do that?"

"To put you off the track. You're pretty good at solving cases but the thought of her being alive is distracting you."

She had a point but the idea of losing my mother again…

Agnes stood and headed for the back door. "I've got to go now. For some reason Mabel wants me to come by the flower shop. I think a window got broken during the storm."

I grabbed her to give her a hug. "Thanks, Agnes. I'm sorry about all of this. If you see Randall again would you ask him to call me?"

Her eyes went wide. "I hope I never see him again."

From the look on her face I wondered if she'd revealed everything that happened that night. I closed the door behind her and then locked it, watching her make her way toward the street. She looked small and very vulnerable.

After moving through the store to make sure all was where it was supposed to be, I locked up and headed home. It was becoming dark when I crossed the street through the park, walking by the exact bench where I'd left my five hundred dollars. I shivered thinking about tonight and doing the same thing again. I hadn't had the nerve to put him off this time with excuses about banks not being open on the weekend. What would happen if Jerry and Sam didn't catch him?

Jerry scowled. "Are you saying your brother killed

Serena?"

He was making us dinner, standing in front of my stove as though he owned it. I loved seeing him there since I rarely cooked and when I did it was simple things like hamburgers or spaghetti. The smell of frying chicken wafted into the air and in a pan on the burner next to the chicken, fried potatoes with thyme and garlic were adding to the mouth-watering aromas. "That's what Agnes seems to think. Apparently he knows Ephraim."

Jerry turned, spatula in hand, his apron spattered with oil. "And what do you think?"

"I don't know what to think. I don't know Randall very well but I'd never imagine him killing anyone. What would his motive be?"

Jerry shook his head turning back to the stove where the grease spat and sizzled. I opened the refrigerator and took out salad makings, plunking everything down on the butcher block next to my wooden salad bowl.

"How was Randall's relationship with your mother?" he finally asked.

The question took me by surprise. I thought about it for a second or two and then said, "My mother drank too much sometimes and I remembered them fighting. I remember one time he called her a whore and she hit him and then he punched her in the stomach."

Jerry looked over his shoulder. "When was this?"

"I think I was around eight. I'm sure it wasn't an isolated incident."

Jerry turned back to the stove, turning the chicken and making it sizzle. "Was she alive when Randall got married?"

"Yeah, but we weren't invited."

"If you've never met Randall's wife how do you

know he has one?"

"Has a wife? Why would he lie?"

Jerry flipped the potatoes over. They smelled divine. "He could be one of those sociopaths who make up a life but are living a completely different one."

"This sounds like cop paranoia to me. He's my brother. I have to believe what he tells me."

"Did your mom meet his wife?"

"Not that I know of."

Jerry turned, facing me as he placed the spatula on the counter. "Don't you think that's kind of odd?"

The more I thought about it the weirder it seemed. How can a mother not want to meet her daughter-in-law? And Mom would never take no for an answer. I was suddenly hot all over and a second later I was shivering. "I hope Agnes isn't right about my mom," I muttered.

"Right about what?"

"That she's dead and someone's messing with my mind."

"Who would do that?"

"How do I know? But it would be easy enough to spray some of her perfume around and leave an ambiguous note. I really hope this isn't the case because I've been looking forward to seeing her again." Tears sprang into my eyes and the next thing I knew I was sobbing. Jerry came over and held me until the food began to burn. He let me go and turned off the burners, cursing under his breath.

After dealing with the food he turned around again. "I think your mom's alive. Wasn't the note in her handwriting?"

I sniffed and wiped my eyes with a paper towel. "I hope you're right."

117

"And what's happening with Agnes? I thought you two were on the outs."

"She dropped by the store this morning and apologized. We've been friends forever, Jerry. I can't just throw her under the bus."

"Did I say I expected you to do that? I was just surprised after your phone conversation."

We both stopped talking as he fixed plates of food and brought them over to the table. I poured dressing on my salad and then sat down across from him. Despite the slightly burned edges the chicken and the potatoes were delicious. I shoveled greens into my mouth, telling myself that it would make up for all the grease on the chicken. But coconut oil was good for you, right?

At the end of the meal Jerry brought up the plan for tonight, something I'd conveniently put out of my mind.

"Sam is staking the place out. He'll be there early."

"I don't even have an envelope for my non-existent money."

"Just use a mailer. We'll have him before he even opens it."

I suddenly realized that Cutty wasn't under my feet begging. "Where's Cutty?"

Jerry frowned. "I haven't seen him."

I jumped up and ran out the door, heading to the back garden and calling his name. He wasn't there and the garden gate stood wide open. I ran down the street calling for him but there was no sign of him anywhere.

When I headed back toward the house Jerry was coming toward me. "I didn't worry about him because of the dog door."

"It's not your fault. The gate's open but I haven't a clue how that happened. It has a special string at the top you have to pull from the inside. I'm going to call the shelter."

"It's Sunday night. I doubt they're open."

I let out a long sigh. "He wouldn't wander. I think someone took him."

Jerry pressed his lips together and shook his head. "Who would take him?"

"How about raspy voice?"

"Get real, Summer. That guy wants money, not a dog."

"It's harassment. He's messing with me. If he hurts him, I'll…"

Jerry put his arm around my shoulders. "Cutty's fine. We'll find him."

A terrible thought went through my mind. Cutty wasn't good with strangers but if it was someone he knew he'd be all over them. Suddenly I had a vision of Randall crouching down and calling to my dog and Cutty's eagerness to please him as he ran forward. I didn't know if I had made it up or if it was truly what had happened.

The next hour and a half I went door to door up and down the street but no one had seen Cutty or anyone suspicious around my house. Normally a few of these neighbors were busybodies, knocking on my door early in the morning or late at night to report seeing something strange going on. Maybe their reticence was due to the cop car parked in front of my house for the past two days. After no luck I checked with the shelter, leaving a detailed description on their lost and found line. But no one called me back.

I left Jerry talking on his cell phone and sat down on the stoop in front. It was dark now and very cold. I was near tears when my cell phone rang.

"Want your dog back?"

It was raspy voice. "Where did you take him?"

"That isn't important—what I want from you is the same as what I wanted two days ago. If you don't bring me the money tonight your dog is toast." I heard a bark in the background and then the phone went dead.

I rushed inside unable to stop the tears. "He's going to kill Cutty!"

Jerry looked up and then spoke a few words into his cell phone and put it in his pocket. "He called again?"

"Just now and I heard Cutty bark." I stopped to think for a minute, realizing that Cutty's bark was not his fearful one. "He knows the person—it's got to be my brother."

"Or your mother."

"Why would my mother do this? That makes no sense and besides, she's kind and loves animals."

"Sam just told me that the ME got the toxicology report back and that Serena was definitely poisoned. It had to be one of your mother's formulas."

"Come on, Jerry. We both know my mother couldn't do that."

"Do we?" Jerry stared at me with his eyes narrowed.

I turned away, my mind on Cutty. "If I don't get my dog back I might go completely crazy." Jerry came close to put his arms around me but I backed away. "I'm mad at you right now. I don't understand why you think my mother had anything to do with this. She may be weird, but a murderer? Do you actually think she's raspy voice? She'd never treat me this way."

"All I'm saying is what Sam told me. I can't rule her out."

"I hope you catch this guy because if you don't I

think you should sleep at your own house." I turned on my heel and went into the bedroom and slammed the door and then threw myself facedown on the bed, sobbing into my pillow. Jerry knocked but I ignored him until I heard him say, "Summer, it's time to go."

When I glanced at the clock I realized I must have dozed off. I jumped up and pulled a warm jacket from my closet and then opened the door where Jerry waited.

"You have to understand who I am, Summer. Cops don't play favorites. I don't want to hurt you, but…"

I held up my hand and headed toward the door. "Don't say another word."

In the car I stared out the window into the dark tree-lined street, my heart hammering in my chest.

When we drove by a dark car with tinted windows Jerry pointed. "That's Sam."

I didn't answer, wondering what, if anything, Sam could see. In my opinion he was too far away. When Jerry stopped the car I jumped out and headed toward the bench, ignoring his whispered, 'be careful.' I was a wreck now, churning out scene after gruesome scene.

There was no one in the park and no one around when I lay the envelope down on the park bench. I heard a short bark and turned to see a figure in the shadows and then heard a curse before Cutty hurtled out of the darkness and jumped on me. His leash was dangling as though he'd pulled out of someone's grasp.

I don't know what compelled me but before I knew what I was doing I was chasing the guy down. He wasn't far ahead and didn't seem to be moving very fast—it was then that I noticed the limp. "Ephraim!" I yelled out, "is that you?"

Behind me I heard running feet and then Sam sped

past me. A second later I watched him tackle the guy, both of them going down in a heap. When I caught up Jerry was there as well, the two cops working to handcuff the man. When they pulled him to his feet Ephraim stared at me worriedly. "I didn't do anything wrong," he said. "I was trying to bring your dog back."

"Save it for the judge," Jerry said, dragging him toward the car.

"Ephraim, are you the one who's been calling me demanding money?"

Ephraim turned, his expression bewildered. "I would never do that."

I tried to ask another question but by now we'd reached Jerry's cruiser and he pushed Ephraim into the back seat. "Sam will give you a ride home, Summer. I'll be back in an hour or so."

"No, you won't," I told him. "I want to be alone tonight." I took hold of Cutty's leash and turned to follow Sam to where he'd parked his car. I put Cutty in back and then climbed into the front seat.

"Trouble in paradise?" he asked, grinning.

I ignored the question. "Is Ephraim the only person you saw out here tonight?"

Sam shrugged and started the car, pulling away from the curb. "There were a couple of others but no one who looked suspicious."

"What does suspicious entail?"

"Skulking, lurking, you know."

"Ephraim was lurking."

Sam sighed. "To be honest I didn't see him until you started chasing him."

"So there could have been someone else. I don't think Ephraim is raspy voice."

Sam frowned. "Who is raspy voice?"

"The guy who's been calling me. Don't you and Jerry compare notes?"

Sam didn't respond and when we reached my house I hopped out, opened the back door for Cutty, thanked him and then watched him drive away. There was something about Sam that I didn't like and didn't trust.

12

I locked every door and every window before heading into the guest room with Cutty for the rest of the night. I told myself this was for safety reasons since the window was too small for anyone to fit through and there was a substantial lock on the door but in truth I didn't want to smell Jerry's aftershave on my sheets. Mischief meowed at the door a short while later and I let her in too, glad to have both my animals with me.

I lay there in the darkness unable to sleep, my mind going to Jerry and how it felt to share my bed with him. I didn't want to blow the relationship but his distrust of my mother and self-righteous attitude made my blood boil. At least I wasn't such a wuss that I put up with things I didn't like, I thought, giving myself a mental pat on the back. But I had to admit that I missed the feel of him next to me, the knowledge that I was protected.

My cell phone woke me the next morning, startling me out of a dream in which my mother was telling me some long-winded story of what she'd been up to for the past five years, but as soon as my eyes opened the dream was gone.

"Can I come over?" Jerry asked after I said hello.

"I just woke up. Give me an hour, okay?"

"I have news and I need you to come down to the station."

"Okay. What news?"

"I'll tell you when I get there."

I took a shower, dressed in jeans and a sweatshirt and then made coffee, trying to decipher Jerry's tone. It had been less than cordial. He was probably annoyed with me. Who could blame him? But then again, I was annoyed with him too.

When he arrived and knocked I opened the door, the familiar butterflies traveling through my stomach. He looked rumpled and exhausted, with dark circles under his eyes. I wanted to hug him but stopped myself. "You look like you didn't sleep either," I said, moving aside so that he could come in.

"You and this case are driving me crazy," he said.

"What's going on now?"

His gaze roamed into the kitchen. "Can I have a cup of coffee?"

"Help yourself." I went to the kitchen and sat down at the table, waiting while he poured coffee and then opened the refrigerator to retrieve the half and half.

"Where's Cutty?" he asked, sitting across from me.

"Backyard. And I put a lock on the gate back there."

"Good plan." He took a sip and then let out a long sigh. "Ephraim swears he's innocent and I have half a mind to believe him, but I think he knows more than he's saying."

"I don't think Ephraim is the guy. I don't know why he happened to be roaming around in the park at midnight with my dog, but..."

"I want you to come down to the station and talk to him. He seems to like you and maybe he'll come clean."

"Sure, no problem, but I don't know why he'd tell me anything he won't say to you."

"Sam wanted to interrogate him the way we do with suspects—you know the drill—good cop bad cop?"

"Sam is the bad cop, right?"

Jerry grinned. "He can pull it off better than I can."

"I bet he can," I muttered to myself.

"What?"

"Nothing. Let me feed Cutty and Mischief and make a piece of toast and then we can go."

"No rush. Make yourself a real breakfast, Summer. I wouldn't mind some eggs this morning."

I began to reply with something sarcastic and then softened when I saw the sad puppy-dog look on his face. "You are pathetic, you know that?"

Jerry grinned. "I missed you last night."

I made a face and then went to the refrigerator to get the eggs.

By the time we finished eating we'd begun to talk. And when we left the house an hour or so later we were holding hands. Jerry admitted to jumping to conclusions about my mother and then told me that Sam was convinced of my mother's guilt.

"What's with Sam, anyway?" I asked him in the car. "How long have you been partners?"

"Less than a year but we get along great. He's a hotshot cop from New York, you know, only transferred here because of his father. I guess he's got some terminal case of something and he wanted to be closer to him before he died."

"I'm sorry to hear that but don't let him convince you of stuff that seems far-fetched. Trust your own instincts, Jerry."

"He's usually right on, but this time…" Jerry pressed down on the gas and we roared away in the squad car, startling several of my older neighbors who were walking sedately along the sidewalk.

"What are his reasons for suspecting my mother?"

"Motive and opportunity."

"What motive does she have for extorting money from me or killing her best friend? And what about the little girl, Merrily?" I shook my head. "We need to find Lila."

"Don't think we haven't been trying. How do we know Serena was her best friend? Did you ever hear her talk about her? Sam thinks..." Jerry trailed off.

"Thinks what?"

Jerry looked over at me. "He thinks Lila's the key to all of it and he's intent on finding her. And when Sam's on the trail he's like a bloodhound."

"There's something off about all of this. Sam's doggedness and conviction that my mother's a criminal seems over the top, somehow."

"Sam has an easier time making up his mind about things. It's what makes him a good cop."

"A good cop is someone who is thoughtful and doesn't jump to conclusions."

"Sam's seen all the evidence, Summer."

"And so have you but you still have an open mind about things—at least I hope you do."

"If it means not losing you I'll do everything I can to keep my mind open," he said, pulling to a stop in front of the police station.

Only a few people worked on Sundays and so when we came inside the station was oddly quiet. But Sam was there, and I detected hostility when he greeted me. Jerry didn't seem to notice, taking me by the hand into the back to one of the interrogation rooms. "Wait here. I'll go get Ephraim."

After Jerry left the door opened and Sam came in.

"So you think you can crack this case?" He laughed. "I've heard all about your little visions but in my opinion good old fashioned police work always wins out."

"What police work led you to suspect my mother?"

Sam scoffed. "She's the only one who seems to know all the players and being suddenly resurrected from the dead doesn't help her case. And why hasn't she come forward?"

"Maybe she knows you plan to railroad her."

Sam let out a laugh and was about to say something else when Jerry came through the door with Ephraim in tow. "Just keeping your girlfriend company," Sam said before pushing by the two men.

Jerry's eyes met mine. "I promised Ephraim we wouldn't listen in on your conversation," he said before depositing the handcuffed man into the seat across from me.

"Can we take off the cuffs?" I asked.

Jerry shook his head no. "Without listening I have no way to know what's happening in here. This is for your safety. I'm giving you fifteen minutes." Jerry looked at me again and then exited, closing the door softly behind him.

Ephraim looked up, his eyes bloodshot and puffy. "Thanks for meeting with me. They think I want money from you but that isn't true."

"First of all, what's your real name? And why did you come to Tarot and Tea?"

Ephraim looked away and then seemed to come to a decision. "My real name is Ephraim Morrow. I'm your brother Randall's father," he said, his eyes meeting mine. "If you want proof of my identity I have a driver's license on me and several credit cards."

I stared at him in surprise. "You're Randall's father? What is Randall's part in all this?"

Ephraim looked uncomfortable, swinging his head from side to side. "I told him not too—begged him, actually—but he wouldn't listen."

"Randall's the one who's been calling me. Did he take Cutty?"

"Both of us did. Your brother, my son, has severe mental problems." He looked at me again and I could see what this was costing him.

"Is my mother alive?"

"That I can't tell you. I haven't seen her."

"Did you plant the note in the store?"

"What note?"

My heartbeat quickened. "Did Randall kill Serena?"

Ephraim looked about to cry. "I don't know. I sincerely hope not but I have to say he's capable of it. He's been in an institution off and on since before your mother's disappearance. I tried to keep him there but the doctors refused to listen to me. Randall is very sick but he's extremely good at hiding it."

"What about his wife, his child? Is he a sociopath?"

"He isn't married and never has been. As far as the name for his disorder--maybe there isn't one. The doctors used the term sociopath and several others, but I don't think they ever understood him the way I do. I've been attempting to keep him from doing bad things for a very long time."

Ephraim couldn't wipe his eyes and so I reached forward and wiped them for him, gently using my sleeve. "Did my mother know about him?"

He shook his head. "I tried to tell her early on but you know how she was. She could only see the good in people."

My heart sank at his use of the past tense. "Why did you help him take Cutty?"

"Because if I hadn't, he would have killed him and left his body at your house to scare you."

I recoiled in shock. "Where is he now?"

"That's the thing. I don't know."

A second after that statement there was a quick knock and then Jerry came into the room. "All done here, I hope."

I looked up. "You have to let Ephraim go. If you don't, Randall could do something a lot worse than extorting money. I think he killed Serena."

Jerry looked from me to Ephraim. "I'll have to talk to Sam about it."

"Forget Sam. Ephraim just told me everything you need to know." I turned to Ephraim. "Can you summarize for Jerry?"

"I'll lead you to him if you'll allow me."

Ten minutes later the three of us were in the front of the station, Jerry talking to the captain about taking Ephraim into the field to search for Randall.

"Sam has to go along," the captain told him. "I'm not letting you out of here with a man who assaulted a police officer without back-up."

When Sam appeared Jerry grabbed him by the shoulder and then the two of them went into the captain's office. Ephraim looked at me.

"Do you think they might release me?"

"They can't ignore the fact that you shot a cop."

"I didn't mean to."

I shook my head. "Doesn't matter whether you meant to or not. Lucky for you the bullet didn't kill him."

A few minutes later Jerry and Sam appeared.

"The only reason you're not behind bars right now is because you can take us to Randall," Jerry told him.

Ephraim nodded his agreement and then we all went out the door and crossed the street to the squad car. Sam opened the back door and pushed Ephraim inside and then slid in next to him. Jerry gestured to the front seat and I went around the car, climbing in next to him. "Are you planning to leave the handcuffs on?" I whispered.

"Hell yes, we're keeping the handcuffs on," Sam answered. "This man shot a police officer and should be in jail right now."

"Which way?" Jerry asked, turning the engine on.

"Take the main road out of town."

We left the village of Ames behind, heading into farmland and driving by rural fields plowed and ready for winter. I thought about my brother wondering what had happened to him. Was he really as crazy as Ephraim indicated? I hoped for all our sakes that we'd find him.

Ephraim led us to a broken down shack that seemed familiar. I wondered if it was the place I'd gone with my mother when I was a little girl. We all got out of the car and then Jerry and Sam told Ephraim to wait by the car before pulling out their guns and heading toward the door. I followed them but not too closely, glancing back at Ephraim who looked worried. "Don't let them kill him," he whispered.

I watched Sam and Jerry go inside and then there was silence for a few seconds before Jerry appeared. "There's no one here," he said.

I went up the rickety steps onto the porch and entered the shack watching Jerry and Sam searching for clues.

"Does this belong to your brother?" Sam asked, holding up a Swiss army knife.

I shrugged. "I don't know what he carries in his pockets."

"It has blood on it."

When he held the opened blade out and I saw the dark dried-out substance marring the metal I felt sick.

"Nothing much here," Jerry announced, heading toward the door. I followed him out, surprised when he jumped off the porch and took off at a run.

"Ephraim's gone!" he shouted, sprinting down the road away from the shack.

Sam ran by me, the two of them disappearing around a bend in the narrow dirt track. I looked down, noticing a pair of footprints heading off the road and into the forest. I saw Ephraim in my mind's eye working his way through closely packed trees. For a moment I thought of going after him but then I saw Jerry coming back. When our eyes met he shook his head.

"Jerry, there are prints…" I began, but by that time Sam was back and the two of them were discussing what to do.

"Jerry…" I tried again.

"Get in the car," Sam ordered, sliding into the front next to Jerry. "He won't get far with hand-cuffs on."

I climbed in the back and a minute later we were barreling down the road away from the shack and away from where I knew Ephraim had gone.

"With that nut-job on the loose you're either staying at my house or I'm staying at yours."

We were at the station where Jerry and Sam had explained everything to the captain who still looked angry enough to spit nails. I nodded, much more glad than I should have been that Jerry and I would be together tonight. When I pictured Randall now I saw a very different person—I knew nothing about the man that Ephraim described who lied to all of us and tried to rape my best friend, not to mention nearly killing my dog. I was right to feel comforted by Jerry's presence in my life.

I tried again to explain the footprints I'd seen but Jerry waved it off as though it didn't matter anymore.

"I nearly got suspended for losing him, Summer, Sam too. We're on desk duty until they catch both of them."

Jerry took me home and then left for his house to pick up a few more things. Apparently two changes of clothes, a toothbrush and his own special toothpaste, shampoo, a razor and aftershave weren't enough to get him through the night. Meanwhile I brought my dog inside and hugged him to me as though I hadn't seen him for a month. Cutty was happy to receive the attention.

After Jerry left I called Agnes to catch her up on the latest news.

"Holy moly! Things are getting even weirder! I wish I'd mentioned his behavior sooner. I just thought he was strange, not crazy. And where do you think Ephraim is? I bet Jerry's mad at himself for letting him get away. Any more news on Serena's missing kid?"

"That's a good question. Jerry's convinced the law firm hired a private eye to find her."

"Oh, I forgot to tell you. When Randall was staying at your house he talked about selling it and taking his half of the money. According to him he's half owner."

"It's true. My mother left it to both of us. If he pursues this I don't know what I'll do."

"He'll be in jail before that."

My mind roamed away, seeing my brother in alleyways and lurking in the shadows by buildings ready to pounce on me the second I walked by. "I hope so."

By the time bedtime rolled around Jerry and I had eaten a dinner of leftovers and drunk several glasses of wine. I didn't bring up the footprints, knowing it would only add another layer of annoyance to Jerry's already irritable mood. When I brought up Randall he assured me that a BOLO had been issued and that he'd be found.

"I'm just sorry it isn't Sam and me out there looking for him. At least I can keep you safe now."

I didn't comment until his expression went from a scowl to calm again. "What about tomorrow, Jerry? What if he comes in the shop again?"

"Keep my number on speed dial and call me immediately if he wanders in, but I doubt seriously he would be that stupid."

"He could have a key. Should I change the locks?"

"It wouldn't hurt. That way the workmen will be around for at least part of the day. I'll come check on you during my lunch break and if you're really worried I could assign an officer to stand guard."

"Jerry, don't beat yourself up about Ephraim. Who would have thought he'd take off wearing handcuffs? He's no spring chicken."

"That's why we should have found him, Summer."

He stared at me with an expression of extreme frustration until I leaned toward him and pressed my lips against his. I felt his tense shoulders drop as he kissed me, his arms wrapping around me as he pulled me close. Shortly after that we headed into the bedroom.

13

The next morning I discovered a dirty plate and a cup as well as a sleeping bag in the back room of the shop. Food had been prepared and I was sure whoever it was had left only moments before I arrived. I immediately called the lock people and told them it was an emergency.

When Jerry called me a few minutes later I told him what I'd found.

"I'm sending an officer over," he said and then the call ended.

The officer ended up being Sam and he arrived at the same time as the locksmith, causing major chaos to the few customers roaming around the store.

"What has happened?" Mrs. Browning asked worriedly.

"Someone's been playing a prank on me," I told her, attempting to smile. "They slept here last night."

Mrs. Browning put her arthritic fingers on my arm. "Oh my dear! But if it was your mother how will she get in?"

"It wasn't my mother. She wouldn't leave a dirty plate and cup behind nor would she sleep on the floor in a filthy sleeping bag. I'm more inclined to believe it's my brother."

"I didn't know you had a brother," she said blandly before heading back to the shelves. No one thought a brother breaking in was anything to worry about but I knew now that Randall was unpredictable and dangerous.

When Sam put his hand on my shoulder I jumped, whirling on him.

He threw up his hands in mock surrender. "Sorry to startle you. Glad you don't carry a gun. Just wanted to say that the locksmith is finishing up and expects to be paid."

"Thanks, Sam. How long will you be here?"

"All day unless something more interesting calls me away. Boring work but I guess someone has to do it."

I went to my desk and wrote out the check for the locksmith, watching Sam swagger through the door and head toward his cruiser. For some reason he rubbed me the wrong way.

Jerry called a few minutes later to report a major robbery on the other end of town. "Sorry, Summer, but with all the other officers out looking for your brother Sam and I have been put in charge of this one. . Will you be all right for a couple of hours?"

"I hope so. I don't expect Randall to come back but I'd feel better if they found him."

"They're scouring the countryside right now. I've got to go."

I placed my cell phone on the counter and watched Sam driving away. He looked pleased with his new assignment. A few people wandered in and bought this and that, keeping my mind off Randall as I rang them up and chatted about their purchases. Around one there was a lull and my nerves began to ramp up. And then Randall walked in.

"Hi Sis, how ya doin'?"

I felt the blood drain from my face. "Fine, Randall. Did you sleep here last night by chance?"

He smirked and then adjusted something on his belt. "Didn't think you'd mind. How about we get out of here for a while?"

When I looked closer I saw a gun hidden under his jacket. My heartbeat quickened as I tried to maintain calm. "The store is open—I can't leave."

Randall came close and grabbed me by the arm. "I think you can. We have unfinished business to attend to and with me along there'll be no more fooling around."

I tried to pull away but his grip was strong and now the gun was pointed at my middle. "What are you talking about?" I asked, stalling for time.

"I'm talking about the money, moron. We're going to the bank together." He dragged me out the door toward a rusted-out beater parked across the street.

"I've got to lock up!"

He scoffed. "None of your clientele would think to steal anything. You'll be back to close up if all goes according to plan."

He pushed me into the passenger side of his car and then went to the driver's side, all the while pointing the gun at me. To say I was scared was an understatement— the look in his eyes was not normal. "Are you taking drugs?"

He laughed, a nasty sound. "I've sampled this and that. The pharmacist, Brent, keeps me on track." He turned the key and the car sputtered a couple of times before coming to life. It backfired as we pulled away from the curb and then Randall put his foot on the gas heading in the direction of town.

"'Did you kill Serena?"

"You mean that woman that got poisoned? That's not my style. I prefer my victims to suffer for a while."

I was staring out the window trying to think whether to jump from the car when he suddenly veered off and headed in another direction. "You know on second thought I think kidnapping you might afford me a bigger payout. What do you think?"

"What is wrong with you? You're my brother! And who do you think is going to pay it?"

He made a face. "That cop you've been hanging out with might come up with some dough. As to your other question I've never felt a bond between us. Mother made me acutely aware of how much she despised me and loved you."

"That isn't true."

The car swerved toward the curb as Randall swiveled to look at me out of his over bright eyes. "Just shut up. I don't want to talk." He waved the gun around as he brought the car under control.

He moved his mouth as though talking to himself as we drove out of town and headed into the countryside. I had no idea what he had in mind. I don't know how much time had passed before he turned right on the same narrow dirt track in the middle of nowhere where we'd searched for him. We bumped along until we arrived in front of the falling down shack. I noticed a rusted-out car in the front yard that hadn't been there before.

"This is my home away from home," he told me, pulling the car around back. "Do you remember this place? Our whore of a mother called it her hideaway. It's where she brought her boyfriends." He got out and came around to open my door, the gun waving loosely in his hand. "Hope you brought your toothbrush," he sniggered, pushing me ahead of him toward the front door hanging crookedly on one hinge.

Inside it smelled like mouse droppings and decay. There was an old iron bed in one corner with a sleeping bag on it and several dirty dishes were stacked on a rickety table on the other side. "Make yourself to home," he said, pushing me toward the bed.

"I have to get back, Randall. If I don't Jerry will come looking for me."

"That inept cop? He and his partner are like a comedy routine. My father had no problem eluding them."

"Ephraim?"

Randall shot me a look. "You know him?"

"Yes, he came into the shop. I like him."

Randall smirked. "You wouldn't like him if you knew what he'd done for me."

I decided to let that go. I didn't want to think that Ephraim was Randall's accomplice since I happened to be in a very vulnerable position. My brother could shoot me, rape me or torture me and my screams would not be heard. "So why am I here?"

"Are you so stupid that you can't figure it out? I need money."

"How long have you been living like this? Did you ever have a house in Boston?"

"I had a house but it burned down. I come out here when I want to get away from people." A second later he grabbed his head. "Shut up!" he yelled, twisting as though in pain.

I was heading toward him when he whirled on me and before I could register what was happening the gun went off, the bullet hitting me in the upper thigh. I screamed and went down.

"Why did you do that?" he whined. His eyes

widened and he looked seriously scared.

"You just shot me."

"No, I didn't. They did."

He mumbled something I couldn't hear as I examined my leg. There was a lot of blood and it hurt like hell but my fear overrode it. When I looked at Randall again he was sitting on the floor with his head in his hands. "They won't leave me alone," he muttered.

"You need help," I said, soaking up the blood with the hem of my skirt. "You need drugs to stop the voices."

"Drugs don't stop them—nothing stops them except when I…"

I didn't want to know the rest of that thought. "Does Ephraim know about this place?"

He seemed to come out of his stupor for a second. "Ephraim? Sometimes he talks about putting me away somewhere but I don't want to go. He's afraid I'll be caught and tell on him."

"Randall, you're sick. You need to listen to him."

"No, I don't!" He screamed this so loudly I had to plug my ears. A second later he lurched out the door and I heard the car start. I heard gravel scatter from under the tires as he pressed down on the gas and sped away.

I searched for a cell phone but of course there wasn't one and then I searched for something clean to tie around my leg. I had to get back to town but it was bleeding so badly and hurt so much that I couldn't imagine walking very far. And from the two trips out I knew town was close to twenty miles away.

I had to be gone when Randall came back because I'd already had a vision of what he planned to do with me. I shivered as his true nature penetrated my consciousness. How had I not noticed that he was completely insane? I hadn't thought of myself as a Pollyanna, but at this moment I had to admit that I'd had blinders on for a very long time.

The only thing I could find that wasn't covered in filth was part of a sheet. I ripped a piece and tied it tight around my leg and then hobbled out the door. Walking down the road was out of the question and so I took off across the field, trying to stay close to the tree line where he couldn't see me when he came back. What if I came upon Ephraim out here? As far as I knew no one had found him yet. He was older and not in the greatest shape. He could be dead somewhere in the woods. And then I had another flash of Randall with one of his victims. I wouldn't live long if he found me, but it was the part in between that had me trembling—what I would have to endure before the blessed release of death. I knew now that torture was the only thing that stopped his voices.

Shortly after I crossed the first field I heard Randall's car coming along the road. I crouched down so he wouldn't see me and then continued on once he had gone by. I tried to go a little faster after that, afraid he would follow my prints and find me.

I had climbed through a barbed wire fence into my third field when darkness dropped over the landscape like a heavy curtain. I'd watched the color leach out of the sky, felt the chill as the temperature dropped, heard the call of birds as they found their warm spots beneath the trees. I had no coat, had come directly from the shop with only my light skirt and gauzy shirt that had become my uniform. Luckily I was wearing boots. I wasn't sure how far I'd traveled but so far I hadn't seen any familiar landmarks. The overcast day had hidden the sun and I hoped I wasn't going in circles.

I was exhausted and my thigh burned and throbbed as though it was on fire. I was afraid to look at it. I had to find shelter for the night. When I saw the haystack in the middle of the field it looked like a temple of solace to my over wrought mind—and I headed toward it. It was the old-fashioned kind with hay pitched up and up until it made a pyramid. Animals had made small caves in its sides, the decaying hay giving off warmth as it rotted. I made one of these caves bigger and crawled inside, pulling hay over me to prevent detection. And then I went to sleep.

I woke to the sound of a tractor, looking out of my hidey-hole to see the farmer plowing up the damp earth along the edge of the field. But when I tried to stand I realized that my leg had seized up. It was swollen nearly twice its normal size and I couldn't put any weight on it. I stood on my one good leg and cupped my hands, yelling as loud as I could but he seemed oblivious as he made furrows from one end of the field to the other.

Finally his systematic plowing brought him close enough to the haystack that he noticed me standing there. He stopped the tractor and jumped off, heading my way.

Kind blue eyes scrutinized me from a deeply lined face. "What's happened to you, little lady?"

"I got shot. There's a maniac living in an abandoned shack about ten miles that way."

I pointed but I didn't know if it was in the right direction. I wondered if I might be feverish. I felt myself slipping into unconsciousness and I knew I had to tell him where I lived so he could take me there. "I need to…" My body seemed to lean for a second and then my legs refused to hold me up. After that there was only darkness.

When I opened my eyes again I was lying in a hospital bed and Jerry was standing next to me. "You're finally awake." He leaned down to kiss me, his forehead puckered in worry.

"What happened?"

"I was hoping you could tell me. You were unconscious when the farmer brought you into emergency. The doc said you were feverish and severely dehydrated and that you'd been shot. Who did this?"

"Randall. He kidnapped me. Didn't he call for a ransom? I don't want to tell you what he had planned." I shuddered. "I got away but..."

Jerry shook his head. "No one called the station. When I called your cell phone and you didn't answer I went to Tarot and Tea. The place was wide open and you were gone. Jesus, Summer--I thought I might lose it."

"What Ephraim told us is true--Randall is seriously crazy. Randall told me Ephraim helps him, and from what I know now..." I trailed off as the horror of my vision rolled through my mind.

"Don't think about it," he whispered. "At least we know he's living in that shack. He'll be put away where he can't hurt anyone else."

"*If* you catch him. He's not stupid. I think he might be a serial killer. And Jerry," I said, grabbing his arm. "He tortures his victims."

Jerry's eyes went wide. "Did he torture you?"

I shook my head. "I got away before he had the chance."

"Did he tell you what he's done?"

143

"No. I had a vision and it was …" I shook my head and tried to get the horrific images out of my mind. "I thought I was a goner for sure. If he hadn't left me alone like that I'd be dead by now or wish I was."

Jerry winced as though even the thought of what I was saying pained him. When his eyes met mine he didn't need to say a word.

"Are Cutty and Mischief okay?"

He nodded. "They seem lonely, though. I guess I'm no substitute for you."

It was a few minutes later that the doc came in. "Looks like you'll be with us for at least one more day," he said, scanning my chart. "That bullet did a lot of damage."

"It just grazed me."

The doctor shook his head. "You obviously have a high pain threshold. It was imbedded deep in the muscle of your thigh. Luckily it missed the bone. We had to operate to get it out." He glanced at Jerry. "Can you stick around for a while? I have a couple of questions for you."

Jerry looked over at me and then back to the doc. "I'm not going anywhere."

Jerry was true to his word and when I fell asleep and woke up again he had pulled a chair up next to my bed.

"I can't tell you how I feel right now. It's my fault this happened."

"It wasn't your fault!"

"I called Sam away and left you there."

When I turned to look at him he had tears in his eyes. I reached out and took his hand. "Jerry, I'm fine. Please don't blame yourself."

An involuntary shudder passed through his body. "We have to find that crazy bastard before he hurts someone else. And after what you said I think Ephraim is involved. I've heard stories about the parents of serial killers condoning what their sons do. And so far five cops haven't been able to track down either one of them."

"It's hard to think of Ephraim in those terms, but..." I let out a long sigh. "Did you at least catch the robbers?"

"What?" His eyes slid away and then back again. "Oh, the case you mean. Sam tracked 'em down."

"How long have I been here?"

"Two days. And don't worry, Agnes is minding the store." He smiled his boyish smile. "I can't wait to get you home."

I thought of his arms around me, solid and tight, my dog and my cat close by, the warmth and coziness of my cottage. "And I can't wait to get home."

It was another full day before they released me and it was only my assurance that I wouldn't go back to work for a few days that made up their minds. There was risk of infection and standing on the injured leg would not help the healing process.

Jerry wheeled me down the corridor and out of the hospital, only letting me stand for a few seconds before he lifted me and carried me to his car. This time it was his ancient Mercedes diesel that I rode in, the one that belched black smoke. I didn't care what it did as long as I was next to Jerry and we were heading home.

Inside my cottage Jerry had to grab Cutty to prevent him from jumping on my injured leg. After that my dog refused to leave me alone for even an instant. He jumped up on the bed next to me and snuggled close, closing his eyes contentedly. It took my cat a little longer, her haughty gaze punishing me for my absence before she jumped on the bed and curled up on the pillow next to my head.

14

The next morning Jerry brought me breakfast in bed, waking me with the aroma of espresso from his machine. The heavy appliance was one of the things he'd found necessary to bring over. I didn't complain, lying back on the soft pillows and feeling like a princess as he served me a steaming cappuccino and pancakes and eggs. Beside me Cutty begged for handouts, his pleading eyes making me laugh. Mischief had left the bedroom once Jerry joined me the night before, more than likely on top of the cabinets in the kitchen, her favorite spot during cold days.

"You'd think I hadn't fed him the entire time you were gone," Jerry grumbled, watching Cutty beg.

"It's so nice to be home again," I murmured, reaching down to rub my dog's ears.

After I finished eating Jerry clapped to Cutty who miraculously listened to him, jumping off the bed and waiting attentively for his next command. "I'll put him in back and then I have to go in to the precinct," he said, sitting on the edge of the bed. "We may have a lead, at least on Ephraim. He was spotted in town yesterday buying supplies at the hardware store."

"I thought you were on desk duty."

"We're short staffed so the captain eased up on us."

"So no sign of Randall?"

He shook his head. "We combed the area around the shack and set up a stake-out but neither of them have come back. Did you know there's swamp all around that place? In the state you were in you could have fallen in and drowned."

I thought about how delirious I'd been, the visions I had of where Randall's victims were buried. I shuddered. If I concentrated I might know where to find the bodies.

"...If we find Ephraim we find his son," Jerry continued, bringing me out of my reverie.

"Ephraim?"

Jerry stared at me with a puzzled look. "Isn't that what I just said?"

I met his gaze. "I hate to say this but I don't want to be alone until Randall's caught."

He sat on the bed next to me and picked up my hand. "I'll make sure an officer is outside at all times. Unfortunately I'm a senior member of the force and I can't be your security detail—except at night," he added, raising one eyebrow.

"And have I shown enough appreciation for your efforts in that regard, Officer Brady?"

"Yes, you have, Miss McCloud," he answered, leaning down to plant a kiss on my lips. It was a while later that he stood and pulled out his cell phone and punched in the station numbers. After arranging the security detail he picked up my empty breakfast tray and left the bedroom. "Keep the bed warm for me," he called out.

I watched Cutty follow him out of the bedroom and then heard the dog door as Jerry urged him into the backyard. I sighed my frustration. It was time to go back to work and get on with my life. I struggled out of bed and limped into the bathroom to take a shower. In the mirror I contemplated my drawn pale face, the dark circles under my eyes. I wasn't back to myself yet but at least I was home and in one piece.

Around eleven I called Agnes to check on the store, glad to hear her chipper voice.

"Are you okay?" she asked, her tone turning somber.

"I'm fine. Jerry's taking good care of me."

Agnes didn't say anything and I regretted bringing Jerry into our conversation. But a second later she was chattering away again.

"That man, Ephraim came in the store this morning looking for you. He isn't part of what happened to you, is he?"

"Ephraim was in the store? He's definitely involved. I had a couple of visions about what Randall and Ephraim have been up to and it's very nasty stuff."

"What are you talking about?"

"Didn't Jerry tell you what happened? Randall kidnapped me. At first he said he wanted money, but then...Agnes, I think my brother's a serial killer."

"Oh my god! I feel sick. What did he do to you?"

"He shot me. He's crazy, Agnes. I'm just glad I got away. If he comes in the store call the police immediately. He's really dangerous."

"You're scaring me! And what about Ephraim? He was in here and there was no one else in the store."

"Call the police on him too. On second thought close the store until all this is over with."

"Sounds good to me. I'm shaking right now. And from the lack of sales lately it won't hurt your business. And by the way, that other man, Douglas, I think his name is? He spent a bunch of time in the shop talking to me. I don't have to worry about him too, do I?"

"As far as I know Douglas is just a kindly older gentleman who knew Serena and my mother."

I heard Agnes sigh. "Glad to hear that at least. I'm closing up now."

I hung up and then gazed out the window at the cop car parked there and then I noticed that instead of the officer who I'd seen earlier another person dressed in a uniform stood next to the car. It was Randall. A second later he burst into the house. Cutty raced toward him barking and snarling but Randall kicked him away.

"You bitch!" he yelled. "They found my secret place because of you!"

"Randall, calm down. I can help you."

"I don't need your help. I have Ephraim. I just called him and he's on his way. He knows a place where they won't find us. And when I'm finished with you they wouldn't recognize your body if they did." He laughed, sending a chill up my spine. "Come along, Sis. Let's take a ride in a *pol-eees* car."

When he reached down and grabbed my injured thigh I let out a shriek of pain. "Does that hurt? Oh, I'm sorry." Cutty lunged for him again and this time he let out a yelp as Randall's foot connected with his ribs.

"Leave my dog alone!" I screamed, bending down to check on him.

But before I could determine his state Randall dragged me from the house. I looked back but Cutty was still lying on the floor.

When Randall opened the passenger door and pushed me inside I saw the other officer in his underwear spread-eagled in the back. By the angle of his neck it was broken, his wide-open eyes staring at nothing. I gagged and turned away, afraid I would be sick. A second later another car moved down the street toward where we were parked. I hoped fervently that it was Jerry but instead Ephraim emerged from the vehicle and hurried toward the cruiser. He opened the back door, pushed the body aside and squeezed in.

"Hello, Summer. How nice to see you again." He held up his hands. "No cuffs," he said smugly. "This time I'll be calling the shots." He reached to pat his son on the shoulder. "Good work. Now let's get the hell out of here before we get caught."

We raced away from town siren blaring and Randall laughing like a madman.

This place was newer than the other shack, with doors that actually closed. It was further away from town and stood by the river. I could hear the water rushing by as they dragged me from the car. Inside it had an antiseptic smell, a metal table in the middle of the room with a smaller higher table on one side. If I didn't know better I would have thought it was a doctor's examining room. Ephraim pulled me with him into an adjacent room and strapped me to a chair. He closed the door and left me in the dark.

In the next room I could hear the mumbled conversation between Ephraim and Randall. What they were saying was like listening to a horror movie. They had been killing women for a long time and until now no one had been the wiser. It was only my visions that had tipped anyone off. Ephraim must have killed Serena but I still didn't have the full story and didn't understand why. So much for my little voice--I'd been dead wrong about the man.

For some reason fear hadn't kicked in. Maybe it was

the pain meds I was on. I was certain that the police car could be tracked and that Jerry would find me. Also it seemed I was on the back burner since Ephraim and Randall had made previous plans. Randall's victims were all big-breasted blondes of varying ages--not surprising considering our mother's physique. If my mother was dead I was sure Randall had killed her. But why kill her over and over again? I still had hope.

Apparently Ephraim found the women for Randall, lured them to wherever their tools were and then assisted with the torture and final killing. And it was Ephraim who buried the bodies. They were a practiced team. It sickened me as I heard them going over what they had planned for the next victim. I hoped Jerry found me in time because if he didn't I'd be in a shallow grave or tossed in the river like all the others.

When they took off in the car together I began to freak out. I could die here without water and food and tied up so tight I could barely breathe. My leg was throbbing again and I hoped Randall hadn't re-opened the wound. But then I thought about the death I would experience at their hands. Dying of thirst didn't sound so bad.

I must have dozed off because when I woke again they were back. And when I heard the high-pitched scream of terror I knew they'd brought their victim back with them. Would I have to witness the horror of this and not be able to do anything about it? Fear kicked in with a vengeance and I screamed, making a muffled sound as I rocked back and forth in the chair, scraping it along the wooden floor.

The door opened suddenly, the light nearly blinding me. "Do you want to go first?" Ephraim asked. He smiled down on me and then dragged the chair with me in it into the other room. "Better yet, you can bear witness and know what's in store for you." He took the gag out of my mouth. "I don't want any screaming out of you, Summer. If you can't control yourself I have several ways to shut you up." He picked up a hammer and then a knife off the table, holding them up and smiling at me. I got the message.

The woman was terror stricken, her eyes pleading with me silently until I had to look away.

Ephraim grabbed my chin and pulled it around. "You need to watch this, Summer. Your mother deserves this after what she did to me and your brother."

I watched them untie her and strip off her dress and underwear before forcing her onto the table on her back. The woman had begun to shriek, the terrified sounds making my ears ring. They ignored the noise, Ephraim holding her down while Randall fastened straps around her arms and legs. She kicked out once, catching Randall in the lower belly and pushing him off balance. But a second later Ephraim grabbed her leg, strapping it down tightly. "You have a long way to go," he told her mildly. "You'll be hoarse if you keep this up."

By now the woman's face was as white as paper, her eyes red-rimmed and bloodshot from crying. "Why are you doing this?" she cried out. "What did I ever do to you?"

Ephraim laughed. "You are a slut and you neglected your child."

"I don't have any children!" she cried out. "You have me mixed up with someone else."

Ephraim stuffed a rag in her mouth. "I'll take that out if you promise not to talk," he told her. "Nod for yes."

A light had been hooked up and attached to one end of the table, illuminating her ivory skin. Her luxurious blonde hair fanned out around her face like a halo. She looked like a younger version of Lila but it was easy to see the differences. Did Ephraim truly believe she was Lila? And that's when I realized that he was just as crazy as his son.

She nodded and Ephraim removed the rag. "That's better, isn't it?"

A vision of what was to come went through my mind and I let out a stifled scream that sounded like some kind of bird distress call, but Randall and Ephraim ignored me as they arranged their scalpels and other instruments of torture out on the table next to where she lay. I prayed for Jerry, saying his name over and over in my mind and seeing him come through the door as though he was really there. But he wasn't there and now they had begun.

The screams went on and on, relieved only when the woman blacked out for a while. They waited, chatting quietly until she came to and then began again. The cuts they made bled, dark lines standing out against her translucent skin as it oozed in uneven lines and dripped onto the floor. I wriggled in my chair and then retched and retched, finally unable to bring anything more up. I felt her pain viscerally as though it was me lying there. Tears ran my cheeks dripping onto my lap. There was nothing I could do but sit there and wait until she died.

Hours had gone by and still they were at it. I couldn't believe she was still alive. But that was the entire purpose—to keep her alive as long as possible and inflict as much pain as they could. I was next and the thought made me writhe and twist to loosen my bonds but nothing I did made any difference. I was shaking so much my teeth were chattering.

I closed my eyes but the sounds of whimpering and crying penetrated nonetheless. She was losing consciousness more often now. I had no idea of time anymore, shaking so hard with revulsion and fear that I couldn't think. When I gagged again nothing came up, my stomach convulsing.

There was a scratching sound outside the house that could have been a squirrel or a rat. Randall and Ephraim both looked up and then glanced over at me before turning back to their victim. She pleaded with them, her voice cracked and weak as she begged for her life. Ephraim laughed and said something to Randall about which instrument to use on her next. I saw the light reflect off the scalpel before his hand moved toward her body. They bent to their work and she was shrieking again and this time I wondered if it would be her last. There was only so much a body could endure.

When she abruptly stopped screaming I craned my neck to see her face. Ephraim and Randall paused and I saw Randall pick up her wrist to check her pulse. Her eyes were closed and shadowed, the skin of her cheeks slack. Her mouth hung open and a trickle of blood ran from her nose. The silence was ominous and I had a strong feeling she was dead. Part of me rejoiced to know that she was finally free. But then I remembered that I was next. I closed my eyes and prayed.

A second later there was a loud crash as Jerry and Sam burst in, guns blazing. Randall looked utterly surprised, falling backward as a bullet tore into his chest. Ephraim was up and running and knocked my chair over as he went by. The chair fell, my head slamming against the floor. I was dizzy and disoriented when another shot rang out. I heard a heavy sound as someone went down and I hoped it was Ephraim and not Sam or Jerry. I must have passed out because the next thing I knew I was lying on the back seat of the squad car. I could hear the wail of an ambulance in the distance. I closed my eyes and slept.

15

I dreamed I was in a cocoon, wrapped in soft wool and warm as toast. Muffled sounds surrounded me, soothing. I felt arms lifting me, soft murmurs as I was placed in water—warm water. I felt gentle hands on my body, washing me, the splash of water before I was lifted and wrapped in something that smelled faintly of lavender. I was dressed in soft pajamas and then placed under covers that smelled like heaven. I was dead—surely I was dead. Nothing in this world felt this wonderful. And then I opened my eyes and looked straight into Jerry's eyes. And he was crying. And then I was crying too.

The next time I woke I was alone in my bed. I panicked until I heard Jerry whistling in the kitchen. And then I noticed Cutty at the foot of the bed and Mischief curled up next to my head.

"Cutty, you're all right." At the sound of my voice he wriggled close and I pressed my head into his fur. I checked him over but nothing seemed amiss.

A moment later Jerry came into the room carrying two mugs. "Perfect timing. You're finally awake."

"How long have I been sleeping?"

He looked at his watch. "Twenty hours give or take? That's after the doc looked you over."

When I pulled myself to sitting a sharp twinge went through my back. "Twenty hours? How is that possible?"

Jerry hurried toward me, placing the mugs on the

bedside table. "Take it easy, Summer, you've been injured."

"Last thing I remember is…" Actually I couldn't remember anything. My mind felt hollowed out and blessedly blank.

"How about you don't think while we drink the lattes I just made." He took one of the mugs and went around to the other side of the bed, pushing a pillow against the headboard to lean against. Mischief jumped off the bed in a huff.

I picked up my mug and took a tentative sip. Delicious. "You are the barista of all barista's," I told him. But when I glanced at him the expression on his face was one I'd never seen before. "What's happened?" I asked him.

He placed his mug on the table and turned to me. "I nearly lost you, that's what happened." His eyes were liquid as they met mine, tears shining.

"I…I thought that…" I didn't know what I thought, only that I knew something had happened.

"It's all okay now." He reached out and touched the side of my face with the flat of his hand, a gesture he'd never made before. It was simple and yet the feeling of it was like being swept up and pressed close.

I had a flash of something horrific and then it was gone. "Jerry…tell me."

He shook his head. "Better if you don't remember."

But as I sipped I began to have flashes and then longer scenes and then finally the full force of the ordeal came crashing into my consciousness. I let out a strangled cry and then I was shaking and sobbing. Jerry held me against him for a long time as I cried and when I was finished he pulled me even closer.

"I love you, Summer. I'm so sorry you had to go through that."

He'd never said those words before and they penetrated deep inside, warming the hollow coldness that had taken up residence in the pit of my stomach. "Did you give me a bath? I have these warm memories of being wrapped up like a baby—swaddled. It was wonderful."

Jerry smiled. "I had to do something. You were barely conscious when we got back and shivering, as though you'd been swimming in ice water. I gave you a bath and then put you in bed."

I reached over and kissed him and then grabbed his hand. "You saved my life."

"Yeah, after putting it in jeopardy. I had no idea what Randall was capable of."

"Is he dead?

"They're both dead by my gun. I may be suspended."

"For saving that poor woman and me?"

"I didn't need to kill them. They were unarmed."

"Except for the knives and scalpels and whatever else they were using to torture that poor woman. Is she alive?"

"She's in the ICU but she's hanging in there. Strong woman."

I stared at the wall. "Like my mom."

Jerry looked down and then picked up his mug and left the room. I wondered what else he'd found out but I was afraid to ask.

I was dizzy when I got out of bed and had to grab hold of the bedpost to keep from falling. Jerry was there a second later, his arm going around my middle. "What are you doing?" he asked.

"I have to go to the bathroom."

Jerry helped me into the bathroom and would have stayed if I hadn't shooed him out. "At least let me do one thing in private," I said. "We aren't to that point in our relationship."

Jerry folded his arms across his chest and leaned against the wall. "So sleeping together, saving your life twice and just admitting my feelings for you don't give me the right to watch you pee?"

I waved my hand feebly. "Get out of here."

Jerry was waiting in the bedroom when I came out again, his smile warming me. "What else did you find out while I was in dreamland?"

His smile faded. "You might not like it."

"I'll find out soon enough so why not be the one to tell me?"

Jerry sat on the bed next to me. "We searched Ephraim's house and found a couple of letters that dated back fifteen years or more. They could have come from that box that was stolen out of the Airstream. In any case he and your mother were not on good terms. She knew all about what those two were doing. Apparently she threatened to go to the authorities. She wanted Randall institutionalized."

"She never mentioned anything bad about him."

Jerry picked up my hand. "She didn't want to worry you."

"You think she's dead, don't you?"

"I don't know, Summer. Everything points to it, but..." He looked away.

"You don't know for sure."

Jerry lifted one shoulder.

"And what about Serena?"

"Didn't you mention something about a book she was writing? There were letters between Serena and Ephraim about it—Serena planned to expose the entire nasty business. Have you heard of someone named Vivienne?"

"I told you about that letter I found, threatening my mother. Did you find something else?"

"Ephraim got a letter from her. It sounded like they were friends. It intimated that there was bad blood between her and Lila but didn't say why."

"So Ephraim killed Serena to keep her from exposing he and Randall in her book?"

"It looks that way but my cop instincts say otherwise. Killers who enjoy torturing don't normally veer off into this kind of murder. But if it wasn't them I have no idea who did it."

"I think Serena was here to pick up that book. I had the strangest feeling that my mother placed it in the store so Serena could find it—maybe it was a way for them to communicate."

Jerry frowned. "Notes passed back and forth in code?"

"Yeah. That would explain why the note was there."

"Unless she was using it as a bookmark."

"Do you remember what page you found it on? That could be a clue."

Jerry glanced at me. "I didn't pay attention."

"Ephraim really fooled me. I thought he was a good guy."

"He was an actor. Apparently that's how he first met Serena. There were a bunch of scripts among those letters and some head shots of the two of them from when they were young."

I let out a long sigh and sank back against the pillows. "So everything he told me was a lie? Will life ever feel normal again?" I began to cry.

Jerry left shortly after this conversation and I hobbled around the house straightening up and trying not to think about the woman still in the hospital. I had to go see her at some point. There was a hollow feeling inside me that I couldn't shake. Even Jerry's pronouncement of love had done nothing to alleviate it. What was wrong with me? For the rest of the afternoon I sat on the couch and stared out the window with Cutty pressed close.

16

It had been over a month since my ordeal and Randall and Ephraim's deaths. We did not bother with a funeral nor did I shed any tears. My leg had healed and any injuries from my fall were only memories now. And yet something was not right. I couldn't pin point what was wrong nor could I answer Jerry's questions about why I never smiled. My dreams were filled with flashes of the torture and I woke screaming a lot of nights. Jerry was good about this, holding me until I could calm down enough to go back to sleep. Cutty never left my side now as though he knew something I didn't. During the day I felt empty and out of control with no idea what to do about it.

I forced myself to visit the woman in the hospital, horrified when I saw the extent of what they'd done to her. When she saw me her eyes went wide as though I had something to do with her torture. Maybe in her mind I did. I told her they were both dead and tried to cheer her up but there was a wild look in her eyes that I had a feeling would be there for a very long time. When she asked me why they'd chosen her I told her about my mother and that my brother had reacted very badly to her behavior when he was a boy. "He must have had a screw loose early on but I never noticed anything. He just seemed like any other teenager."

"How many others?" she asked hoarsely.

I shook my head. "We'll never know." But I did

know. I'd seem the graves in a vision. And there were more than I could count.

I felt sick when I left the hospital as though I was partially responsible for what had happened to her.

"You need professional help," Jerry told me a week after my visit to the hospital. "It's like you have PTSD. Look at yourself in the mirror—you're ashen and your eyes look dead. I've tried but nothing I do seems to make any difference. You're not the same person you were and I can't have a relationship with a ghost."

I knew exactly what he was talking about but I couldn't bring myself to contact a shrink and go through it all again. Reliving the experience was just too painful. For days after our talk I moped around the house staring out windows and sitting on the couch for hours without moving. I had no energy at all.

It was a week and a half later that Jerry insisted that I go back to work. Agnes had contacted him to say that she was unable to continue filling in, and besides that, paying Agnes was cutting into the income I needed to pay my bills. He was right, of course. But once I returned to the shop and my clients faced the specter I'd become they began dropping away. I think I scared them with my blank stares and how I sat at my desk without moving for hours. Underneath my inability to function something was nagging at me that said the story wasn't over.

It was the end of October and I'd been going through the motions, dragging myself to work and coming home to fix a lackluster meal. Jerry stayed away a lot now, going out with Sam and coming back after I was asleep.

We hadn't spoken deeply about anything nor had we made love.

Cutty greeted me as always, his tail wagging as though he hadn't seen me in months. When I went into the bedroom to put on my sweats I noticed the closet door hanging open and when I reached to close it I saw that Jerry's side was empty. In the bathroom his things were gone as well and the kitchen revealed an empty space where his espresso machine had stood. I should have expected it but the shock was like someone had punched me in the stomach. I went to the sofa and collapsed, trying to make sense of what to do. Should I call and beg him to come back? I knew why he'd left but I couldn't promise that things would be different. I didn't have the energy or the will to do much of anything.

I didn't sleep that night and spent a lot of hours crying and thrashing around. In the morning the bedclothes were in a tangle and I was red-eyed and exhausted. I took a shower and dressed and headed into the kitchen for my usual espresso, shocked again by the machine's absence. I'd grown used to my life with Jerry, our morning coffee ritual, our evenings spent snuggled on the couch together reading or talking. But the past week or so he'd been oddly absent during these times, with excuses about work and his family who I had yet to meet. We'd been planning Thanksgiving with them and I'd been excited about the significance of this step.

Part of me was relieved that I wouldn't have to bring myself out of my malaise—it would have required energy that I didn't have. But another deeper part was crying out in pain. Maybe I should consult a shrink after all.

Three more weeks went by without any word from

Jerry. I kept expecting him to show up or call so that we could hash things out. My sleep was virtually non-existent and I wasn't eating properly because I always felt sick. When I did sleep my dreams took me to dark places and I would wake in a cold sweat.

It was a week and a half before Thanksgiving and I'd had another sleepless night in which I tried to make sense of my new reality. I woke early with a burning desire to change my life. I knew that unless I did something drastic Jerry wouldn't be willing to try again. I punched the numbers that I'd taken from the web into my cell phone—the psychiatrist who specialized in unresolved trauma. And when the secretary answered I made an appointment for the next afternoon.

It was around eleven when I heard the chime of the bell on the front door of Tarot and Tea. I looked up from my computer to see Douglas Weatherby bend his tall frame to come inside--my first customer of the day. Tabby was in the front and took one look at him and hissed before hurtling toward the back. I'd never seen him act that way.

"My dear, you look dreadful," Douglas said, his gaze worried. "You may be healed on the outside but I can see that you still suffer."

I tried to smile. "I have to admit I haven't felt myself since it happened. How do you know about it, anyway?"

Douglas smiled. "You know small towns. Everyone loves to gossip. You were the main topic of conversation for several weeks. And of course I was called into the police station to give a statement."

"What did they want from you?"

"I'm Jonathon's brother and I knew all the players,

including your brother, Randall."

I stared at him, surprised. "Did you know what he'd done?"

"I'd heard rumors from your mother but she never said anything too specific. She never wanted to say a bad word about anyone." He looked sad, his gaze going into the distance.

"Did you and my mother…?"

"Did we have a love affair? Yes, my dear, we did. Your mother was a free spirit. And in answer to your other question I loved Serena as well. The reason I came in today is to ask you a little favor. I want you to publish Serena's memoir."

"Me? Do you have her notes?"

Douglas's gaze slid away. "Your mother and I spent time in that Airstream when she first bought it years ago. I knew about the papers and hoped that's where I'd find them. A few things were missing but the bulk of Serena's journals were there. The publisher is expecting the manuscript. Will you do this?"

"But now that they're dead what's the point of it all? I mean didn't she write it to expose Ephraim and Randall?"

"Her story is much more than that—it encompasses her life and includes your mother and everything that happened over the years." He smiled and reached out to touch my face. "You really don't know much, do you?" And then he turned and headed for the door.

"Wait!" I called out but the door had already closed behind him and when I ran outside he was gone.

I glanced at Bookers wondering if that's where he'd disappeared. I could easily imagine him spending hours browsing through books no longer in print.

I had no more customers for the rest of the day and when four o'clock rolled around I closed up early and headed for home.

The next morning I stopped in Starbucks on the way to the shop and ordered a cappuccino before walking the last two blocks. When I reached Tarot and Tea I put my cup on the stoop and fished in my purse for the key. When I pushed the door open it pressed against something heavy barely opening enough for me to slip inside. The cardboard box from the trailer had been deposited against the door. Douglas must have dropped it by. But how did he get in?

I dragged it over to my desk and opened it, examining the stack of papers and folders. An hour later I had my answer about Serena's journals because her entries were laid out chapter by chapter. All I had to do was copy it into a computer, print it and give it to the publisher listed at the top of the first chapter.

I was typing away when Mrs. Browning arrived. "My dear girl, the roses seem to have returned to your cheeks!" she exclaimed.

I smiled and stood, rubbing my lower back. "I lost track of time."

"What is it that you're working on?"

"An old friend of my mother's wants me to publish Serena Weatherby's journals. All her notes are in this box."

"Serena Weatherby?" Mrs. Browning seemed to pale. "Goodness, what a job."

"Not really. All I have to do is turn it into a Word document and print it out. It's already written."

Mrs. Browning reached out to pat my arm. "I won't interrupt you further. I only wish to see what new books you have." She turned and headed toward the stacks.

I watched her for a moment before turning back to my work, eager to read more about Serena and my mother as young women. According to this they'd been quite promiscuous in their younger days with stories that almost made me blush. Of course this was way before I was born. My brother Randall was a small boy at the time and with Ephraim lurking around, this behavior of my mother's surely impacted Randall's life. By Serena's account, Ephraim did not take kindly to what the two of them were up to. Maybe that was the reason they'd been driven to torture and kill. Possibly it was Ephraim's influence that had turned Randall into the monster he became.

Mrs. Browning arrived at the counter with a book about Celtic goddesses and several packets of chamomile tea, her favorite. "I love this series," she said, putting the book on the counter. "I have the one on Greek goddesses at home."

"I'm glad," I said, ringing her up. After she left I was back to work again, my fingers flying across the keys.

I took a break at lunchtime reading through the several chapters about the early days I'd already transcribed. This encompassed the beginning of Serena's acting career and the first time she met my mother, which was in a dance class in New York City. They'd become instant friends and everything that came after seemed to include Lila, as though that moment had changed their lives forever.

By skipping ahead I knew that my mother and Serena did indeed have a threesome with Douglas. They both loved him and had only good things to say. He was quite a bit older, a man who according to Serena, was a courtly gentleman of varying tastes who didn't balk when things were outside the norm. The lengthy descriptions of their interactions were written in a rather old-fashioned style that barely kept it from turning into erotica. I was no longer transcribing at this point but when my cheeks began to burn I decided it was time to take a break and go back to where I left off.

When I went to make tea and glanced at the clock I was surprised by how much time had gone by. I was due at my appointment in less than a half an hour. There were no customers in the store when I locked up and put a sign in the window that said I'd be back in an hour and a half.

I hurried down the sidewalk wondering what I would say to the shrink about why I had come. My mood had improved considerably since beginning work on the book. *Maybe Jerry will like me again,* I muttered to myself. But immediately a little voice chastised me. This wasn't about Jerry. It was about my life and my happiness. Until I worked through whatever was troubling me there was no point in having a relationship.

I waited in the sumptuous lobby wondering how much money this man made a year. It reminded me of the lawyer's office in New York with thick richly colored carpeting and expensive furnishings. I hoped my insurance would cover the sessions.

Only a few minutes went by before the door to the office opened and a man appeared. "Summer? I'm Doctor Holgren." Since I was the only person in the waiting room his hawk-like eyes pinned me like a bug.

I nodded and headed his way wondering why doctors greeted their patients by their first names and introduced themselves by their honorific. It certainly put the power solidly in their court. He looked to be in his mid-forties, trim and slightly balding.

His office was less imposing than the waiting room with modern abstract paintings on the walls and simple Japanese style furniture. He gestured to a wooden chair with a black leather seat and then sat in a chair facing mine and picked up a clipboard and a pen.

"What brings you in, Summer?" He held his pen poised as though ready to write down every word I spoke.

I watched his face for signs as to how to proceed but his expression was blank. He wore a white shirt, plain navy tie and dark trousers, his receding brown hair combed carefully into place. He had a kind aspect but I had the feeling that who he was had been well concealed. I no longer trusted my intuition and had also lost faith in people. "I had a near death experience around two months ago and I've been--I guess you might say--depressed, since then. I'm getting better now, though."

He didn't register surprise or interest. "And to what do you attribute feeling better?"

"I have a project going and it's captured my imagination."

He nodded and wrote something down. "Tell me about this near death experience."

I shuddered and looked down at my hands clasped in my lap before stuttering my way into the past. By the time I finished I was crying. "And my boyfriend, the cop I mentioned, he left because he said I had to do something to help myself. He mentioned PTSD."

Dr. Holgren ignored my tears, not even offering a tissue. He wrote something else down before he said, "This could be a diagnosis for what is going on with you.

If you'd like I can prescribe some anti-depressants."

"I don't want to take anything."

"What exactly do you want, Summer?"

"I want to feel better, to be my old self, to feel happy again."

"What you went through will always be with you. You will never 'feel like your old self', as you put it. You've been changed by that experience. It takes a long time for the psyche to heal after something like you described. I suggest you say as much to your boyfriend since he obviously understands PTSD. I'm writing a prescription for you and you can take it or not. But I highly suggest that you use it for the time being. It's only a temporary measure until the trauma takes a back seat to your current life. It sounds as though you've moved forward with this project you mentioned. The more you engage in life the better you will feel."

He handed me a slip of paper and rose from his chair. "Come see me in a week or two after you've been on the anti-depressants." And then he showed me to the door.

I gave my information to the secretary who took everything down.

"I'll bill your insurance but I can't guarantee they'll pay."

I nodded, looking at the bill for two hundred dollars for twenty minutes. I was in the wrong business.

Relief flooded through me the minute I walked outside. Not only had I made it through the appointment but I also had a reason to contact Jerry. The doctor had told me to. I pulled my cell phone out and punched in his number.

"Hello?"

"Jerry? It's me, Summer. I just saw a psychiatrist and he suggested I call you."

"Really? Why, exactly?"

"He said since you knew about PTSD you should understand what was going on with me."

I heard a long sigh. "Summer, it isn't that I don't understand—anyone would be traumatized by what you went through. It's just that I couldn't live like that anymore. You were like a ghost. I need a real woman in my life, not someone who's barely there."

"I'm here now."

"Are you? For how long?"

"Jerry, please. I just want to see you. I have some news you might find interesting." There was silence on the other end. "Are you still there?" I asked.

"I'm here. What do you suggest?"

"Let's meet for dinner."

We hung up after I talked him into meeting at Grub and Grins at six thirty, but I didn't feel good about how I'd coaxed and prodded to get him to say yes.

I dressed carefully for my date with Jerry, covering up the circles under my eyes with make-up and brushing on copious amounts of blusher. I dressed in a long black skirt and sage green sweater that came down over my hips, an outfit I knew he liked. In the kitchen I fed Mischief and Cutty and told them I wouldn't be gone long. Jerry had promised to pick me up but when I saw his car coming down the street I panicked. I was as nervous as a cat.

I grabbed my winter coat and hurried out, locking the door behind me. I teetered down the walkway, regretting my decision to wear heels. By the time I reached the car he had come around to open my door.

"Thanks," I said, sliding in.

I watched him walk around the car and slide in on his side, my heart doing funny little dances with the beats. He gazed at me. "You look good, Summer."

"Thanks, so do you." We stared at each other for a second before he started the car and pulled away from the curb. The ride was made in silence and I despaired of this going well. I could feel my nerves eating away at my empty stomach. It seemed like a year since we'd seen each other but in reality it was only a month.

In the restaurant we found a small table in the corner away from the bar and the T.V. We ordered wine before perusing our menus. "What's been going on with you?" I asked.

"Same old same old. Cop business, beer with Sam after work. The usual."

"Have you gone out with anyone?"

Jerry scoffed. "What do you think? Jesus, Summer, you can be such a ditz."

"Thanks a lot. I don't think asking if you're dating is ditzy. How would I know?"

Jerry shook his head. "Do you remember anything I said before I left? I'm not available for dating at the moment. Maybe it you piss me off enough tonight I'll be more inclined."

I sat back and stared at the T.V. There was a game on. When the wine came I lifted my glass and took a sip. I was afraid to open my mouth for fear of what might come out.

"Summer, you said you had some news. Why don't we talk about that?"

I nodded and placed my glass on the table.

"Remember the elegant gentleman I told you about, Douglas? He came in the store the other day. He wants me to transcribe Serena's book and I've been doing it."

Jerry frowned and stared at me. "Douglas Weatherby?"

"Yeah, Jonathon's brother."

"Summer, he's dead."

"What? No. He's not dead. He delivered the box that was stolen from the Airstream. It has all her papers in it."

"I've read through all the information about the Weatherbys. Douglas Weatherby died years ago. He was killed in a car accident."

I shook my head feeling like the world was spinning out of control. "It can't be. I've seen him around town several times. Were there pictures? This guy is really tall and has a squarish face and gray hair. He's very elegant and old-fashioned."

Jerry looked annoyed. "Douglas Weatherby lived in Ames more than twenty years ago. Sounds like the same man but I'm sure it couldn't have been."

"I'm not crazy. I'm sure I mentioned him earlier and you didn't say anything. I'm telling you, this man…"

Jerry put his hand up. "I know you think you saw this guy, Summer, but I suggest you keep seeing the psychiatrist. You need him." He pushed back his chair and stood. "I've got an early day tomorrow so I think I'll beg off now. I'll give you a ride home."

"Forget it, I'll walk." I picked up my glass and took a hefty swig as Jerry threw some bills down. And then I picked up his glass and finished what was there. He stared at me, shook his head and walked out of the bar.

I fought tears as I ordered another glass of wine. When it came I dialed Agnes. It was a testament to our friendship that she listened to me and responded since I'd basically dropped her as soon as Jerry and I became intimate. We hadn't spoken for weeks and I hadn't even thanked her for helping me out with the store. She walked into the bar less than fifteen minutes later, her concerned gaze finding me in the back corner.

"What is going on with you two?" she asked, slipping into the chair next to me.

"I wish I knew. He doesn't trust me at all and he treats me like I'm an idiot. He's never acted this way before. And what he said about Douglas Weatherby can't be true unless the guy I met is an imposter. What should I do?"

"First we should order food and a bottle of wine." Agnes opened the menu took one look and waved to the waiter. When he came over we ordered a pizza and a bottle of red Agnes picked out.

She put her elbows on the table and gazed at me. "Have you thought about signing up on one of those sites?"

"Agnes, I can't do that! I'm in love with Jerry!"

"Does he know that?"

"I haven't said it in so many words but he's got to know."

"And has he told you the same?"

"He told me he loved me after that last horrible incident but I didn't say it back because I couldn't feel anything. I've been completely numb until just recently when I started working on the book."

"What book?"

"I didn't tell you? We have a lot of catching up to do."

An hour later she shook her head in amazement.

"Your life is beginning to remind me of a soap opera. But I think I know why Jerry's mad."

"Why?"

"Because he bared his soul to you and he feels guilty that you got hurt. He's a man, Summer, and men are not good with emotions. And as far as this Douglas person, I think you better find out what's going on before you go any further. If this guy's another imposter you need to be careful. Jerry's probably worried about you on top of everything else."

"He didn't act worried, only annoyed. Douglas seems honest to me but lately I've been wrong more times than I've been right."

"I met him too and I liked him. That's the other thing—you need to trust yourself again. I wonder if the anti-depressants that doc prescribed would help?"

"Have you ever taken them?"

"No, but I know people who have. Some liked them and some didn't. It depends on your body chemistry, I guess."

"The last time I took them I didn't feel like myself—it's like they numbed me out and right now I feel numb enough without adding something else." I sighed and looked down at my plate at the half eaten piece of pizza. It did not look appetizing. "But maybe the type he prescribed are different. I can give it a try and see if they help—I can always stop if I don't like them." I raised my gaze to hers. "I feel like I've been living in a bubble ever since my mother disappeared."

"You kind of have. That's why I was worried when you got together with Jerry—I was afraid you'd glom onto him as a replacement. And then the idea that she's alive just made it worse."

I stared at my friend who was gazing at me worriedly. "I don't know what to think anymore."

"Maybe talking to the shrink can help. I would love to have my old friend back—you know, the free-wheeling one who isn't afraid of anything?"

I shook my head. "I've never been like that—you have me mixed up with my mother. But I'm not pursuing a relationship with Jerry until I'm all here. Funny thing is, I didn't know I wasn't until the past few days. Reading that book has opened my eyes. You wouldn't believe the stuff those two were into—talk about free spirits! That's how I want to feel—capable of anything."

"You're talking free love and all that?"

I laughed. "No. A free spirit on my terms."

"A free spirit on your terms wouldn't be a free spirit, Summer. First you'll need to loosen up. I suggest a night out at The Keg. There's a good band playing this weekend."

17

I was angry when I woke up the next morning—at myself as well as Jerry. This was the first time I'd felt like this in a couple of months and although anger probably wasn't the best emotion to feel, at least it galvanized me into action. Even after too much wine the night before I actually had energy.

I took a shower, dressed, and made myself an omelet and toast before I fed Cutty. He seemed more exuberant than usual as if he noticed my change in mood. I left the house early, planning to go by the drug store on the way to Tarot and Tea to fill my prescription.

As I walked along I was aware for the first time in weeks of sounds going on around me: the call of a cardinal, the roar and hum of cars, the chattering of children on their way to school. My mind turned to the night before. How rude and inconsiderate could Jerry be? At this moment I had no desire to see him again and labeled him 'jerk of the highest order' in my mind. Some harsher expletives arrived on the heels of this thought and I grinned to myself. This was new for me.

At the door of the drug store I paused, a realization going through my mind. I had essential oils at the shop and lots of literature about the healing benefits. Many of these were good for depression and to increase energy. Before I succumbed to the effects of chemicals I might as well give them a try. That way I'd have first-hand experience when I recommended them to my clients.

I walked by the drug store, my step light. Everything was going to be okay.

In my shop I perused the collection of oils, reading through the literature the company had provided. And then I chose clary sage, frankincense and lavender, which were all good for anxiety, insomnia, fear and stress. To this mix I added wild orange to lift my mood, adding two drops of each into a diffuser.

In the back room I filled up the diffuser with water, found a glass jar and added one drop of each herb to it and filled it up with water as well. I would surround myself with the scent and take it internally to boost the effectiveness. By the time I had the diffuser going and had taken several large gulps of my oil infused water my first customer walked in.

Douglas Weatherby was in his usual outfit, his wide smile irresistible. "Hmm...what a pleasant aroma," he said, looking toward the diffuser on the counter. "This will pick up your business."

I gazed at him, puzzled. "How did you know business was down?"

"My dear girl, it's obvious to the most unskilled observer," he answered, gesturing toward the full shelves and lack of customers. "The store is just as it was last week. Now tell me, how is the book going?"

"It's going great. I love Serena's style and reading about my mother as a young girl is opening my eyes."

Douglas cocked his head to one side like a bird. "They were quite the pair. Have you reached the part about your brother?"

"He's born if that's what you mean."

"Ah. When you come to it, try not to let it upset you.

You know how it turns out." He smiled, heading to the essential oil section. " I think I'll try this one today," he said bringing one of the small bottles up to pay for it.

"Ylang ylang?"

"It was a favorite scent of your mother's, that and patchouli."

"I didn't know she was into essential oils."

"Oh yes, my dear—very much so." He began to say more and then stopped himself. "When do you think you'll have the book completely transcribed?"

I smiled, taking the money he handed me. "If it stays this quiet it won't take me long. It's very absorbing."

Douglas glanced around the empty shop before turning back to me. "You won't have much time today I'm afraid." He picked up his little package and left the store, the bell tinkling as he pulled the door shut behind him.

I puzzled over his words and was just getting out my computer when several people entered. I'd never seen them before and they were dressed in extremely old-fashioned dresses and suits that seemed similar to the elegant clothing Douglas wore. They nodded to me before working their way systematically through the store, ending up at the counter with many things in their hands. I rang them up one by one, shocked that it wasn't ten yet and I'd just sold more than two hundred dollars' worth of merchandise. When they left I hurried to the door, expecting an old Rolls Royce or some other vintage car to carry them away, but they were already out of sight.

Customers came in fits and starts all day long, which made it hard to get any transcribing done. When three o'clock came around I made a decision to take my computer home and work there. Just before five I counted up the days earnings, gratified to see that I'd done more than a thousand dollars. If business kept up like this I wouldn't have to take a mortgage out on my house to repair the storm damage.

It was cold when I left and I was glad I'd brought my down jacket and wool scarf along. Clouds were massing and I was pretty sure another big storm was on the way.

I made a salad for dinner, throwing in some cooked shrimp. Cutty sat beside me begging, his liquid gaze melting my heart. "Okay, just one," I told him holding out my hand. He took it delicately, his expression puzzled as he tried to decide if he liked it or not. In the end he decided yes and begged for more. In the meantime Mischief had noticed and was now meowing. I broke off a small piece for her and then hurried to finish, my mind already on the book and anxious to begin work. After a cursory cleanup I sat down at the table and opened my computer. When my cell phone rang a second later I frowned in disgust, picking it up to see who dared disturb my concentration.

"Are you ready?" Agnes asked.

"Ready for what?"

I heard an annoyed sigh. "We made a date to go to The Keg."

I'd forgotten what day it was in my haste to read Serena's journal. "I just sat down to…"

"No excuses, Summer. I'm on my way over."

I hung up and went into the bedroom to search for something appropriate to wear. I picked out a pair of jeans and a western shirt I'd recently purchased from the secondhand store, pulling on my cowboy boots. When

Agnes arrived she took one look at me and shook her head before dragging me with her into my bedroom.

"Slinky low cut top, Summer. Where would I find one?"

I held my hands out. "Not sure I have one."

But somehow Agnes found something suitable buried underneath several layers of T-shirts. It was a deep orange with a gathered neckline that was low cut and very flattering. "Wear this skirt," she ordered, pulling a skirt I never wore off a hanger. It was purple and tighter than I felt comfortable in but when I put it on I realized I'd lost some weight.

Agnes held out her lipstick and I dutifully smeared it onto my lips.

"You can wear your cowboy boots," she conceded.

I pulled on a heavy coat and a scarf and followed her out to her car.

When we walked into The Keg I noticed that several male heads turned. I assumed they were eying Agnes since she was gorgeous and always looked perfect in her black outfits. But when a man came up and asked me to dance I realized that it was not only her they were paying attention to. As the evening wore on I forgot my troubles, enjoying myself way more than I expected.

Sam turned up at some point coming over to our table and asking Agnes to dance. I watched them on the dance floor surprised to see how good a dancer he was as he led Agnes in a version of the swing. There was something appealing about them together with their opposite hair color. Sam in jeans and a western shirt was very different from Sam in a uniform.

I searched for Jerry but didn't see him and before I could fret about him another guy asked me to dance.

When we left two hours later I was giddy and slightly tipsy from the wine we'd consumed.

"I told you you'd enjoy yourself. If Jerry wants to stay away that's his problem but don't let him keep you from having fun, Summer. You're way too young to hole up in your house every night."

"Since Sam was there I thought I might see Jerry."

"Sam's interesting in a cop sort of way," she said, cocking her head. "He seems too big city to fit in here for long."

"I've never felt comfortable around him—he has an air of superiority."

Agnes glanced at me. "I think he's insecure," she said. "He doesn't know how to act in a town where everyone knows everyone else. And his father's sick."

"What?"

"Yeah. That's why he moved here. From what Sam said he doesn't have long to live."

I stared into the darkness thinking about my unfeeling reaction to Sam. Jerry had mentioned Sam's sick father and I'd forgotten all about it.

I closed the store early next day just to get home and read Serena's journals. I made myself a cup of tea and settled on the couch.

Ephraim and my mother met during a random bus trip from Ames to New York. My mother lived in New York but had grown up in Ames and she had come to see her aging parents who I never got to meet. In his day job Ephraim worked for a candy company and had traveled to Ames to elicit orders for the New York store. They struck up a conversation on the bus ride back and when my mother discovered that Ephraim was an actor and knew Serena she was immediately enchanted. From then on they were inseparable. My mother had always longed to be an actress but didn't have the gift.

My mother became pregnant a few months into the relationship but when Ephraim asked her to marry him she said no. It was not long after the birth that my mother decided she'd had enough of him. She'd had a water birth with candles and a midwife despite Ephraim's insistence that she have the baby in the hospital. In Serena's opinion Ephraim was an overbearing man who hoped to clip Lila's wings. That would never have worked, I thought to myself, reading on.

After they split up Lila was accommodating with the baby, allowing Ephraim access when he wished, but her subsequent love affairs grated on Ephraim's nerves. He wanted to report her to the authorities for child neglect but somehow Serena and Lila convinced him not to. It seemed they had used magic to change his mind but the description had been ripped out of the manuscript. I kept going.

During that time Serena and Lila belonged to a coven and were studying witchcraft. Ephraim knew nothing about this. They participated in séances and went to meetings on the full moon where they danced naked and performed rituals. All of it sounded innocent enough but the day Ephraim discovered what they were up he went berserk. He threatened to take the baby away and contacted the authorities who actually made a surprise home inspection. Luckily this happened on a day when my mother was at home doing domestic activities. After that it was all out war between Lila and Ephraim.

In the meantime Serena was having troubles of her own, married to one man after the other, the marriages lasting for a year or less. Again there were passages missing from this section as though someone had ripped them out to prevent anyone from reading it. From what I could glean these men all had one thing in common— they were sociopaths who preyed on others. Serena spoke at length about what she planned to do to these men, she and my mother whipping up spells left and right and using voodoo they learned from a Jamaican woman who was a member of their coven. No deaths occurred but from the descriptions there was plenty of pain. Serena justified it, saying that these men deserved even worse— and as I read on I began to agree with her. Why she continually picked sickos to have a relationship with was a mystery since she and my mother both seemed very intuitive. I wondered if it was solely to punish them. There were a couple of references to a woman named Vivienne who seemed less than excited about what Lila and Serena were into to, but nothing to indicate exactly who she was.

I finally reached the part in which Serena and Douglas met. Douglas happened to watch her in an off-Broadway production of Romeo and Juliet in which she was cast in the lead. He came back stage, introduced himself and that was the beginning of their love-story. Of course I knew from reading ahead that they formed a threesome with my mother a few years later.

Reading on I found out that they moved in together when Randall was a toddler. They shared a house in New York. Ephraim was far from giving up on his custody battle and haunted my mother with constant threats and accusations. It was shortly after that that Serena, Lila and Randall and Douglas moved to Ames hoping to put some distance between them.

For a while things were calmer but when Serena and Lila formed another coven and conducted their rituals and ceremonies out by the river, the townspeople began to protest. Several newspaper articles were pasted into her journals with titles like: **Disappearing cats and dogs!** followed by lengthy descriptions of sacrifices that had absolutely nothing to do with Serena and my mother. I read through one from a supposed eyewitness who claimed he saw ghosts flying about and heard the screams of human sacrifice. All this did nothing to increase their popularity. It was around this time that my mother bought the building that eventually became Tarot and Tea. Her parents had died by this time and she used her inheritance for the investment and then the three of them, and baby Randall, moved in.

Eventually it was Douglas who changed hearts and minds. He debunked the newspaper reports and began organizing garden parties at their new address, turning their occult practices into party favors. Soon they were the talk of the town and had people begging for Tarot and palm readings. The front room was used exclusively for this purpose, with candles and furnishings to set the mood.

It was around nine o'clock when I had to reread a paragraph several times to have it penetrate into my brain. Serena's words rang out as though she was standing next to me in my living room.

Douglas Weatherby was killed in a car crash today. He's always been a fast driver but we never worried about him because he was such a good driver. From the account from witnesses, a delivery truck veered into his lane sending him careening down an embankment. The other driver was fine but our dear sweet and loving

Douglas was killed instantly when his head hit the windshield. Lila and I went to identify his body, both of us overcome with tears. I've never felt so sad about anything in my life. The shock has driven me to take a short hiatus from this work and Lila is completely heartbroken.

I sat back, staring at the words in longhand. Jerry was right—the man who I knew as Douglas Weatherby was an imposter. But what was he after? I turned the page of Serena's manuscript to see what happened next, finding several newspaper clippings glued to the page. When I opened them up to read the obit, a picture was included. I peered at it closely. It was the same man I knew, the same man who had bought essential oils from me yesterday morning.

I didn't read any further, my mind attempting to grapple with this new revelation. The man I'd seen was either a ghost or Douglas Weatherby's twin brother.

My cell phone rang early the next day and I answered it hurriedly without checking to see who it was.

"Summer?"

"Hi, Jerry."

"I think you'd better come down to the station."

"What happened?"

There was a long pause. "Just come down, would you?"

"I have to go to work."

"I'll pick you up and deliver you to the shop afterwards."

I looked at the clock--it was barely seven-thirty. "Okay, just let me put some clothes on."

"I'll be there in fifteen minutes." He clicked off

abruptly. What in the world was going on now? He sounded deadly serious.

I was waiting outside trying to keep from freezing to death when he drove up. The wind was fierce but so far there had been no rain or snow. I opened the passenger side of the patrol car and climbed in. "What's this about?"

"We have some news about Ephraim and Randall and also more details on Serena but I want you to see it for yourself."

"I have some news too—you were right about Douglas. He was killed in a car crash in 1977. But the man who came into my store looks identical to the picture I saw. Was he a twin?"

Jerry glanced over. "Not that I know. So you're still sticking to your story about this guy?"

"It's not a story. He was there yesterday. Agnes has met him too."

"Do you have a credit receipt? Maybe we can track him."

"No. He always pays in cash."

"That's convenient."

"What are you saying—that I'm delusional? I'm really tired of your attitude, Jerry. Is this Sam's doing?"

"Sam has his opinions but I'm a free agent. I call 'em as I see 'em."

I stared out the window trying to keep from screaming at him. How could I have been in love with this...this...I let the word I never said out loud drift through my mind, feeling better. When we reached the station I hopped out and hurried inside, afraid that if I looked at Jerry I might have to smack him.

Inside the station he grabbed my elbow. "Come with

me," he ordered.

I wrenched away. "I'll follow you."

He led toward a desk in back where Sam was sitting with a female cop. They both looked up as we approached. "Summer, the ghost buster—how nice to see you." Sam smirked.

"Very funny," I said slanting a look at Jerry. "Thanks for telling my secrets."

"Had to verify things with my partner," Jerry answered, his expression bland. He pulled out a chair. "Sit. We have some pictures for you to look at."

On the desk was a large book like the other one where I'd found my father. But this one was open to a picture of my mother. And she was holding a number.

"Did you know your mother was incarcerated?"

I stared at the picture, shocked by the tangles and greasy look of her normally glossy hair, the bags under her eyes. She looked like a floozy. "No. When was this?"

"The year you were born," Sam said. "She was pregnant with you when they picked her up for child abuse. You were born in the slammer, Summer," Sam said smugly.

"I...what?" I glanced over at Jerry who nodded.

"Apparently she left your brother alone one too many times. Ephraim had lodged several complaints against her and this one happened to stick. When you were born child services took you away. And then Ephraim came forward and took care of you until a foster family was found."

"Foster family? I don't have any memory of that."

Jerry perched on the edge of the desk watching me. "You were a newborn, Summer. Lila was out by the time you were eight months old and petitioned the court to get you back. They were lenient because she promised to marry your father."

"But she never did."

"Actually that's not true. She did marry him. They were together until he was caught for breaking and entering. Unfortunately a death accompanied that crime and even though it wasn't proven beyond a shadow of a doubt, your father was put away for twenty years for second degree murder."

I thought about my mother, remembering how she tucked me in and sang me to sleep. I had no memory of a man in our lives other than the few times I saw my father. "Who was my foster family?"

"Now that's the interesting part. I don't know how they managed it but from what we can glean it was Serena and Douglas and it seems very possible they were married at the time. They lived in the house where your mother started Tarot and Tea."

Some memory moved quickly through my mind, evaporating before I could get hold of it. "Did Serena have a daughter? I remember playing with someone."

"Yes. Apparently she's the one who's named in the will. Unfortunately no one knows where she is."

"They haven't found her yet?"

"Not that I know of," Jerry answered, looking over at his partner. "But we're not privy to what's happening in the courts."

"So is my mother alive or dead?"

Jerry glanced at Sam and back to me. "I was hoping you could tell us. Your father hasn't turned up and we think the two of them are trying to exact revenge for what was done to him."

"You mean for going to jail?"

"We found newspaper articles and old police records that indicate that he never stopped professing his innocence," Sam answered. "According to his statement the body was already there when he broke in."

"That was before DNA, right?"

"Yup. 1980."

I tried to puzzle through all the information. "So you brought me down here…why?"

"To explain what we've found out. We need your help to find her."

I shook my head. "I don't know where she is. I haven't heard from her since that one note she left and there's been no more sign of her since those two were killed."

"Remember the robbery a few weeks back? Someone broke into the house of the retired homicide detective who was in charge of Frank's case. And the only thing they stole was files."

"That doesn't sound like revenge to me."

Jerry frowned. "There's more to it than that but it's police business for now. We've put out a Bolo for both of them. Just help us locate your mother, okay?"

Sam put a hand on my arm. "Tell that friend of yours I enjoyed dancing with her the other night."

I felt Jerry watching me as I answered. "Didn't you two exchange phone numbers?"

Sam looked down. "I'd had a couple of beers and I wasn't thinking straight. Do you have it?"

I was acutely aware of Jerry's eyes boring into the back of my head as I gave Sam Agnes's number. Sam wrote it down on a square of paper and stuffed it into his back pocket. I waited for Jerry to say something but he only exchanged a look with Sam and then bent to ask the female officer a question. Apparently the meeting was over.

When Jerry and Sam began to talk I headed toward the front. I paused at the door wondering if Jerry planned to give me a ride back but he and Sam were still talking, the female cop as well.

A cop at the front nodded to me, gesturing toward a patrol car. "Jerry asked me to give you a ride to work."

The two of us ran through driving rain to get to the car. By the time he dropped me at the store the rain had turned to snow.

"Thanks." I climbed out and hurried inside wondering if I should close for the day. The sky was steel gray and the flakes were small—not a good sign.

It was cold in the shop and I cranked up the heat before re-filling my diffuser. I brought it to the front and turned it on, letting the scents do their magic. A second later the door opened and five people hurried inside, stamping their feet to get the snow off their boots. They were all strangers to me.

When one of the women brought up her various things to purchase I asked her how she found out about Tarot and Tea.

She laughed. "Douglas has spread the word that you have the best occult store in miles. He's your biggest fan."

"You know Douglas?"

The woman, who had long wavy gray hair and deep brown eyes, regarded me for a second or two. "We all know Douglas," she said, pulling out some bills.

By the time they'd all left I was five hundred dollars richer. And fifteen minutes later a few of my old customers who had abandoned me trooped in. "We heard you were having a sale," one of them said.

"Um, no sale. What are you looking for?"

"I think I might try those essential oils," Mary Porter told me, smiling. She was in her fifties, a person who browsed but rarely bought anything. Mostly she wandered around drinking from her Starbucks cup that she always had along. "A friend of mine said they work for insomnia."

I nodded. "Lavender's the best. Let me help you." I went ahead of her to the display showing her the booklet and the lavender. I turned as another older woman appeared.

"I heard they were good for women's problems, you know..." she seemed to blush.

"Hot flashes?" I asked.

She nodded, looking around furtively. "With the cold weather they're somewhat welcome but they come at the most inconvenient times. "

I consulted the pamphlet and then pulled out clary sage, geranium and peppermint. "Any or all of these can help."

She took all three and headed toward the counter.

Even with the continuing snow the day continued with sale after sale. The way things were going I would need to place another order for the essential oils and diffusers. When five o'clock rolled around several shelves were completely empty.

I closed out the register and put the cash into the envelope to take to the bank before making sure Tabby had enough dried food to last if I didn't get in the next morning.

When I left the store the snow was still coming down

and lay crisp and white along the sidewalk. A light wind blew it off the branches as I walked in the direction of the trailer. I pulled my wool scarf tighter and readjusted the satchel that held my computer, wishing it wasn't so heavy.

The lack of cars and people on the streets left a silence that seeped into me quieting my inner tension but my cell phone rang dispelling the calm mood. I stopped and dug into my bag to retrieve it. Agnes.

"Did you fill your prescription?"

"No, I decided to go the natural route first. I've been using the oils and I feel a lot better."

"You sound better. Want to go to The Keg for a beer tonight?"

"In the snow? I can't. I have to work on the book. I promised Douglas I'd get it done. Jerry called me down to the station today. He wants me to help them find my mother."

Agnes sighed. "So Jerry still thinks she's alive?"

"Some evidence came to light. He didn't go into detail. I'm inclined to agree with you but I'm heading to the trailer to see if she's been there. And Jerry expects me to come up with her old haunts but I can't remember a thing."

"I know one—remember when she took us out to that little lake? There was like a shack out there where we changed into bathing suits and then we all went swimming. And come to think of it there was a woman along who…" Agnes broke off and I heard her gasp.

"What is it?"

"Summer, we were really young. I thought we didn't meet until we were sixteen. And the woman—I think it was Serena."

"I remember the shack but I don't remember much else. How old were we?"

"Like maybe six?"

"That's weird, Agnes. Do you remember anything else?"

"Not right now but I'll let you know if I do. I kind of remember how to get there though."

"The weekend's coming up. Shall we check it out?"

"If it isn't snowing."

"Before you go, Sam asked for your number today."

Agnes made a funny sound that could have been a nervous laugh. "Maybe I'll go to The Keg without you." And then she clicked off. Agnes never said goodbye like normal people.

When I reached the trailer the door was wide open—someone had been inside and not bothered to replace the bungee cord. The wind had come up and I shivered, but mostly it was nerves that caused it. I pulled the door closed behind me as well as I could, immediately noticing the aroma of roses. In the corner I saw a bag that hadn't been there before, but when I rifled through it I saw that it was mostly men's jeans and shirts and a couple of sweaters. I concluded that someone had been squatting here since there were several dirty plates and cups on the tiny counter by the sink. A pair of slip-on black Capezios caught my eye and when I examined them I was sure they were Lila's. I had half a mind to wait for her to come back but it was too cold. I found a piece of paper and wrote her a note:

Mom, if you're really around I would dearly love to see you. The mystery of whether you're alive or dead is becoming tedious. I love you, Summer.

I propped it on the counter and then pulled the door

shut as best I could and headed home. Snow was falling again and I hurried along the darkened sidewalk, hunched over like an old woman. Just outside the chain link fence that enclosed the parking lot a shadowy figure ran by, but when I moved in that direction there was no one there and no footprints.

Cutty was covered in snow when I arrived home, his little body shivering from the cold. "Why didn't you come in?" I asked him as I rubbed him down with a towel. I fed him dinner and heated up some leftovers for myself, my gaze going to the window. Snow fell steadily and it was definitely sticking. If this kept up it wouldn't be easy to get to the shop in the morning. Luckily the electricity hadn't gone out yet. As that thought went through my mind the lights flickered and went out. "Dang it."

A second later my cell phone rang. "Are you all right?" Jerry's voice asked.

"I'm fine but the electricity just went out."

"That's why I was calling. Mine went out about fifteen minutes ago. Do you want me to come over?"

"No, Jerry. I have a fireplace if I get cold, candles and a warm down comforter on my bed. This house is old with thick walls. I'll be fine."

"You should get a generator."

"This doesn't happen often enough to warrant the expense. I was hoping to work on the book tonight but I doubt that's going to happen."

"Call if you need anything." And then he clicked off.

I groped my way to the drawer where I kept the candles and pulled them out. Lucky for me I had a gas stove where I could light them because trying to find the matches in the dark would not be easy.

I finished eating before opening my computer, using a candle to help see the screen. It was bright enough but I'd neglected to turn it off the last time and the battery was running low. I turned if off. When I called Agnes to make sure she was all right she was on her way to The Keg.

"Are you sure you won't join me? I'm walking and it's beautiful out here."

"I'm already in my PJ's but thanks for the invite. I hope they have electricity--half the town is down. Have fun." I clicked off and then blew out candles and headed into the bedroom.

Carrying the candleholder made me feel like one of the original owners of this house. I thought of ghosts, wondering if the image in my mind was someone from the past. The man was dressed in a long nightshirt and wearing a little cap. If so he was a benign presence. But it was what I actually saw a minute later that sent shivers up and down my arms. My mother, dressed in a skimpy nightgown, ran across my bedroom, her finger to her lips as she glanced at me. I watched her transparent form disappear through the back wall. "Mom?"

I thought I heard the words, 'I'm watching out for you,' but it could have been the wind. Cutty jumped up on the bed, his ears pricked forward as he watched the place where she'd disappeared. A second later the candle flame wavered and nearly went out as cold air came through the gaps around the window frame.

I sat there for at least an hour waiting for her to show herself again but finally my eyelids began to droop and I pulled the down comforter around me and fell asleep.

When I woke in the morning the snow was pristine and sparkling in the sunlight. More than a foot lay on the ground—it was like a winter fairyland outside. My electricity was still off and so I figured the shop was without power as well. No reason to open. I had to shovel my walkway and call the electric company and if the power came back on maybe I could work on the journals for an hour or so. I could see my breath inside the house and dressed warmly, adding heavy socks, a sweater and a scarf before I heated water for coffee. After coffee I crumpled paper and placed kindling and a couple of logs on top and lit it with the matches I'd found in the cupboard next to the refrigerator. Soon I had a cheery roaring fire going. I watched Cutty and Mischief gravitating toward the warmth, both of them settling in on the floor.

The rumble of a snowplow moving along the street broke the stillness and I turned to the window watching cars with their tall hats of snow moving along behind them. The day had begun.

The electric company assured me that they were doing everything they could—thousands were without power. I just had to be patient.

It was around ten that my doorbell rang. A florist delivery truck was idling next to the curb. I opened the door but by then the driver was climbing back into his truck. A thin cardboard box with a green ribbon tied around it had been placed on my stoop. Opening it revealed a dozen vibrant orange roses with a note attached. *Please forgive me*, it said. *I've been a fool.* It was signed Jerry.

I found a suitable vase and put them in water before rereading the note. My eyes welled with tears. This was how he courted me the first time. We had spoken about the meaning of rose colors and I knew that orange represented passion, excitement and desire. He'd never sent this color before. Mostly he'd sent white roses and yellow daisies and purple hyacinths. I had a feeling the conversation with Sam about my night out with Agnes had pressed him into action.

I reached for my cell phone and thought better of it. Let this gesture settle, I told myself. I didn't want to push ahead until I was sure the time was right. I wasn't ready to take up where we left off—not with everything that had happened between us. I was still angry and frustrated. And on top of all that I had to find my mother and get to the bottom of what was going on. And that's when I remembered my visitation. I stood there unable to think for several long moments. Unless I was completely crazy my mother was a ghost. Would I see her again?

Around noon the electricity came back on. By then the fire had burned down and my animals had disappeared to their normal places to rest. I stared at my computer but for some reason I felt anxious to get to the shop. I packed my computer into the satchel, donned my warmest boots and jacket, adding mittens, a hat and scarf. Just before I left I gave Cutty a dog bone as a peacemaking gesture. Mischief eyed me from her place on top of the kitchen cabinet as though any recognition of my existence was beneath her dignity. I stuck my tongue out at her as I opened the front door, pulling it closed behind me.

School was canceled and kids were out making snowmen and having snowball fights. There was a holiday feel in the air. I remembered that Thanksgiving was coming up. Jerry had invited me weeks ago, but now...I put the thought out of my mind enjoying the beauty of the trees and listening to the whump of snow falling off the branches.

When I reached the shop footprints indicated that several customers had come and gone. I unlocked the door and put the open sign in the window and then went to check on Tabby. As soon as I opened the door to the kitchen I saw the note on the table. *My darling girl, I got your message. It isn't safe yet for me to come forward so please don't look for me. But once we unravel the mystery you won't be able to get rid of me. I've missed you so much! Love, Mom.*

What?

Before I could puzzle over this I heard the bell chime and hurried into the front. Douglas was just ducking his head to enter the shop. He pulled the door closed behind him, his gaze meeting mine. I noticed that he was dressed as always, his clothing without a wrinkle, and not a flake of snow on his shoes.

"Hello, dear girl. I came to say goodbye."

"Goodbye? I thought you lived here."

His eyes swiveled sideways for a moment before they met mine. "I did but that was long ago. It's time for me to move on now. I've done what I came here to do."

"What was that?"

Douglas smiled. "I met you, for one thing. And now Serena's journal will be in the world for all to see. It's an important story and I will always be grateful. Your life is about to open up, Summer."

"Douglas, I know who you are now," I stammered hurriedly. "Jerry saw some old records from when I was first born. He told me you and Serena took care of me when my mother was in jail. And last night I saw my mother walk through my bedroom wall. I need answers." I stared into his gray eyes watching them grow misty.

He put his hand on my arm, the first gesture of this sort he'd made. "Dearest girl. The past is gone. Everything that is happening now is part of the mystery that surrounds us all. You'll soon know the truth. Take care of that friend of yours who sometimes minds the store." He smiled but there was sadness in his eyes. He turned toward the door but what happened after that I wasn't sure.

"Wait a second!" I called out. But the door was shut as it had been and I was positive I hadn't heard the chime of the bell. I opened the door and ran outside but there was no sign of him anywhere.

I brushed away the tears running down my cheeks. According to Jerry Douglas had stood in for my father when I was a baby. I hadn't read far enough in the journal to know if this was true. And then I thought of the year of his death—1977. I wasn't born until 1978. A shiver moved from my toes up to my head. I thought about what he'd said and all the myriad things he hadn't said.

It was sometime later that a delivery truck pulled up. This time the flowers Jerry sent were white and red roses mixed. Their aroma was heavenly. Red for passion and love, white for friendship. I thought back to the masses of flowers I got from him every day during the short time we dated. I knew he'd deny it, but he was a true romantic. My heart longed for him but I couldn't succumb to his charms yet. I'd just had a visit from another ghost.

18

"What?" Agnes's exclamation hurt my ear. "I'm not kidding, Agnes. He's a ghost."

"I'm not saying I don't believe it. I'm just shocked, is all. He seemed perfectly normal aside from his interest in me."

"What interest?"

"I already told you. He asked me where I lived, what I did when I wasn't here, how my life had been so far. He asked me what my earliest memory was. He hugged me goodbye, Summer. And I'd just met him."

"That's kind of weird because he told me to look out for you."

"Okay that's even weirder. What did he mean by that?"

"I have no idea. I was going to ask him but he seemed in a hurry to get away. Maybe the journal will shed some light on it. And in all the excitement I forgot to tell you the weirdest part of this story. My mother's ghost was in the cottage last night. She said she was watching out for me. I saw her walk through my wall."

"I have goose bumps all over." Agnes was quiet and I could hear her breathing. "What's up with you and Jerry?" she finally asked.

"He's sent me flowers twice now but until he can accept the way I think I can't get back together."

"What if he never accepts the idea of a ghost? I don't

know many who would."

"I can't be with someone who doesn't believe in things he can't see. There's too much out there we don't understand. Before all this I thought I was open-minded but in reality I was a complete skeptic. But after Douglas and now my mom I'm way ahead of Jerry."

"Good luck," Agnes said. "A cop is the last person to have an open mind. If your mom's a ghost who wrote that note?"

"That's what I've been wondering. And there was another one today in the shop. She said not to look for her because it wasn't safe and something about unraveling a mystery."

"I'm glad I'm not you right now."

"Douglas said that I'd soon know the truth. I hope he's right."

I was on my way home from the shop when Jerry's cruiser stopped beside me on the road. "Can I give you a lift, pretty lady?"

Clouds had massed again and the wind was blowing hard. I welcomed the offer. I climbed into the passenger side and pulled the door shut. "What brought you into this neighborhood?"

Jerry grinned. "I have a friend who lives around here. At least she used to be my friend."

"She still is. How can a girl resist roses?"

Jerry turned to look out the windshield as we moved slowly along the street. "I'm sorry, Summer. I know I've been acting like a jackass. These past few weeks have been really hard."

"What's going on?"

"I didn't tell you everything that day at the station. This case with Frank and your mom has brought up some very nasty business that involves my father."

"Did you know this when you moved out?"

He nodded looking abashed. "I told you already that Frank Messer always insisted he didn't kill that man. And the ME at the time lied about the victim's time of death, and there were also lies about the gun and who it belonged to. The arresting officer brought forward a witness who committed perjury during your father's trial."

"So they pinned it on my father. Did they know who killed the guy?"

"Someone on the force at the time."

"But who, Jerry? Who railroaded Frank?"

Jerry looked away for a second and then pulled over to the side of the road. He left the car idling, the heater blasting warm air into the interior. "It was my Dad."

"Your father? Wasn't he a detective?"

Jerry looked pained. "Pop was Chief of police at the time. The man my dad killed knew he was a dirty cop. Pop shot and killed that man long before your father broke in. Pops is going crazy now that Frank is out of jail and all of this is coming to light. And he remembers Lila from the early days and how she refused to give up. He knows his head's on the chopping block."

No wonder Jerry had been so weird for the past few weeks. "Lila isn't alive, Jerry. I saw her ghost walk through my bedroom last night." I looked over at him to gage his reaction but he was staring into space as though he hadn't heard. "Whoever is writing those notes is not my mother," I continued, reaching into my satchel to pull out the latest one. "According to this she doesn't want me to look for her—something about unraveling a mystery."

Jerry turned his attention back to me, reaching for the note. After reading it his gaze met mine. "This was in the store?"

"It was. But after last night I'm sure she isn't among the living."

"Summer, the electricity was out, you were using candles which means weird shadows were dancing off the walls. I'm sure you imagined it."

"I don't think shadows were responsible for seeing Lila walking through my wall. And she said she was looking out for me."

He turned and stared into space, his lips pressed together. "My father's old and in a very fragile state. I'm not sure he can make it through a trial."

"You think it will come to that?"

"He will be indicted for this, Summer."

I'm sorry, Jerry. I know how this must hurt. Are you going there for Thanksgiving?"

"Yes. My mother needs me. His arrest has been put off until after the holiday since his health is so poor. Only a retired Chief of police would receive this sort of treatment."

I reached over and touched his arm. "Just for the record, Jerry, I love you. I know I didn't say it before. I've been so angry since you left. And then the way you behaved in the restaurant that night..." I met his gaze. "You hurt me."

Jerry reached forward and took my face in his hands. There were tears in his eyes. "Can I come back now? I can't afford to buy any more roses."

"Even though I just told you I saw a ghost?"

He grinned. "I promised I would keep an open mind.

I don't believe you really saw a ghost but I'm not going to discount it either."

Okay. At least he wasn't dismissing it altogether. When our eyes met I saw his pain and stress, his brown eyes soft with yearning. A second later I was pressed against him our lips meeting in a kiss that nearly brought me to tears. When he finally released me it felt like something heavy had been lifted off my chest.

As he pulled away from the curb I smiled to myself wondering how he would take another ghost in the mix. I'd told him about Mom but I hadn't yet mentioned what I'd seen in the journal about Douglas's date of death.

He kissed me again before dropping me off. "I have to go to Pop's tonight. My brother just came into town."

"I haven't even met them yet. "

He shrugged. "Now is not the right time." I watched him drive away and then went inside.

The first thing I did after greeting Cutty was to call Agnes. "Are you all right?"

"I'm fine. Are you going to fuss over me now like a mother hen?"

"Agnes, I trust Douglas and if he's worried then something's going on or will be going on. I wish you'd move in with me for a week or two."

"What's with you and Jerry now? I thought I saw his car heading toward the shop."

"He's moving back in but you can still come. I have an extra room."

"Did you tell him about your mom?"

"I did. He didn't believe or disbelieve, at least that's what he said, but he's got his own troubles right now. You know the crime my father supposedly committed?

Well, it was Jerry's father who did it and the entire police department backed his lies. It looks like they're going to indict Jerry's father."

"So your Dad was in jail all that time for a crime he didn't commit?"

"He broke in and stole stuff but he didn't kill anyone. His sentence would have been a quarter or a third of what it ended up being. According to Jerry his dad is old and frail. Jerry's a wreck."

"Maybe being a wreck will make him more open to paranormal happenings," Agnes said.

I laughed. "So give it some thought, okay? I'd feel a lot better if you were close by and not on the other side of town."

"I wish Douglas had been a bit more explicit."

"He told me all would be revealed."

"Soon?"

"He didn't say."

At the shop the next morning I kept hoping Douglas would walk through the door. There were so many questions bubbling up in my mind. Every time the bell jingled I looked up eagerly but it was never him. In all likelihood he wasn't coming back. I heard funny noises a couple of times during the morning hours that seemed to emanate from upstairs but with customers roaming around I couldn't investigate. By the afternoon I'd concluded that I had a squirrel up there, which meant I would need to call pest control.

I was in a melancholy mood when I left the store, my mind casting back over the past few months. The snow lay in uneven patches along the sidewalk making it difficult to keep from slipping even with my hiking boots on. I had gotten my hopes up about Mom being alive and now I had to accept that she was gone.

I heard a car pull up alongside me and turned to see Jerry behind the wheel of his old Mercedes. When I climbed in I noticed that the back seat was filled with his stuff.

Jerry shrugged and grinned. "I didn't want to waste more time moping around my house. Are you okay with this? You look kind of sad. I don't want to push myself on you if you're not ready."

"I'm fine. I've just been thinking about Mom and Douglas Weatherby."

Jerry shook his head and glanced at me before turning back to the road.

"I didn't truly believe in ghosts until just recently, Jerry. You'd believe too if you'd seen Mom and spoken with Douglas."

"I had a couple of weird experiences when I was younger but I figured it was because of pot use or one of those hallucinogens I took back then."

I thought of the pictures I'd seen of younger Jerry, imagining him holed up in some room smoking pot with a bunch of other kids. It was easy to do. "What's really weird is that Douglas told people about Tarot and Tea. I understand a ghost being see-through and ethereal like Mom was but this one was corporeal and had money."

"Past tense?"

"He came to say goodbye and when I went after him there were no footprints in the snow." I watched Jerry for a negative reaction but he only looked thoughtful.

"Hard for me to believe in ghosts," he muttered. "Maybe Douglas had a twin after all. Have you checked in Serena's book?"

"I'll look tonight but I'm telling you Douglas was definitely not of this world. And I swear some of the people he sent to the store were ghosts too."

"What?" Jerry frowned.

"I've never seen any of them before and they were dressed in clothing that hasn't been fashionable for thirty or forty years." Jerry didn't respond to this, his attention seemingly on the road. "I hope you don't mind if I work for a while tonight," I continued. "These journals are irresistible."

Jerry's mouth quirked. "As long as you come to bed at a reasonable hour."

"I'm definitely planning an early night," I replied. Maybe this would work out after all.

19

We made dinner together and sat at the table to eat. The espresso machine stood in its allotted spot again and something about seeing it there gave me a little thrill. Or maybe it was visualizing Jerry's arms around me that was sending chills up and down my spine. After dinner we cleaned up and then Jerry went to the couch to read the newspaper while I sat at the kitchen table and opened up my computer.

I hadn't gotten very far when a passage popped out. "Look at this!" I yelled, pointing to a paragraph in Serena's hand. Jerry put down the newspaper and came into the kitchen to read over my shoulder.

With a little help Douglas has come back to us. Lila is skeptical but she's beginning to believe what I've been telling her all along. There is magic in the world if you know how to harness it. At the same time little Randall is turning into quite an obnoxious child, pulling the wings off butterflies and stepping on any bug he comes upon. I've argued with Lila about this but she ignores it, chalking it up to little boy behavior. And Lila is such a creature lover. She has a blind spot when it comes to her son. Ephraim is equally unconcerned, that is when he's around, which isn't often. Lila has met someone and I think this new fling may stick for a while. His name is Frank and he is a looker. The only fly in the ointment is Vivienne who's decided that Frank is more her style. So far Frank prefers Lila, but I could see this turning into quite a fight.

In the meantime I'm acting in several plays and having my own fun playing with Douglas and flirting with his brother.

"What in hell does she mean, 'harnessing magic'? Is she saying she brought the dude back to life?"

"It kind of sounds like it."

"This is too weird for my Italian/Irish blood. Contrary to Irish lore I wasn't brought up by fairies."

"My mother never mentioned a word about any of this and she loved talking about her spiritual awakenings and her connection to the goddess. She told me about astral traveling and seeing little light beings in the corners of the room but she never mentioned bringing anyone back to life."

Jerry listened to me and then hit his forehead with his palm. "Crap. I just remembered Thanksgiving. I know I invited you but under the circumstances I…"

"I wouldn't come even if you begged me. When your father finds out I'm Frank Messer's daughter he'll have a heart attack."

"Don't say that. He has a weak heart already." Jerry made the sign of the cross.

"Are you Catholic?"

"Italian mother and Irish father—what do *you* think? A better description would be lapsed Catholic. I gave it up years ago."

"We've known each other for years—how did I miss that?"

"It doesn't come up in normal conversation and you haven't met my parents. If you'd been to their house you'd figure it out pretty quickly."

"Crucifixes all over the place?"

"Yup, and statues of saints as well as a million brothers and sisters."

"Really? I wish all this hadn't happened. I was looking forward to meeting everyone."

"Once you do you'll regret that thought, believe me. I wish it hadn't happened too, but for different reasons."

"How many of you are there?"

"I've got four brothers and three sisters. They'll all be there because of Pop."

"I'm sorry, Jerry. The stress must be very hard on him."

Jerry scoffed and shook his head. "He brought it on himself. The worst of it is realizing the person I looked up to most in life was a dirty cop."

"You never suspected anything?"

"I was a little kid when all that went down. If Frank hadn't been released it never would have come out."

"I wonder if my mother disappeared so she could pursue it for him." My eyes met Jerry's and neither one of us spoke for a full minute. "Do you know how she might have done that?" I finally asked.

"If she got hold of the court records from the trial she might have seen something, especially since she knew what she was looking for, but I don't see how she could have managed that."

"Maybe Douglas helped. He certainly helped me."

"I thought you told me you'd seen her ghost."

"Maybe someone killed her just recently."

Jerry yawned and stretched, raising his eyebrows suggestively. "I'd love to put my mind on something more pleasant. Any ideas?"

Heat rose into my cheeks. I closed my computer and took the hand he held out.

The next morning Cutty was incensed that he'd spent the night locked out of my bedroom. When I came out to make coffee I gave him lots of love, inviting him in when I brought Jerry his cappuccino.

Jerry smiled, looking appealingly rumpled and sleepy. "Haven't felt this good in a while," he said, taking the cup I held out. "Unfortunately I need to go back to the real world."

"It's Saturday."

"Doesn't matter. I'm on call and this stuff with Pop isn't helping." He looked wistful. "At least I escaped for a night."

"Will you have to testify?"

"Hell no. I told you before I was a little kid when this happened."

"Yeah, but didn't you say you've known about it for a while now?"

Jerry's shoulders drooped. "I tried not to believe it. I know you're not crazy about Sam but he's the one who got me to see the truth."

"I have a friend like that too," I said, thinking of Agnes. "If you're going to the station I'll go to the shop. I was considering playing hooky today."

"Wish we could," Jerry said, getting out of bed. I admired his butt as he headed toward the shower.

I was in the shop when the call came in on the landline.

"This is Brandy Wine from the D.A.'s office. Is Lila McCloud available?"

Brandy Wine? Who would name a kid that?

"Um...no. This is her daughter, Summer. I haven't seen my mother since she disappeared five years ago."

"Well, she filed a complaint with our office. We're just following up on our findings."

"What kind of complaint?"

There was a pause and I heard papers rustling. "It has to do with a man named Frank Messer who was recently released from prison. Your mother is suing the department for, according to her, putting an innocent man in jail."

"Frank Messer is my father."

"Can you tell me where I can find him? Do you have a phone number?"

"I've never met the man."

There was another pause, longer this time. "If you see either of them could you ask them to call, please? Our office has uncovered several discrepancies that need to be cleared up."

"Does this mean her suit is being settled?"

"It's not quite that simple. Here's my number."

I took down the numbers and hung up wondering why Jerry hadn't mentioned any of this. Surely he knew about the suit. My mind careened down a winding path that emptied into a blank white space and for a moment I wondered if I might faint. I grabbed hold of the counter to steady myself. All my ideas about ghosts had been dashed when I met Douglas. Could Serena and my mother have managed another sleight of hand to bring her back to life too? I had to get home and read that journal through to the end.

When I called Jerry I got his answering machine. I left a short message asking him to call me and hung up. After that I paced around the empty shop trying to decide what to do. In the end I closed early and walked home.

I was sitting on the couch reading when my cell phone rang.

"Sorry Summer. I was busy. What's up?"

After I told him about the call there was utter silence. "Jerry, did you know about this?"

He hesitated for a minute before saying, "It's kind of a long and complicated story. Can we do this when I get back?"

"It sounds like you've known about my mother all along. You think she's alive. What do they want from her?"

"I can't talk about it right now. I've got to go." The phone beeped as he severed the connection.

I skipped to the last part of the manuscript, trying to ignore the nerves that had settled in my stomach. Something was seriously off about all of this and I wasn't sure I wanted to find out what it was. The image of my mother's ghost went through my mind. I had no doubt about what I'd seen. So how could she be alive?

And then I reached the part in Serena's story that happened just before Serena came to Ames the last time.

I told Lila a long time ago not to fool around with Vivienne in this way. Lila and Vivienne were always up to no good and playing tricks on people. I thought their falling out would stop her but there were times she said she just had to get away. I knew it might come to this and now it's too late to help her. With a small amount of black magic I've discovered some of what they have in mind. They know I'm trying to stop them. I felt sorry for him until I realized that he has a serious criminal streak. Of course she's as bad as he is, something I warned Lila about over and over. I thought he'd given it up but from what I've seen lately I was dead wrong.

I have to travel to Ames to see Douglas about these journals. And I hope I can find the book Lila left in the store for me. With her help I managed to get rid of Jonathon in a way that was virtually undetectable. Douglas begged me to leave him but how could I? I'd only married the man because Douglas was a ghost by then and I couldn't count on him to support me. My acting days were long over by then and I'd used up most of my savings.

The man deserved to die painfully over and over for what he did. In the final edit of my journal I must write this part out since I would rather not be taken to jail over it. Even if they never discover how I did it being in a jail cell for more than one hour would be the end of me.

I've had a recurring nightmare that someone is going to do me in. I guess I deserve it after what I've done but I want to make sure my daughter has what she needs and understands why I had to do what I did. I'm still in awe that she was conceived at all. She's my other reason for visiting Ames.

Douglas has been gadding about Ames and talking with everyone he meets. He seems intent on helping Lila's daughter with the store for some reason. Maybe he's nostalgic for the old days when the three of us were together. He must know that his time on this earth is limited. I would have expected him to spend more of it with me but he's always been the social one. I'll miss him when his time is up.

The date on this page was the day before Serena's death and I read it carefully.

I saw Ephraim this morning before I went into Lila's old store. He seemed particularly upset with me about the

217

book, wanting to know details about what I'd included about him and Randall. I told him not to worry. But in reality he has plenty to worry about. I have an entire chapter dedicated to Ephraim and Randall and their psychopathic behaviors. I've tried for years to get them arrested and put away but the police refused to follow up on it.

I'm nearing the end of the story now although I could add many more pertinent details. I just hope my publisher has a good editor and can whip this into shape. They begged me for it since I'm somewhat famous in certain circles, insisting that it would sell like hotcakes. Once I copy it I'll edit out the nasty parts and send it off. I've been as honest as I can and I hope I haven't gotten anyone into trouble as a result. (Except those who deserve it, of course)

I'm signing off for now but I will continue this tomorrow…Several things have just come to mind that I must include in the story.

But tomorrow never came for Serena. I let out a sigh thinking about everything she'd written. If Ephraim had any inkling of what was in the book he had plenty of motive to kill her. As far as my mother, I wasn't sure what was going on—who was Vivienne? And it sounded as though Serena had done something to hasten Jonathon's death but apparently the autopsy had not revealed what it was. And where was this mysterious child?

The book was to be edited by the publisher, which meant there was no reason for me to transcribe it. Douglas's entire purpose was for me to read it and know the truth of what had gone on over the years. Serena's ambiguous style left me with many questions when it came to my own family, but it would expose the respected family of Weatherby for what they were as well as several other men who shouldn't be allowed to reproduce. As far as ghosts, I didn't know what to think.

When Jerry arrived home I was waiting for him. I had opened a bottle of wine, hoping it would soften whatever he had to say.

He came into the living room and sank down on the couch. When I held out a glass of wine his fingers closed around it, his eyes meeting mine briefly before he took a sip. He sighed and put the glass on the table before turning to me. "I guess you figured out I've been lying to you."

When I began to respond he held up his hand. "Let me get it all out before you say anything." He picked up his glass and took another swallow. "I've known about Lila's complaint for several months now. She filed the first one shortly after Frank went to prison. The DA's office is just now taking it seriously."

"How is that possible?"

"I told you before they didn't want to investigate because of the internal chaos it would create. Everyone on the force knew about it."

"You didn't tell me this, but go on."

"It was decided that nothing would be done until my father retired. Your father was already serving his sentence and there was no reason to think he'd manage to re-open the case."

"Did he re-open the case?"

"Your mother did. She was furious."

"After or before she disappeared?"

"This was way before. Maybe ten years into Frank's sentence. By that time she had a lawyer and she'd filed several more complaints."

"You weren't on the force then, were you?" I asked hopefully.

"I had just joined. I was twenty-four at the time and had the idealism that all junior officers have. I was sure that everyone on the force was there purely to do good." Jerry took another swallow of wine and replaced the glass on the table. "My father was the chief at the time and well respected. I tried to stay under the radar since I didn't want people to think I was getting preferential treatment because of him. I heard some talk around the station about the case but I ignored it. The DA was a tough old guy who'd put away many a criminal. And he didn't want to hear about any improprieties in a past case."

"Was the talk related to my mother?"

Jerry nodded. "Your mother caused an uproar. To this day the name Lila McCloud sends shivers down spines. She refused to give up even though the DA dismissed her over and over again. But Lila kept coming back, insisting that he re-open the case and revisit the evidence. She had a lawyer but she fired him and hired a top notch criminal litigator from New York."

"So why wasn't he released?"

"Because the prosecution proved again that he'd done it."

"But what about the DNA evidence, the gun? Everyone on the force knew that he didn't."

"Pretty much, but who wants to go up against a chief who's been there for twenty-five years? They stacked the jury. I tried, Summer. I talked to Pop. I even visited Frank in jail. What I didn't know at the time was that everyone was protecting Pop. They all knew what happened."

"But you said he was dirty. How could they support that?"

"A lot of them were into bad stuff. They didn't want their drug deals to go bust—they were making too much money. But there were a few who insisted that Pop retire. He hung in there for as long as he could but finally it was too much for him. When he had his heart-attack that was kind of it for his career."

"Did you know Frank was innocent?"

"He wasn't completely innocent, Summer. He was a small town crook who broke into houses and stole things." He turned to look at me. "You have to realize this was my father. I couldn't go against him, bring him up on charges like some of them wanted. I supported your mother as best I could and I even talked to the DA myself a couple of times. He was old school and wouldn't budge—said it would ruin our credibility if it came out."

I poured myself another glass and re-filled Jerry's. "And now?"

"My father retired five years ago and a new chief came in—a woman. But what really changed things was when the new DA was elected. Myra Proctor is not into good old boy politics. She cleaned house. That's why all of this is coming up again—because of her. But your mother made a big mistake when she sued the entire department. It's one thing to get a settlement for wrongful incarceration but now she's put herself in the line of fire."

I let out a long sigh and sank back against the cushions. "I kind of wish you'd told me all this before."

Jerry shrugged and looked away. "I didn't have all the pieces until recently and with everything else that was going on I didn't want to tell you that your Mom was alive and could be arrested."

"Arrested?"

"She sued the entire police department under a false name. Why she did this I'm not sure. If she had come forward as herself the suit would have stuck."

"I'm still wondering how I saw her ghost if she's alive." I stared into space. "Serena's journal brought up Vivienne again and hinted that Vivienne and Frank are together, not my mom." When I turned my gaze to Jerry he was frowning.

"Who in hell is Vivienne?"

"I wish I knew. Read this and see if it makes any sense to you." I handed him the journal pages, making sure it showed the last couple of entries. "Serena was having premonitions about being killed, Jerry."

Jerry began to read and then stared at me. "What the hell?"

"Keep reading."

A few minutes later he looked up. "This isn't very clear, is it? It sounds like this Vivienne person was there from the get-go. And now Frank's involved with her? Serena alluded to them being up to something, but what? Maybe she was talking about the lawsuit. This makes me think Ephraim and Randall killed her."

"I'm not so sure. Maybe Mom's ghost will appear again and give me some clue," I said, sighing.

"So this makes you believe your mom's dead?"

"She pretty much spelled it out, Jerry."

"I don't see that but now I'm really wondering who Serena's daughter is."

"Me too. What's going on with the case now?"

"The DA is definitely willing to re-open it. They've

already begun the paperwork against my father and any others still on the force who knew what was going on."

"I hope you're not included in it."

Jerry grimaced. "I wasn't part of the team at the time."

I stared at the floor "If there is any chance my mother's alive she may have to stay in hiding forever." I gazed at Jerry but he didn't reply. A second later he rose from the couch and headed toward the bedroom.

I sat there thinking about my mother's ghost and what she said. *I'm looking out for you* certainly pointed toward me needing to be looked out for. Why? And who the hell wrote those notes? I looked up as Jerry came out of the bedroom carrying his suitcase. "What are you doing?"

His eyes looked watery. "Didn't think you'd want me around after what I just told you."

"I don't hold you responsible for any of this, Jerry. I don't want you to leave."

"I'm responsible for a lot of it. Mostly for not coming clean at the beginning."

"After what happened to me with Ephraim and Randall? How could you? I would have completely freaked out."

Jerry put his bag down. "You did anyway."

"Did you leave before because of all this?"

"Partly. I knew I'd have to tell you sometime. But what I said about not wanting to live with a ghost was true."

I laughed at the irony. "Am I a ghost now?"

Jerry smiled and headed toward me, sinking back down on the couch. "I don't think a ghost could make me feel the way you do."

"Are you talking sex or just generally?"

"Both." He leaned toward me and whispered, "I'm glad you want me to stay—I'm not sure I can live without you, Summer McCloud." And then he put one hand behind my neck and pulled me toward him. Our lips met in a kiss that I knew I would remember for a long time.

20

When the man arrived from the pest control the next morning I led him to the stairwell behind a door in the back. The second floor of Tarot and Tea had been closed off since my mother bought the cottage and only housed boxes and extras Lila had left behind when she moved. I'd stuffed a couple of extras on the steps but I hadn't ventured upstairs in years. The timing of Lila's move must have had to do with her relationship with Frank and the need to have a place of their own. I was yet to be conceived. Had Serena been here then? I didn't remember reading about it in her journals.

I moved the boxes on the stairs aside and led the way up the enclosed stair well. Luckily I had a flashlight to guide our way. The door at the top was usually locked but this time it stood ajar. I pushed it open expecting to find the storage boxes my mother had left and lots of cobwebs but instead I found a fully functional living room, well-equipped kitchen and a bedroom and bathroom that contained many bottles of shampoo, face creams and two toothbrushes. I stared around in surprise before the pest control guy said, "So where is the rodent problem?"

"I...maybe what I heard was people," I answered, noticing a full ashtray and a couple of dirty wine glasses sitting on the coffee table.

"Why did you call me, lady?"

I turned to him. "It's a long story but someone's

pulled a trick on me."

He pressed his lips together and shook his head. "I have other calls to make." He headed for the stairs and I heard him clomping down, his heavy footfalls growing fainter as he moved across the shop. I heard the jingle of the bell as he opened the door and then the windows rattling as he slammed it shut.

In the bedroom the bed was rumpled and unmade and lingerie lay strewn here and there as though hastily removed. The closet held women's clothing as well as a man's trousers and shirts. I recognized several items belonging to my mother. When I heard the bell I hurried downstairs closing the stairwell door carefully behind me.

"You look like you've seen a ghost!" Mrs. Browning stared at me.

I tried to smile, steadying myself against a bookshelf as I moved toward the counter in front. "Can I help you with anything?"

Mrs. Browning waved her hand. "No, dear, just browsing today. Has Douglas been in?"

"How do you know Douglas?"

Mrs. Browning looked surprised. "He lives at the retirement center. We all do."

"What? Who lives there?"

Mrs. Browning laughed. "Where did you think all those new customers came from? Douglas told them all about your store. He's such a nice man."

I couldn't speak for a moment but then I asked, "Is he still there?"

Mrs. Browning looked sad. "I'm afraid not. He had to move back to New York—something about a friend in need."

I sat down heavily in one of the chairs I'd placed

against the wall. "Have you seen my mother?"

"Why no dear. My understanding was that she had died. Is this not so?"

I didn't answer and Mrs. Browning turned away, heading to her favorite place by the goddess shelves. I heard her humming.

The day was a blur as I tried to make sense of what was going on. First thing I did after Mrs. Browning left was to call Jerry and tell him my latest findings. "And according to Mrs. Browning Douglas was living at the retirement center."

"And your mother and Frank upstairs?"

"That's what it looks like to me, but how they moved around up there without me hearing them is a mystery. Those old floorboards creak. And what about the ghost I saw?"

Jerry ignored the ghost comment concentrating on the reality of what I'd seen upstairs. He was in full cop mode. "Is there another entrance?"

"Yes, but I thought it was closed off years ago."

"Summer, I've got to go. Investigate for me, would you? Looks like we're getting close."

I had a few more sales after that and when there was a lull I hurried upstairs again. But this time when I entered the living room my mother was standing there, a smile on her face. She was wearing a gauzy lightweight dress more suited for the summer. Her hair had more strands of gray in it but other than that she looked the same.

"I wondered how long it would take you," she said, moving toward me. A second later I was held against her ample bosom.

I was crying when we pulled apart. "Why didn't you tell me? You let me mourn your death—I was miserable for years!"

Lila put her hand on my cheek. "My sweet girl, you've had that handsome policeman mooning over you—how could you be miserable?"

"What have you been doing? Jerry told me all about the lawsuit and everything. He says you could be arrested."

Lila laughed and reached down to take a cigarette out of the box on the table. She lit it with the lighter lying next to it and puffed, letting the smoke out slowly.

"And when did you start smoking?"

She smiled, drawing in more smoke and sending a thin stream of white toward the ceiling. "Come sit down and tell me all about your life."

Suddenly I was filled with anger. "You expect us to just take up where we left off? You abandoned me," I said, glaring at her. "I have a store to run. " I turned toward the stairwell.

"Don't you want to meet your father?"

I ignored her and continued down the stairs. I was shaking all over.

It was twenty minutes later I heard the chime of the bell and a tall older man entered, his gaze trained on me. "Summer McCloud, I presume." He held out his hand. "I'm your father, Frank Messer."

I gazed into hazel eyes the same color and shape as my own. He had a beard now and his hair was fully gray but I recognized him from the mug shot. A few seconds later I heard footsteps hurrying down the stairs. Lila opened the door and came toward us. She was barefoot and I saw the familiar toe rings.

"Hello, darling," she said, reaching up to kiss Frank on the mouth. "Our daughter is quite annoyed with me at the moment." Her amused gaze met mine. "I did this for you, sweetheart," she said. "I had to clear Frank's name before you met him."

"But his name isn't cleared yet. And he's a petty thief." I stared at my father who didn't react to my outburst.

"I've been working on this for nearly twenty years," my mother continued, ignoring me. "That police department has been a cesspool for over a quarter of a century. It's only Frank's case that brought it to a head. Can you imagine being in jail for all that time for a crime you didn't commit?"

"Why did you feel it necessary to disappear to accomplish this?"

"I always told you your father was gone, Summer. I couldn't find it in my heart to tell you he was in jail. I know now that this was not the wisest decision I've ever made, especially considering everything that's happened." She reached out to touch my arm. "I'm so sorry about Ephraim and Randall. If I had known what they were capable of I would have done something years ago. You didn't need to go through that."

"You mean like kill them?"

Lila's eyes went wide. "Of course not! I meant alert the authorities."

"I heard that you tried."

Lila shook her head and looked up at Frank. "Not hard enough. I can be very forceful when I want to be."

"Tell me about it," Frank said, smiling. He hooked his arm around her neck and pulled her close.

When the bell on the door chimed again I cursed

myself for not locking up. I let out a sigh of relief when Jerry walked toward us.

"After Summer's call I thought I might find you here," he said, focusing on my mother and Frank. "I should haul you both off to jail but I think Summer might be unhappy with me if I did."

Lila hesitated and then moved to hug him but Jerry put up his hands. "I'm here in an official capacity, Ms. McCloud, or is it Mrs. Messer?"

"I never took Frank's name," Lila told him. "But you know you can call me Lila. Now as far as jail goes, can't we come to some kind of agreement?" She smiled coquettishly and wound a lock of her hair around her finger.

I watched in amazement as my mother flirted with my boyfriend. Jerry didn't react to her maneuvers, his gaze turning to me. "What do you think, Summer?" he finally asked.

"I don't see any reason to put her in jail. She hasn't done anything illegal except keep her identity a secret and pretend to be dead. Is that against the law?"

"It is when you file a suit against an entire police department. I do have to admit that this entire corruption scandal wouldn't have come out if it wasn't for your mother."

"See? I knew we could come to an understanding," Lila said. She headed to the door and put the shut sign up and turned the lock. "No point in alerting the entire town to my presence."

An hour later we were all upstairs. Frank had asked me question after question, embarrassing me but also making me feel very much wanted. While we chatted

Jerry and my mother had their heads together plotting. Finally Lila rose from the couch and went into the kitchen. "Who wants wine?" she called out.

I went in to help her, taking a wedge of Gorgonzola cheese from the refrigerator as she uncorked a bottle of red. "Crackers?" I asked. She pointed toward a cabinet. When she brushed by me I noticed that her perfume was different from what I remembered. "What perfume are you wearing?" I asked her.

She looked startled for a second and then she smiled. "I got tired of that rose fragrance, Summer. This is more my style now."

Out of the corner of my eye I saw a gossamer form slip across the room. I turned just before she disappeared through the wall. But what I saw sent a shiver of fear up my spine. It was my mother and she was shaking her head no.

"What is it, Summer?"

I stared at her. "Who are you?"

Her eyes went wide. "I'm your mother of course. Who else would I be?"

"What's happening with the wine?" Frank called out.

"It's coming," she called out in a girlish voice I didn't recognize. And then she picked up the tray and headed into the other room.

There was a lull in the conversation while everyone sampled my mother's quiche she'd added to our snacks. I'd never known her to cook anything—she wasn't domestic by nature. I suddenly remembered picking up the scent of cooking food in the past week or so but I'd assumed it was coming from the bakery.

"What happened to Merrily, Serena's little girl?" I asked her.

Her eyes slid sideways before she waved her hand in the air dismissively. "She's all grown up now. I'm not sure what she calls herself but I know it isn't Merrily."

"But she's the one Serena left all her money to, isn't she?"

The woman who I'd decided was not my mother glanced at Frank. "Yes," she said cautiously. "I know Serena wanted to support her."

"So where is she?"

"How would I know?" she said, her tone belligerent. "The girl's been out on her own for years now. She's your age, Summer."

I let that go and went on. "In her journal Serena didn't mention whether she and Douglas stayed in this house after you started the shop or if they moved back to New York."

She frowned and glanced at my father. "Do you remember, Frank?"

Frank smiled, placing his hand on her knee before turning his attention to me. "Lila's memory isn't what it once was. They stayed for a while and then moved back. By that time your mother and I were living in the cottage. You were only a gleam in my eye at that point."

"What about Randall?"

"He was with us and sometimes with Ephraim. I knew early on that he had problems but your mother refused to see it."

"Weren't you in jail by then?" I asked my supposed mother. "I heard that's where I was born."

Lila's mouth opened. "Well, yes. Wasn't Ephraim responsible for that?" She glanced at Frank who continued. "Ephraim accused your mother of child abuse, Summer, but it wasn't true."

"What about the birth, Mother? How did that go in jail?"

She looked like a deer caught in headlights. I saw her swallow before she answered. "It wasn't pleasant, Summer, but having you was worth it."

"Did they let you keep me?" I asked even though I knew the answer.

Her gaze went to Frank who answered for her. "That time in your mother's life was very difficult. She doesn't like to think about it."

"You do know I have Serena's journals. Douglas brought me that box of papers and asked me to transcribe them." I stared at her, waiting to see her reaction.

"Douglas? Where is he?"

"He was here. Serena said you two brought him back to life. How exactly did you accomplish that?"

She paled and took a hefty drink from her wine glass. "I, um...it was a long time ago. I haven't done that sort of thing for a while."

"We would love to see Serena's journal, Summer. Does it mention her daughter?" Frank asked, leaning forward.

Jerry hadn't said a word and I glanced at him before turning to Frank. "She mentions her but apparently the authorities haven't located her yet."

"Well, that's too bad. You know if they don't find her your mother is next in line to inherit." He looked at the fake Lila and smiled. "We could use that money right about now. It'll be a while before we get anything out of that police department. Do you know how much time has to go by before they give up trying to find Serena's daughter?" he asked, looking at Jerry.

"I think you'll have to ask the law firm that question.

By the way," Jerry continued, "we need you to come down to the station."

Fake Lila looked puzzled. "Why?"

"Because of the lawsuit. There are questions that need to be answered."

I glanced at Jerry again and then leaned toward fake Lila. "Once we tell your old clients you're here they'll be lining up for readings."

When her eyes met mine they were wide, the rest of the color draining out of her face. "I don't do that anymore." She reached for another cigarette and Frank leaned forward to light it for her.

"What about the coven, Mom? Becky's mom, Valerie is anxious to have you back. I'm thinking about joining."

The look of surprise and utter confusion that crossed her face nearly made me laugh.

"I've changed, Summer. You must understand. I haven't engaged in witchcraft since…"

"Since you killed my mother?"

Jerry and Frank stood at the same time. "How dare you talk to your mother like that!" Frank shouted.

Jerry took hold of my arm. "What's going on?"

"I'll tell you in the car." I grabbed his hand and hurried to the stairwell. Over my shoulder I saw fake Lila grab hold of Frank's arm, the pleading expression on her face making me feel sick. Frank shook her off and then yelled. "You better have a good explanation for your behavior, young lady!"

I went down the stairs two at a time and then hurried toward the front door.

"Wait, Summer! What the hell is going on?"

I didn't answer, rushing out the door and toward his

cruiser. He pulled the door shut checking that it was locked, his expression clouded with confusion. I was already inside with my door closed when he climbed behind the wheel. "Do you want to tell me what's going on?"

I looked back at the shop. "Start the car and let's get out of here." I felt sick to my stomach, tears threatening to spill over. I'd asked every deity in the universe to give me my mother back and now...now I had to face reality. Mom was dead.

Once we reached the cottage I left Jerry standing in the kitchen and went to take a shower. While the water sluiced down my back I let my tears flow. By the time I came out I was composed enough to talk about what I knew to be true.

After I explained everything Jerry shook his head. "How is it possible for someone to look that much like your mom?"

"She either had a lot of plastic surgery or she's my mom's twin. My question is how do we prove it? They admitted being here because of Serena's will. If the missing daughter isn't found they'll get away with it."

Jerry still seemed unconvinced, a scowl marring his features. "Tell me again what tipped you off?"

"Wrong perfume to begin with and this woman smokes and cooks. Mom did neither. Also she has different gestures and speech patterns. And I know my mother would never give up magic or doing readings. It was her life's work."

"So you think they're here to get their hands on the money."

"I do and I also think one or both of them killed my

mother. This must be the Vivienne that Serena mentioned in her journal. I better keep it under lock and key. Jerry, do you think it was this woman who sued the department? From the journals Frank and Vivienne got together early on."

"Could be. But as far as hoping to inherit, the estate will stay open until the law firm is convinced Merrily is dead or the statute of limitations runs out."

"What if the law firm knows who she is?"

"From what I heard they didn't seem to. Will you be okay if I run down to the station? I need to talk to the captain about Frank and whoever she is." Jerry smacked his hand against his head.

"What's wrong?"

"Tomorrow's Thanksgiving. I'd forgotten all about it."

"Are you considering moving back to your house during the trial?"

"Hell no!" He turned to look at me. "I'm only going over there for the day. I hate to ask but I'm going to need your support. This trial is going to be a real shit storm."

"I'm here for you, Jerry. I'm only sorry that my father's case is the reason this is going down, especially in light of how I feel about him right now."

Jerry grimaced and headed toward the door. "Pop did this to himself. I'm more worried about my mom. She's a wreck. I'll be back in a couple of hours," he said, opening the door. "Be careful, Summer. I don't trust those two."

21

As soon as Jerry left I called Agnes.

"Are you sure she isn't your mom?" she asked.

"I'm positive. You'd know as soon as you talked to her for more than a minute. And every time I asked her a question she had to get Frank to answer for her. Nope. This is not Lila. Can we get together tomorrow for some sort of Thanksgiving? Jerry's going to his folks and I'm not invited and I don't want to be alone."

"I don't have plans but I have to tell you the weirdest thing happened. I was at the flower store and Douglas Weatherby came in. He wanted to know what I was doing for Thanksgiving and if I would be seeing you. I told him I didn't know. He seemed worried and like he wanted to tell me something but then a customer came in and he left. When I asked he told me he lives in an old age home on the north end of town."

"Fake Lila asked about him and I made the mistake of mentioning the journal. Now I have to worry about that as well."

"Safety deposit box?"

"I guess I could get one."

After I got off the phone I looked up 'old age home in Ames, Ct.', but nothing came up aside from the local medical center.

The next day Agnes arrived dressed in black tights

and boots and a long-sleeved dark dress. With her dark red lipstick and pale skin she looked like she belonged in a vampire movie, but in a good way. We fixed our meal as we chatted, catching up on all the details of the past few weeks.

"I'm still mystified about that man's interest in me," she said, uncorking the bottle of wine she'd brought over. "It was actually kind of disturbing after everything that's happened."

"Mrs. Browning told me he'd gone back to New York. When did you see him?"

"Day before yesterday."

"The last time I saw him he said goodbye. You know something else weird? Serena's daughter hasn't come forward. Jerry said he was sure the law firm would hire a private eye to find her. I'm convinced that Frank and that woman are hoping to inherit."

"It's a sizable estate, isn't it?"

"Sounds like it."

"So why can't they find her?"

I shrugged and took the glass she held out. "I guess she was raised by someone else—a foster family--but surely Serena would have that information which means the lawyers would have it. And according to the journals Douglas is her father."

"Really?"

I stared at Agnes and she stared at me. "Agnes, it could be you," I finally said.

"Me? How is that possible?"

"You had foster parents. Do you remember what they called you?"

"What they called me? My name is Agnes Manning."

"Does the name Merrily strike a bell?"

"No, should it?"

I shook my head and continued chopping vegetables. "I think it's very odd that Douglas came to the flower shop, especially after saying goodbye to me. If he's your father he would want to get to know you, right?"

"He's not my father. My foster parents told me my father died a long time ago. And if he was, why wouldn't he just tell me?"

"And your mom?"

"They never mentioned her and I didn't ask. I was kind of in a daze when I was a kid."

I laughed. "I remember. It's probably why we became such good friends."

I thought about what she'd mentioned about being at the shack with my mother and Serena when we were both young girls. "I think you should be hypnotized."

Agnes frowned and stared at me. "Why?"

"You need to find out if you're an heiress."

Agnes laughed. "Wouldn't that be nice? I'm about to be evicted because I can't afford my rent. And if Mabel doesn't give me more hours I'm SOL"

"Why didn't you tell me? I can lend you some money. I didn't pay you enough when you watched the shop for me."

"You paid me plenty and I know you don't have extra lying around. I'll figure it out."

"I wasn't kidding about hypnosis. I know someone who does it. And I'll pay."

Jerry called me right after Agnes had gone home. "I have to stay here over the weekend. Will you be all right?"

I didn't need to ask how his Thanksgiving had gone. "You tell me. My mother isn't my mother and I have no idea what those two are up to."

"I've assigned a detail to watch the cottage."

"What about Frank and that woman?"

"The captain was hard to convince, Summer. You should have heard her laughing when I said the woman could be Lila's identical twin. She said it sounded like some cheesy episode from an old cop show. She finally agreed to bring them in for questioning but she won't do it until after the holiday weekend."

"They know I'm on to them, Jerry. They could be gone by then."

"Don't you think I know that? There's nothing I can do."

❖

Jerry didn't come home until late Sunday night. He looked haggard and exhausted and barely said anything before heading to bed. He was asleep before I could get one word out of him about the weekend.

In the morning Jerry was up early and on the phone with someone from his family. I could hear him talking about his father. When I came out of the bedroom he looked over at me briefly before moving into the living room to continue his conversation. I made espresso and was already halfway through my cup when he finally came into the kitchen.

"Sorry, that was my sister Eliza. She's completely freaked out about Pops. Says she's sure he's going to do himself in."

"Sound like the weekend was rather stressful," I said mildly.

Jerry shook his head and raked his fingers through

his hair. "It was seriously horrible. Pop was completely morose the entire time and everyone was bent on cheering him up. How do you cheer someone up who's about to serve time?" Jerry let out a heavy sigh. "And my mom," he shook his head. "She made the dinner pretty much single-handedly and managed to maintain her usual poise. She's amazing."

I hoped I would never have to compete with this woman Jerry loved so much.

"So what happened here?" he asked.

"Agnes came over. I'm calling a hypnotist today. I really think she's the long lost daughter."

Jerry turned from making espresso. "Something new come up?"

"Douglas has sought her out twice now, once at my shop and once at the flower shop. He wanted to know all about her life. She's the right age and now that I think about it she resembles Serena. The hypnotist might jog some early memories."

"We still don't know who killed Serena. I've ruled out Ephraim because of the poison. I can't imagine him having access or even knowing about it."

"You never told me what it was."

"I didn't? It was ricin—made from the castor bean plant. It's deadly."

A terrible thought went through my mind but I pushed it away. "Who would gain from her death? Or was it simply to keep her from publishing? If that's the case then Ephraim or Randall would have to be at the top of the list."

Jerry shook his head. "We may never know. The ME released her body a week and a half ago."

"After all this time we still haven't solved the

murder."

"We?" Jerry laughed. "Maybe we can be a team, Summer—your visions combined with my detective skills."

"Except I don't trust my visions or my intuition anymore. I've been wrong too many times lately."

"You've also been under a lot of stress." He smiled and sat down next to me. "We've discussed the cure for that, haven't we?"

"Don't you have to get to work?"

Jerry looked at his watch. "Not for another hour."

Jerry dropped me at the shop on his way to work. "That almost made up for all the lonely hours without you," he said, giving me his sweet puppy dog smile.

I laughed. "Almost?" I reached to give him a kiss and then opened the car door and slid out.

When I walked into the shop something didn't feel right. For one thing I felt in danger despite Jerry telling me there was a plain-clothes cop watching the apartment. But when my first customers appeared I forgot about it. As the hours went by and I didn't hear anything from upstairs I began to relax.

During a lull I called my friend Marcy who hypnotized people. She was very good and had done some work for the police department when witnesses couldn't remember details of what they'd seen. I made an appointment for the next day.

"You have an appointment tomorrow at noon," I told her later when I called.

"Wish you'd checked with me. That's my busiest time. Maybe Mabel won't mind filling in for an hour or so." She sighed. "It probably won't matter much longer anyway. I have to quit and find something better."

"But you love that job! You need to talk to Mabel about increasing your hours."

"I already did. She doesn't have the money. It's time to get real."

I was in the shop packing up my mail orders when the door opened and Douglas came in. He looked older, his expression worried instead of his usual smile.

"I should have gone when I planned, but my task is not complete. You are right about Agnes, my dear. She is my daughter." He glanced toward the door in back. "You can't allow them to get away with it." I was about to say something when I heard a noise on the stairs and turned. At first I thought it was my mother's ghost who appeared in the open doorway but then she spoke and I knew it was the poser. "What's going on?" she asked in an irritated tone.

"It's Douglas," I said, turning to meet his grey gaze.

"What are you talking about?"

When I looked back I knew she couldn't see him. She closed the door and I heard her footsteps moving up and then all was quiet.

When I looked for Douglas he was no longer there.

When Jerry arrived right after five o'clock to pick me up I was waiting for him outside. The weather had turned unseasonably mild with less wind and temps in the high forties. It felt balmy after what we'd gone through before Thanksgiving.

"The arraignment is set for the end of this week. My mother wants me home but I told her I couldn't do it." He looked about to cry.

"If you need to go, go. I'll be fine and your mother needs you right now. I can't imagine how she must feel."

"Are you sure? I don't want to go but she sounded seriously stressed out. I'm afraid she's going to have a nervous breakdown."

"I'm sure."

I told him what had happened in the shop with the poser and Douglas.

His look of concern frightened me. "Is Agnes scheduled yet?"

"She has an appointment with Marcy tomorrow."

"Marcy? That gal's good. The department has used her a few times."

At home Jerry packed a bag and gave me a quick kiss. "I'll call every day. Let me know what happens with Agnes. And don't worry I have an officer watching out for both of you."

I fed Cutty and Mischief and made myself something light to eat, hardly tasting it as I chewed. A thought kept presenting itself and I kept pushing it away.

My dreams that night were filled with my mother and Serena. They were using recipes from the book to kill people. And then my mother changed into the poser, her mouth open in a leer. I woke myself up with a scream. Cutty lifted his head to stare at me curiously and then went back to sleep. I dozed fitfully for the rest of the night, feeling worn out when six o'clock rolled around. My plan was to work at the shop and then close up at lunchtime. I had promised Agnes I would go with her to her appointment.

22

Agnes was very nervous and kept asking me what to expect. "It's basically about getting really relaxed," I told her. I'd never been hypnotized but Marcy had told me all about it.

Once we reached the office Marcy was ready for her, ushering her into a darkened room. "You can come in too if you like," she invited.

I looked at Agnes who nodded her head vigorously.

Marcy had Agnes lie down on the couch while I sat in a chair across the room.

Marcy talked with Agnes for a few minutes explaining the method she would use before beginning a guided visualization.

I closed my eyes as Marcy began to speak, letting my mind wander into what she was saying. I was descending into darkness but I was perfectly safe and relaxed. I went down several flights of stairs until I came to the bottom and found a door that led into the past. But the room I entered didn't have windows or doors and I felt trapped and frightened. A note lay in the middle of the table but when I opened it there was nothing on it. I opened my eyes and took in a deep breath of air.

Marcy continued in her singsong voice guiding Agnes. Finally she began to ask questions. Where are you? What do you see? Agnes sounded very young when she answered, her voice high and quavery.

"Ask her name," I whispered.

Marcy glanced at me before her attention went back to Agnes. "What is your name?" she asked.

"I'm Merrily Weatherby," she answered in her high child-like voice.

Shortly after this Marcy brought her up the stairs and then told her to open her eyes.

"What did you see?" Marcy asked.

Agnes pushed herself up to sitting. "I saw Douglas and Serena. I was with them. They loved me."

"How old were you?" Marcy asked.

"Four or so? Maybe younger?"

"Did they say anything that you can remember?"

"They told me I had to live with another family. That my mother couldn't take me with her where she was going and my father was unable to care for me properly in his condition."

"Condition. What condition?"

Agnes's gaze met mine. "I don't know."

"Is there anything else you remember?"

"My mother told me she would come for me when she could. But she never did." Agnes wiped at her eyes with the tissue Marcy gave her.

"Maybe that's why Serena was here," I said.

Marcy looked over at me. "Is this related to the murder I read about a while back?"

I nodded. "Serena Weatherby was Agnes's mother."

"Do they know who killed her?"

I shook my head.

I paid Marcy the fifty dollars and then Agnes and I left the office, taking the cassette tape with us.

I put my arm around her shoulders. "How do you feel?"

"Kind of shaky. It was very weird. And now she's

gone and I'll never get to meet her."

"At least you've met your father. I think Serena's murder was less about the book and more about you. Whoever killed her didn't want her to find you. Or maybe I should say they didn't want you to know about her. I can feel it in my bones."

Agnes smiled wanly. "So you're getting your mojo back?"

I lifted my brows. "Maybe. I have to call Jerry and let him know about this. You're coming into a lot of money, Agnes."

23

After Agnes dropped off the cassette and explained the situation, the police department contacted Jacob and Elliot. When we got a letter back saying that there was no real proof of her identity I decided to take matters into my own hands. I called Becky and told her I was ready to join the coven.

I went to the bakery before work and spoke to Becky, telling her what was going on. Her eyes widened in shock as I explained who was living on top of the shop.

"I saw someone go up there but I assumed it was workmen. I can't believe this!"

"I need to talk to some of the original members of the coven. Are there any left?"

"Of course. My mother was in it and Mrs. Browning and…" She looked away for a moment, her eyebrows furrowed in thought. "Oh, and Marguerite Powers."

"When do you meet?"

"Once a month on the full moon." She looked up at the sky. "Tonight, actually. If you meet me here around eight I'll take you."

"Thanks, Becky." I hugged her and then headed into the shop to feed the cat and make sure everything was where it should be. After filling Tabby's water and food dish and giving him some love I left the shop and walked around back, climbing the stairs toward the outside entrance.

"I know who you are," I said when she opened the door.

She stood in the doorway dressed in a silk robe that gaped open, her hair in tangles. Her eyes narrowed. "If you must be belligerent please let me have a cup of coffee first."

I followed her into the kitchen. "Where's Frank?"

"Do you mean your father? My goodness, Summer, when did you become so ill-mannered?" She turned to the stove where a teakettle whistled and then poured hot water into her French Press. "He's gone to New York on business."

"Cut the crap. We both know you aren't Lila. Did you get plastic surgery or are you her twin?"

"Prove it," she said staring me down. There was a hard look to her that I hadn't noticed before.

"Were you the one Randall was upset about? How long have you and Frank been together?"

She smiled. "Frank always loved me best. When Lila got pregnant he told me he'd fix it but she was determined to have the baby even after she got dragged off to jail. By the time she got out Frank and I were married. You can't imagine the fuss she made."

"Did you kill her?"

"Do you think I'd admit it if I did? Give it up, Summer."

"What about Serena?"

"What about her? She nearly drove us crazy with her antics. She and Lila were like two over grown children with their ridiculous ideas. Bring people back from the dead? Puleez."

"Just one thing before I go. Are you twins?"

She smiled widely. "Can't you tell? You must have read about me in Serena's journal. By the way, Frank managed to move it to a safer place."

"What?"

"Yes, dear. He's a master at sneaking into houses, you know."

When my cell phone rang I jumped. "Where are you?" Jerry asked.

"I'm talking to the..." at that point something heavy came down on the back of my head. My legs gave way and then there was nothing.

When I woke I was lying on the couch and Frank and Vivienne were watching me. "Ah, finally," Frank said. "I didn't think I hit you hard enough to put you out for that long."

I pushed myself up to sitting rubbing the back of my head where a lump had formed.

"What are we going to do with you, Summer?" Frank asked, watching me with his head cocked to one side. .

"I can't prove anything so it's safe to let me go. And according to her," I pointed at the poser, "you confiscated any evidence I had."

"Her name is Vivienne and she's your aunt. I'm surprised Lila never mentioned her." He took hold of Vivienne's hand and brought it to his lips. "She's the love of my life."

"And yet you had a child with Lila," I said.

He laughed. "It was hard to tell them apart sometimes."

"Did you kill Serena?"

"That's for the police to discover, Summer, but I doubt they're clever enough to figure it out. Right now

I'd like to discuss your little friend. I really wish you hadn't gone to the hypnotist but in the long run it won't make much difference. Everyone who knows the truth is long dead."

"How do you know about that?"

Frank laughed. "I know everything that goes on in this town." He glanced at Vivienne and then back to me. "I've been following her for a few days now."

"The police are watching out for her."

"Do you expect that to scare me?" he chuckled. "It hasn't worked so far, has it? I'm a master of disguise after being around your mother's acting friends. I have a police uniform hanging in my closet." He turned his back to pull off his trousers and shirt and then reached into the closet for the uniform. Once he was dressed he turned to Vivienne. "Tie her up and put her in the closet. I'm going after Agnes."

I struggled against her but in the end Vivienne was stronger. She tied my arms behind my back and then pushed me into the closet. When I screamed she stuffed a rag in my mouth and shoved me against the back wall where I lost my balance. I tried to kick her from where I fell but she was too quick for me, the rope going around my ankles before I could connect my foot with her body. It seemed she was very adept at this.

Once Frank had left the apartment Vivienne pulled out some clothes and took off her robe, her eyes on me as she changed. "Don't expect leniency from Frank just because he's the sperm donor, Summer. He never wanted a child and especially a child with her."

Once she was dressed Vivienne closed the closet door leaving me in darkness. I heard the door to the outside open and close and then there was silence.

It seemed like hours before I heard the sirens. I listened to the sound of footsteps running up the outside stairs and a few minutes later the closet door flew open. "Jesus Christ!" Jerry yelled, pulling the rag out of my mouth. He bent down to untie me. "Why in god's name did you come up here without talking to me?"

He pulled me close and then pushed me away to stare at my face. "What are you trying to do, Summer— give me a heart attack?"

I tried to smile but I could barely mange to move my lips at all. "They did it, Jerry—they killed my mother and Serena, I'm sure of it. And if we don't stop them they'll kill Agnes too."

"Sam has Agnes. She's fine."

I was standing now, rubbing my wrists where the ropes had cut in. "What happened?"

"They attempted to kidnap her but luckily Sam was in the apartment. Unfortunately they got away."

"Can we get out of here? This place is creeping me out."

"A bunch of your customers were hanging around down there. I told them the shop is closed until further notice."

"But Jerry…"

"No buts, Summer. We need to catch them before you come anywhere near here again."

"But I still don't know how they killed either one of them."

"I know how they killed Serena. The ME said he found a tiny puncture wound on the back of her neck. He took a sample to save."

"Has he done anything with it?"

"No. He's waiting for us to come up with the murder

weapon."

"I think we should search for it." I began opening drawers. "What size are we looking for?" And then I saw my mother's old jewelry case. I lifted a small cardboard box out of the case and opened it to see my mother's collection of antique hatpins. Several were wrapped in gauze. "Like a hatpin?" I asked.

Jerry pulled some gloves out of his pocket and pulled them on to examine them. I remembered my mother using them when I was small and admired how pretty they were with their jewels and beads.

"Looks about right to me." He grabbed my hand as I reached out to pick up one of the pins. "Do not touch anything, Summer. There could be poison on them."

We left the apartment and Jerry carried the jewelry case to the cruiser, placing it carefully on the floor in the back. "I'm taking you down to the station so you can make a statement. There's already a BOLO out for them."

"Where's Agnes?"

"Sam took her to the station. You'll see her in a few minutes."

"What's happening with the trial?" I asked as we drove, trying to put my mind on something other than Frank and Vivienne.

"I'm coming home tonight. The trial is in full swing and two of my brothers and one of my sisters are here now. My mother can do without me."

"I actually have a date with a friend."

"What friend?"

I laughed at his worried tone. "A girlfriend. We're..." I realized suddenly that I didn't want to tell Jerry about the coven. "She might have some old letters that could help prove who Agnes is."

"Hmm. Are you going to her house?"

"Yes," I lied. I knew we'd be out by the river where they always did their dances. I only hoped Vivienne and my father didn't know about it. "I won't be home till late. "Did I tell you Frank and Vivienne stole the journal out of the cottage?"

"When did that happen?"

"I don't know. Vivienne told me they had it."

"I stopped by the cottage when I was trying to find you and the journal was sitting on the kitchen table."

I breathed out. "I'm so glad. I guess they were trying to threaten me. Is another storm coming in?" I asked, looking up at the dark mass of clouds.

Jerry leaned forward in his seat to see the sky. "I wasn't paying attention on the way here but by the looks of things, I'd say yes. Does that mean you'll postpone your date?"

When I shook my head he looked disappointed.

A few minutes later we pulled up to the police station. Inside I saw Agnes in a room talking with Sam. "What happened?" I asked her, rushing through the open door.

Agnes smiled at Sam. "Sam saved me."

Sam laughed, his usual smirk replaced with a soft expression I'd never seen on his face. "It was a good thing I was there," he said, turning to me. "When Frank broke in the uniform threw me until I recognized him from the mug shot. But before I could get my gun out he was long gone."

"Your gun wasn't on your person," Agnes said. "It was sitting on the bedside table."

Sam turned beet red and then turned to Jerry who

had just come in. "So what's the plan, buddy?"

"Bedside table?" I mouthed, watching Agnes.

She gave me a lopsided grin. "Did you give your statement yet?" she asked me.

"She's just about to," Jerry said grabbing my arm. I let him pull me away watching Sam loop an arm around Agnes. Their heads were together when we left the room.

After I made my statement Jerry called the ME who made a special trip.

I went with Jerry to the autopsy room, the smells of alcohol, disinfectant and some darker odors assaulting my nostrils as soon as we were inside. Jerry handed the ME the box of pins. "We think the murder weapon might be one of these."

Daniel took the box. "Looks about the right size. We'll need to send it to the lab. I'm not messing with ricin."

"How long will that take?" I asked.

Daniel was an older man and looked tired. He ran thick fingers through his graying hair. "Shouldn't be more than a day or two."

"Can you put a rush on it?" Jerry asked.

"Sure, I can do that. Are you bringing someone in?"

"I'm hoping to."

Jerry pulled the cruiser up in front of the cottage. "If you're going out I may as well get some paperwork done down at the precinct. Keep the door locked and please be careful tonight." He leaned over to kiss me before I got out of the car.

Cutty came bounding out as soon as I opened the door, licking my hand and running in circles. It was few minutes later that a cruiser pulled up outside. For one horrible second I imagined Frank behind the wheel but then I saw Sam get out and go around to open the passenger door. And then he walked Agnes up the path.

"Can I sleep on your couch?" Agnes asked me when I opened the door. "It's supposed to snow tonight and the thought of worrying about a murderer and not having any electricity does not make me feel very safe."

"I'd stay with her but I'm on duty tonight," Sam said. "Jerry will be here, right?"

I nodded. "It's fine with me."

After Sam left Agnes flopped down on the couch and put her head back. "Whew! What a day. Do you have anything alcoholic to drink?"

"Would you like wine, beer or hard alcohol?"

"Anything that will calm my nerves."

I brought over two glasses of wine and sat down beside her. "So what's the deal with you and Sam?"

She moved her head to gaze at me. "He's the cop who got assigned to me, Summer. You know we met that night at the Keg. I thought he was cute and I guess he felt the same way—one thing led to another and then…" She pressed her lips together her eyebrows going up.

"You had sex already?"

"It wasn't right away, I mean we talked on the phone and we met again at The Keg and then he was hanging around my apartment. One thing led to another. He's pretty hot, Summer. And you should see him with his clothes off. He…"

I plugged my ears. "Lalalalalalala."

She laughed. "Too much for your sensitive soul? All I can say is I like him and he's incredible in bed."

I unplugged my ears and waited for more but her eyes had glazed over. She turned to me. "I know now why he was so adamant to catch your Mom."

"Why?"

"Your mom gave his dad some herbal remedies years ago that Sam is convinced caused his cancer."

"What?"

"Yup. I told him that couldn't be true."

"Mom didn't advertise herself as a healer, Agnes."

"I know that. I just thought you might like to know why he was so down on your mom."

I shook my head. "Not exactly an open mind, is it?"

Agnes shrugged. "Moot point now."

A few minutes went by and then I asked, "Do you want to go to a witch's coven with me tonight?"

Agnes sat up and stared at me. "What did you say?"

"You heard correctly. I'm meeting Becky at eight o'clock."

"Becky Henderson of the bakery?"

I nodded.

"What about the snow?"

"I haven't heard from her so I assume it goes on no matter what the weather. I'm only going because I want to talk with people from the early days who can vouch for your identity. It would be helpful if you were there."

"Do you have a heavy snow jacket I can borrow?"

I smiled and nodded. Agnes always was up for a good adventure.

Agnes and I left the house around seven-thirty, trudging in snow boots through around five inches of accumulated slush Becky was waiting when we arrived at the bakery, her bright hair covered by a dark hood attached to a long wool cape. She reminded me of a character from a fantasy story, ready to slip unseen through the forest to the little hut where the witches lived.

"I wondered if you'd come," she said, glancing at

Agnes.

"I invited Agnes along. I hope that's all right."

Becky smiled. "The more the merrier."

Becky drove south along the highway, heading toward the river, windshield wipers on high. "Older people come out in this kind of weather?" I asked.

Becky grinned. "You'll see," she answered enigmatically.

Becky turned onto a narrow dirt road and then cut the engine. "We'll walk from here," she said, sliding out. Agnes and I followed suit and then the three of us continued down the snow-covered road. "I hope we don't get stuck out here," I muttered.

"No worries," Becky said brightly.

A forest of hardwoods lined the path on both sides thinning out and disappearing as we neared the river. I could hear it before we saw it, the rushing sound loud in my ears. Snow was still coming down, the flakes sticking to our coats. When the path made a sharp bend to the right the scene took my breath away. Over fifty people had formed a circle one hundred feet from the riverbank. They reached upward toward the moon, which was nearly invisible due to the cloud cover and snow. But the circle where they were standing was clear and no snow fell on them.

"What the...?" Agnes gazed at me from under the hood of the jacket I'd lent her, her eyes wide.

Becky laughed. "I told you. They are invoking the goddess. One of us will be called to the center of the circle. Come." She gestured to us to follow her as she slipped between two people and lifted her arms.

I moved next to Becky and Agnes pushed in beside me. We lifted our arms and joined in the chant that

repeated the words over and over:
Oh, goddess moon, we feel your magic,
We bow to you and take in your power
to use only for good.

We said this over and over until one of the women in the circle fell to her knees. The chanting stopped as the woman next to her helped her up and into the center of the circle. A man joined her, his features obscured by his hood. For the first time I noticed the altar set up on a wide stump, the three bowls and three unlit candles. They both kneeled in front of the altar and the man lit the candles and then raised one of the bowls, his eyes on the moon, which was now bright and huge in the dark sky above us.

"Blessed be, creature of earth!" he cried out. "Let all malignity and hindrance be cast forth and let all good enter herein, in the names of Aradia and Cernunnos!" And then the woman picked up another bowl and lifted it high. "Blessed be creature of water! Wash away all impurities in the names of Aradia and Cernunnos!" The man took something from his bowl and added it to hers and called out, "As water purifies the body, salt purifies the spirit!" And then they both rose to their feet and walked together around the circle sprinkling the water and chanting the words together: "I conjure this circle to be a place of love and joy, the boundary between worlds that shall contain and direct the power in the names of Aradia and Cernunnos!"

It was shortly after this that the music began, singing and people suddenly producing instruments from under their cloaks. Everyone danced, arms lifted toward the moon. It was very weird to see the snow falling outside of our circle as we danced—strange and otherworldly. Agnes and I joined in, both of us giving ourselves over to the drum rhythms, the flutes and tambourines. I tried not to focus too closely on the creatures that seemed part human, part animal with deer antlers and heads on human bodies. Some time had gone by when I saw my mother among the dancers and moved in that direction. "Mom?"

She smiled at me and held up her hand in a wave and then evaporated. I turned to Becky dancing next to me.

"She comes and goes," she whispered, smiling.

"But I want to ask her some questions!"

Becky shook her head and turned away. It was a long time before the dancing came to an end and I got the chance to question some of the older members of the group.

"Yes, of course I knew Serena," Mrs. Browning told me. "And I knew all about Merrily. She talked about her daughter all the time."

I turned to Agnes standing behind me. "Well, this is Merrily only with a different name. But how do we prove it?"

Mrs. Browning put her hand out and touched Agnes's arm. "You look very much like your mother did when she was your age," she said.

After talking with several others we came to the conclusion that despite many of the older members of the coven knowing about Agnes none of them had a clue how to prove it to the authorities. Unless we found some document in that box of papers we were SOL and I had already searched pretty thoroughly. We walked along the road in the snow feeling disheartened. Just before we reached the car Douglas appeared. "They have them," he told me solemnly.

"Who has what?"

"Vivienne and Frank have the documents proving Agnes's identity. You have to find them." He turned to his daughter, enfolding her in a hug. "I'm very sorry I wasn't able to raise you," he said. "I'm not always solid," he continued with a sad smile, pinching his arm. "I couldn't very well take you to school and disappear in front of the teachers. Know I'll always be looking out for you even if you can't see me." And then he slowly faded away, melting into the snowflakes.

When I glanced at Agnes she was crying.

It was one o'clock in the morning by the time we got back to the house. Before I opened the door I noticed that the lights in the living room were on. Jerry was waiting up.

He stood as soon as we entered the house. "Where in hell have you been?"

"I told you I'd be late, Jerry. You shouldn't have waited up."

"Summer, with everything that's going on right now there's no way I could go to sleep." He glanced at Agnes.

"Sam dropped her off because he was on call. She's staying here until Frank and Vivienne are caught."

Agnes glanced at me. "Or until I get my police detail back."

"So where have you been all this time?"

Agnes and my eyes met before I answered. "We lost track of time, Jerry. It's the first time we've had a girl's night out."

Jerry frowned and headed toward the bedroom. "I've got to get some rest. With Pop's trial coming up and my own schedule I've got a busy day ahead."

261

"Why didn't you tell him the truth?" Agnes asked once he closed the bedroom door.

"That we went to a witch's coven and talked to a dead guy and danced around with creatures who looked like they belonged in a fairytale?" I shook my head. "Jerry's been pretty good about this stuff, but I don't want to push it. And besides, a girl has to have some secrets."

Agnes laughed. "This is a pretty big one."

"Are you going to tell Sam?"

She stared into space. "I don't think so, at least not right now."

"The bed's made up and there are towels in the bathroom. Sleep well," I told her before heading toward the bedroom. When I opened the door Cutty squeezed in quickly as though afraid of being shut out again.

Jerry was asleep when I crawled into bed next to him, but when I cuddled close he threw an arm around me and pulled my body against his. "Don't ever scare me like that again," he muttered, and then he began to snore.

24

The snow petered out sometime during the night and when we woke in the morning the sky was blue, shining on the trees and the grass where several inches of snow lay sparkling like crystals. But despite the sun the temperatures had dipped and it was bitter cold.

Jerry called Sam before he left for the station, asking him to pick up Agnes and take her to the flower shop. He told Sam to watch over the shop and then bring her home later. When Sam arrived Agnes hurried outside and climbed into the squad car next to him.

"Ready?" Jerry asked me, heading out the door to the other squad car. I followed him, pulling the door closed thinking about the eyeful my neighbors were getting. Two squad cars? I was positive rumors were flying fast and furious up and down the block.

"I'll call as soon as I hear anything," Jerry told me once we reached Tarot and Tea. "If something happens before that call 911. I have someone assigned to you," he assured me, pointing to a plain dark blue sedan parked across the street.

The toxicology report arrived around ten and Jerry called me to let me know that Daniel had matched one of the hatpins to the puncture wound. Several other hatpins in the box were primed and ready for use.

"It had remnants of ricin on it, Summer. The captain finally okayed my request to pick those two up."

I clicked off feeling a sharp pain in my stomach. I looked around my shop hoping that customers wouldn't be freaked out when the police arrived. Part of me didn't want to believe that my father and my mother's sister could do such a thing. I took in a deep breath trying to maintain some semblance of normalcy but when I heard the sirens my heart came into my throat.

"Why are the police here?" Mrs. Browning asked, gazing out the display window.

I watched Jerry and another officer race around the building with guns drawn. "Did you know about Vivienne?" I asked her.

Her mouth opened and she stared into the distance. "Why yes I did. She and your mother were always switching places and confusing everybody."

"Vivienne is living upstairs with my father and impersonating Lila. It looks like they killed Serena."

Mrs. Browning took hold of my arm. "Oh my dear, that can't be so. They may have pulled some pranks back in the day but nothing quite that serious."

I stared at her in surprise. "How long since you've seen Vivienne?"

Mrs. Browning turned toward me, one finger going to her chin as she thought. "It must be close to twenty years now."

"I think they killed my mother as well. Were they both part of the coven?"

"Vivienne would have nothing to do with it. She wasn't a believer in such things."

I heard heavy footsteps from above and then the sound of someone descending the staircase. Jerry opened the door and came into the shop. "They're gone," he told me. "There's not a stick of furniture or anything to indicate they were ever here."

"What?" I followed him back upstairs. Instead of furniture there were boxes stacked in all the rooms. It smelled musty like an attic. My gaze met Jerry's. "You were up here—how is this even possible?"

He shook his head. "Beats me. As far as Agnes goes, the ME told me to bring her in. We can match her DNA to Serena's."

"Will that be conclusive?"

"I certainly hope so."

25

When Christmas rolled around I was still reeling from the effects of what I'd learned and trying to come to terms with all of it. Jerry and the force were hard at work trying to locate Frank and Vivienne, hoping to bring them to justice. We spent the day with Sam and Agnes drinking champagne and talking about all the strange happenings of the past months. Neither Agnes nor I mentioned the monthly meetings we were still attending.

Between Christmas and New Year's Agnes was given a DNA test, which proved her connection to Serena. After the ME contacted Jacob and Elliot she received a letter from the law firm stating that she would indeed be inheriting. Of course it would take months to fully settle the estate.

My cell phone rang early on New Year's Day, interrupting what was proving to be a very satisfying interlude.

"Why are you answering it?" Jerry asked grumpily, rolling over.

I made a face at him and said hello.

"I just spoke with Jonathon's daughter, Regina," Agnes said, excitedly. "I told her I was planning to share. Did you know how much money I'm getting?"

Jerry nuzzled my neck. "How much is it?" I asked, trying not to giggle as his hands moved across my bare skin raising goose bumps.

"Twenty million dollars, Summer. I can buy the flower shop from Mabel. She told me she wants to retire. I can buy a house!"

"That's great news, Agnes!" Jerry was at it again and this time I couldn't ignore what he was doing. "I've got to go. I'll call later, okay?"

I clicked off and flung the phone off the bed and let Jerry ravish me.

I called Agnes back later in the day to find out the rest of the story. By now Jerry was up and showered, about to head off to see his family. I still felt the effects of what we'd done earlier, my body tingling all over as I watched him leave the house.

"So what did Jonathon's children say when you offered to share?"

"They were so appreciative, Summer. They told me Serena bewitched their father into penning the new will."

"That might or might not be true," I muttered.

"From everyone we've talked to, including Douglas, my mother was a powerful witch. She knew voodoo. I'm sure she killed Jonathon but from what you showed me in her journals he certainly deserved it."

"And she paid with her life."

"Frank and Vivienne killed her because of me, Summer. They didn't want her to find me. I wish I had known her, although I feel sort of pissed off about her abandoning me. Why did she do that?"

"I don't know, Agnes. I think she had to because of her financial situation. She loved Douglas, not Jonathon. But from what I've read, Jonathon would never have married a woman who had a teenage daughter, especially with Douglas being the father. And Jonathon had grown children of his own. I wonder if he abused his own kids?"

"I would love to read the journals, Summer."

"Agnes, now that we know who you are, I think you should write a forward to the book. You don't have to go into detail about the ghost stuff but you could say something about how you feel now that you've discovered your heritage."

"That's a good idea. Hey, Summer, do you want to take a drive north of town and see if we can find where Douglas was living?"

"I would. When do you want to go?"

"How about now?"

After we hung up I straightened the house and then took Cutty for a quick walk. When I went by my neighbor Betty's house she was out in the garden holding a small bundle. She waved and I waved back. I'd been so involved in my own life I had no idea when the baby had been born. I would have to bake something to take over.

Agnes was parked outside the cottage when I got back and I opened the back door to let Cutty jump in. "You don't mind, do you?"

"Heck no," she said, looking at my dog over her shoulder.

She drove carefully along the unplowed streets heading north. When we reached the outskirts of town she consulted her map. "From what Douglas said it should be around here somewhere." She climbed out of the car and I followed her, grabbing Cutty to take him along.

When I noticed what looked like a large apartment building in the distance I grabbed her arm. "Maybe that's it."

We took a left off the main road and headed that way. There was a big empty field between it and the main road and I let Cutty off the leash watching him tear off through the snow.

Agnes stopped in her tracks. "That place has been abandoned for a very long time."

I looked up taking in the derelict Victorian style building. It had once been grand and elegant but now the doors hung crookedly and the roof had collapsed in several places. The paint had peeled off, revealing gray boards that were filled with dry rot. We continued closer.

I walked up rickety stairs and opened a door into what had once been the main entrance. On the wall was an old fashioned list of who lived here with buttons next to their names to press if they had visitors. I ran my finger down the list seeing someone named Emilia Browning. Farther down was the name Douglas Weatherby.

When I glanced at Agnes her eyes were wide.

"When do you think they lived here?"

I shivered as I felt a presence move past me. "A very long time ago."

26

I n late February, a month before the trial was due to begin, Jerry's father committed suicide. He was found hanging in his walk-in closet, a rope tied around the heavy ceiling fan, a chair pushed over next to him. This was a terrible blow to the family since they were all staunch Catholics and believed that suicide was a mortal sin. I didn't see Jerry much for those weeks following the tragedy. I was glad to be left out of it since I wouldn't have known what to say.

With Jerry gone Agnes and I continued our full moon ceremonies. It was after one of these that I spoke with several members of the coven discovering that Lila and her twin sister Vivienne exchanged places often, moving in to replace the other one for a week or two whenever it suited. I wondered about the alcoholic version of my mother, the one who had affairs that she didn't hide from her son. Was that actually Vivienne? Maybe the child abuse charge had come about during one of these times. During those years Frank was not yet in the picture—it made sense. No wonder Randall had gone nuts. It was like having a schizophrenic mother.

By the time I was born Frank was already with Vivienne and she and my mother were estranged. I still had no explanation for the time at the river when I walked home alone. Maybe my mother had demons of her own.

Being part of the coven had increased the shop's

popularity and I was doing a rousing business. I could barely keep my products in stock.

Becky arrived one morning to drop off my mother's Tarot deck she'd borrowed. "I think you should learn to do the Tarot," she told me. "You've been having more visions which proves you're getting in touch with that part of yourself. I can teach you the basics."

I shook my head. "I'd rather save it for police work, Becky. I'm hoping Jerry and I can collaborate on cases."

"Does he know this?"

I sighed. "To tell you the truth I haven't seen him much since his dad died."

"Well, if that doesn't work out you should use your skills for Tarot readings."

That night without prior warning Jerry used his key to let himself into the cottage. When I looked up from my book and met his gaze I knew something was very wrong. I stood to greet him but when his arms went round me I could feel tension in his shoulders. And the way he held me, as if I might disappear, alerted me even more. "What's going on?"

He pulled away and looked down at the floor. "Mom wants me to move in with her for a few months."

"And you said?"

Jerry pressed his lips together trying to meet my gaze. "I told her I would. She's very fragile right now and I just can't abandon her."

"What about your brothers and sisters?"

"None of them live here." He took in a breath and let out a long sigh his gaze finally meeting mine. "I have to do this, Summer. It won't be that long."

"Jerry, we just started this relationship. So many

things have happened to interrupt it. Maybe we were wrong to think things could work out between us."

Jerry moved close and wrapped his arms around me again. "I love you, Summer. That isn't going to change. Can you be patient with me?"

"What happened to 'you can't live without me'?"

"I'll come over as often as I can. We can still be together, just not living in the same house."

"Are you staying here tonight?"

He shook his head. "I can't. She's been drinking too much and I have to get back and make her some dinner."

"When will I see you again?" I asked, following him into the bedroom. He collected his clothes and toiletries, throwing them into the battered suitcase he'd left here.

"I'll call," he answered. And a moment later he was gone.

I stood there feeling numb for a long time and then I sat down on the couch and began to cry. I should have known from the way he spoke about his mother that she would eventually come between us. I suddenly hated her. And somewhere inside I knew this was her way of keeping Jerry away from me. She wanted him to herself. My cell phone rang and I grabbed it off the table hoping it was Jerry saying he'd changed his mind.

"Do you and Jerry want to meet us at The Keg later tonight?" Agnes asked.

Crying, I tried to explain what had just happened.

"I'm coming over," Agnes said, and then the line went dead.

When I answered the door Agnes took one look at me and went into the kitchen for a bottle of wine. "What a bastard!" she said, uncorking the red I'd been saving for a special occasion. "Why are men such dickheads?"

I laughed despite my tears. "Maybe because that's the part of their anatomy that does the thinking? But in this case I don't think that applies." I looked up. "At least I hope it doesn't. I tried to feel sympathetic but I think his mother is manipulating him."

"Have you met her?"

I shook my head. "I doubt I ever will now."

After a glass of wine Agnes talked me into going out with her. We met Sam at The Keg. When the subject of Jerry's mom came up Sam said,

"His mother is a strong woman."

"If she's so strong why does she need him to move in?"

Sam frowned. "I've met her and I do have to say that she's a little over the top when it comes to Jerry. He's obviously her favorite and she fawns over him, giving him compliments he doesn't deserve." He laughed. "Jerry has a big enough head without that."

I had to laugh. I'd never noticed Jerry having an ego problem. We left the subject of Jerry and talked and laughed for the rest of the evening. When it was over I couldn't remember much of what we'd talked about but I did feel better.

It was three weeks after my night out with Sam and Agnes that my cell rang very early in the morning. I had not seen Jerry since the night he left. I was learning to cope and wondering if I would ever hear from him again so when I saw his name on the screen I felt nervous.

"They found Vivienne and Frank," he said as soon as I answered.

"Did they arrest them?"

"They were dead, Summer. They drowned in the

river. Someone discovered their bodies."

"Where?"

"You know the place where the river takes that big bend south of town? Apparently their bodies got caught in the debris from the winter storms."

I did know that place. It was right by where the coven had their meetings. "How long had they been dead?"

"Hard to say. I hate to do this to you but could you come down to the station to identify them?"

"If you come and get me."

An hour later I was in the squad car heading to the station. "How's life with your mother?"

Jerry slanted a glance my way. "It's not fun. She's driving me crazy."

I turned away, looking out the passenger window. He pulled up to the curb in front of the police station and cut the engine. "Listen, Summer, I hate what I did to you. And I miss you so much it hurts. I've been trying to come up with a solution for my mom and I think I may have one."

When I didn't look at him he grabbed my arm. "Please, Summer, give me a chance."

I turned, meeting his gaze. "I haven't met your mother, Jerry, but she knows you're in a committed relationship. I think she's manipulating you--she doesn't want us to be together."

Jerry's eyebrows pulled together. "That's what I was trying to tell you. I've hired a woman to live in."

"What did your mom say?"

"She doesn't know yet but I'm planning to tell her tonight."

"And if she doesn't go along with your plan?"

Jerry frowned, staring out the windshield. "I'll have to confront her. I talked to Celeste, my sister, and she said the same thing you just said. She told me I have to stand up to her. You do know I'm the baby?" He glanced over at me with his puppy dog look combined with a sheepish grin.

"I should have figured."

I followed him into the station and downstairs to the autopsy room afraid of what I was about to see.

Daniel's gaze was sympathetic. "Are you ready for this?"

"Is anyone ever ready to see a dead person?"

He nodded his agreement and moved the sheet aside so I could look down on the bodies. Sticks and weeds clung to them both and their hair was filled with mud and green slime. Vivienne was white and bloated, her blonde hair so tangled into knots that I was sure it could never be combed out. Her resemblance to my mother was uncanny and before I knew it I was crying.

Jerry held me until I could control myself and then I nodded to the ME. "It's definitely Frank and Vivienne."

"It's better this way," Jerry said, smoothing my hair back. "Now it's really over."

"How do you think it happened?" I asked Jerry as we walked up the steps.

"I don't know. It seems a little suspect."

"You mean like somebody might have killed them?"

"We'll never know."

Jerry moved back the following day after having it out with his mother. When I asked how it had gone he shook his head and refused to talk about it. I'd decided I liked Celeste and wanted to meet her the next time she came to town.

On the next full moon I told Jerry that Agnes and I were working on a project with Becky and wouldn't be home until after midnight. This time he smiled and told me he wouldn't wait up. What I learned that night at the coven confirmed some of my earlier suspicions. Vivienne and Frank had definitely not died accidentally.

Look for the next Summer McCloud mystery when Summer and Jerry combine their skills to track down more murderers!

Read the first chapter here:

Saffron and Seaweed
1

I donned my helmet and climbed on the back of Jerry's recently purchased *Indian* motorcycle with some trepidation. The model was called *Indian Chief* and his was painted solid black. He'd had it customized to accommodate a passenger but there wasn't a whole lot of room. If I'd been bigger it wouldn't have worked at all. He'd also managed to retrofit a couple of saddlebags on the sides to carry what we needed for our weekend away.

"Are you set?" he asked.

"I think so," I said, but my words were drowned out by the engine as he put it in gear and we roared away.

I held on for dear life as he took curves at sixty miles an hour racing east toward the coast and away from the town of Ames, Connecticut. This was the first time we'd taken a trip together and I was excited. My friend Agnes was staying in my cottage while we were gone, promising to take care of Cutty my dog, and Mischief my cat. I'd even closed my occult shop, Tarot and Tea, to give us an extra day to explore the beach town of Watch Hill, Rhode Island where we were headed.

"Want to stop at the casino?" he asked over his shoulder.

"No!" I called out. I'd been to the casino many times before and with the heat and humidity of this day in July I was ready to get to the ocean. The leather jacket I'd worn for protection was too hot by far.

We stopped around noon to get gas and find a place to eat and I slid off, feeling the strain in my thighs and lower back from the ride. I pulled off my helmet and ran fingers through my damp hair. "How much further?"

Jerry had just put the gas nozzle into the tank. "Maybe an hour?"

Jerry was a homicide detective on the Ames police force and the two of us had been together for a little over a year now. Our first case had involved my father and Jerry's father and several ghosts, one of them being my mother. It had been a disturbing few months with both of us getting shot and several other near-death experiences.

After the stress wore off we'd decided that we liked working together, my visions and his detective skills seeming to be a good combination. He didn't mention our plan to his fellow cops knowing it wouldn't have gone over well if he explained that his girlfriend was psychic and saw ghosts. Lately nothing much had happened in Ames other than a few burglaries and traffic accidents. I was itching for a real murder to sink my teeth into.

We ate at the dairy queen and then climbed back on the bike taking off with another loud roar.

It was three in the afternoon before we rolled into the

wealthy beach resort of Watch Hill. We'd taken the scenic route, driving by elegant mansions that could house dozens and heading by the Ocean House where room prices began at three hundred and went up from there. The completely rebuilt monolith sat on a bluff overlooking the Atlantic Ocean. Beyond the hotel the road narrowed and curved dropping us into the village and on toward the Watch Hill Yacht Club.

Jerry pulled into the parking lot in front of the yacht club and cut the engine. What do you think? Take a walk on the beach and go for a swim?"

I brightened immediately, pulling off my jacket and helmet. "I have my bathing suit on under my clothes."

He raised one eyebrow, a pirate look that I found very sexy and then his gaze went from my T-shirt to the cut-off shorts I was wearing. "I thought…" he began.

"That we'd go skinny-dipping? Do you think there's a secluded beach in this town? Look around, Jerry, and tell me what you see."

Jerry scanned the crowded parking lot, the cars rolling slowly by the shopping strip and restaurants, the people in bathing suits going in and out of the yacht club and heading toward the cabanas. He made a face. "Too bad." He took my hand. "Let's head out to the point."

Napatree Point was a spit of land that stuck out beyond the harbor separating it from the ocean on the other side. The day was hot and still and I longed to get into the water.

"What do we do about our stuff?" I asked looking down at the expensive customized leather bags he'd purchased to hang on either side of the bike.

"They lock, Summer. It would be pretty hard for someone to get them off." He looked around at the

Mercedes, BMW's, and Porsches in the lot. "And who here would care to?"

I pulled off my T-shirt, watching Jerry take off his leathers. He wasn't terribly tall, with a solid body and broad shoulders. His brown hair was windblown, his face dark from the sun. Even after a year I still got a little thrill when I looked at him.

He stuffed his leathers into one of the bags. When his gaze met mine his mouth quirked. "And what are *you* thinking about," he asked.

"Nothing," I answered looking away. Maybe it was the heat or maybe it was because we were away from Ames but right now I wanted to run my hands all over his body and have him run his over mine. I thought about the privacy of water. "Let's go," I said, pulling him across the parking toward the dunes in the distance.

The sand was hot and I ran toward where the surf had come up and cooled it down. A lot of people were out today, the high-pitched cries of children, barking dogs and the sound of the waves crashing suddenly on the beach mingling into a summer medley in my mind. I walked down the beach away from the crowd to there the strip of land narrowed and came to an end.

"Wait for me!" Jerry called, hurrying to catch up. He grabbed my hand.

We climbed the dunes and headed toward the point where we hoped there'd be less people. As soon as the land narrowed the wind began to whip. I watched sailboats heeling as they moved in and out of the harbor, the sailors pulling the sails down quickly before finding their moorings. There looked to be an invisible line where the calm water gave way to waves with whitecaps. When we reached the place where the land ended I raced down and plunged into the cold water, Jerry right behind me. We swam out beyond where the waves were breaking and then floated on our backs for a while until Jerry grabbed me and pulled me under the water.

I opened my eyes as he pressed against me, our lips meeting in a kiss. Everything was green, light slanting through the water and casting rippling shadows across our skin. We bounced together as waves moved past, our bodies undulating loosely like flotsam. I could hear the deep muffled rumble of the waves, see the tendrils of my brown hair waving like seaweed, feel Jerry's body against mine. His hands moved under my bathing suit top and I felt it slip off and drift away. We rose to the surface laughing and gasping.

"My top!" I yelled, trying to locate it. Jerry grinned as I dove to find it. I let the waves take me closer into shore hoping it was being washed along with me but when I reached the beach I didn't see it. I stayed under the water as much as I could, scanning for other people, but most were down the beach where'd come from and where the water was calmer.

I giggled when I felt Jerry's leg against mine, turning to grab him, but my fingers closed around something that felt squishy and strange. It was not Jerry's leg, It was the arm of someone who was very dead. I let out a piercing shriek, forgetting that I was nearly naked as I stood up in the shallow water.

Jerry swam toward me. "What in hell is the matter?" And then he saw the body rising and falling as the waves moved it in and out.

To contact the author:

nikkibroadwell@comcast.net
(mailto:nikkibroadwell@comcast.net)
www.wolfmoontrilogy.com

Other Books by Nikki:

Wolfmoon Trilogy:
The Moonstone
Saille, the Willow
The Wolfmoon
Gypsy Trilogy:
Gypsy's Quest
Gypsy's Return
Gypsy's Secret
Just Another Desert Sunset

For more information please visit:
www.wolfmoontrilogy.com

Made in the USA
Columbia, SC
26 July 2022

64006799R00174